THE GOOD DREAM

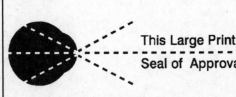

This Large Print Book carries the
Seal of Approval of N.A.V.H.

THE GOOD DREAM

DONNA VANLIERE

THORNDIKE PRESS
A part of Gale, Cengage Learning

GALE
CENGAGE Learning

Detroit • New York • San Francisco • New Haven, Conn • Waterville, Maine • London

GALE
CENGAGE Learning®

Copyright © 2012 by Donna VanLiere.
Thorndike Press, a part of Gale, Cengage Learning.

Thorndike Press® Large Print Basic.
The text of this Large Print edition is unabridged.
Other aspects of the book may vary from the original edition.
Set in 16 pt. Plantin.

LIBRARY OF CONGRESS CATALOGING-IN-PUBLICATION DATA

VanLiere, Donna, 1966–
  The good dream / by Donna VanLiere.
    pages ; cm. — (Thorndike Press large print basic)
  ISBN 978-1-4104-4717-3 (hardcover) — ISBN 1-4104-4717-0 (hardcover)
  1. Tennessee—Social life and customs—20th century—Fiction. 2. Single women—Fiction. 3. Feral children—Fiction. 4. Family secrets—Fiction.
  5. Large type books. I. Title.
  PS3622.A66G66 2012b
  813'.6—dc23
                                                            2012018209

Published in 2012 by arrangement with St. Martin's Press, LLC.

Printed in the United States of America
1 2 3 4 5 6 7 16 15 14 13 12

For Olivia King,
who is the bravest girl I know

ACKNOWLEDGMENTS

Special thanks to:

Troy, Gracie, Kate, and David for giving me so much material to write and speak about. Life is sweeter because of you!

Jennifer Enderlin, Sally Richardson, George Witte, Matthew Baldacci, Matthew Shear, Lisa Senz, Rachel Ekstrom, Sara Goodman, and the St. Martin's sales staff for your love of books!

Jennifer Gates and Esmond Harmsworth for years of friendship and belief.

Mary Weekly for great help, patience, and grace.

Jamie Betts, Jessica Cate (congratulations!), Julie Cranston, Pam Dillon, Angela Hutchins, Travis King, Betty Rich, and Dallas Starke for your heart.

IVORIE

I didn't set out to be an old maid. When I was in my early twenties there was, according to my mother, "still hope for me." But when I got into my late twenties the hope all but left Mother's eyes. "Lord have mercy, Ivorie," she would say. "What is going to happen to you when your pop and I leave this earth?" I was, in her opinion, doomed to a bed-of-nails existence without a man.

Mother had always been fire and sizzle but there was something used up about her the last two years of her life. Her arthritis grew worse; gnarling her small, freckled hand into the shape of a claw and taking care of Pop wore what was left of her away. One afternoon, she came to me in the garden, where she rested that crippled hand atop her cane and looked at me with those sad, cornflower-blue eyes. "What about Lyle Hovitts?"

I nearly toppled the basket of beans I was

picking. "That melon-headed man with the fat stomach and stumpy legs?" I threw my head back and laughed. "Mother! What have I done to you?"

She waved a bony hand in the air and rolled her eyes. "I'm just saying, Ivorie. You're a pretty girl."

I wiped the sweat off my face and squatted back down to my work. "Well, I don't know why every pretty girl in Greene County isn't lined up outside Lyle Hovitts' door. What girl wouldn't want that old, saggy butt crawling into her bed every night?"

"Oh, Lord have mercy, Ivorie! It's too close to Sunday for such talk."

I laughed and tossed another handful of beans into the basket. "You started it, Mother. Lyle Hovitts. I'm surprised you didn't say Garth Landis."

"There's nothing wrong with Garth Landis."

"He's a tall, lanky goon! He's got that sloped nose and those gangly arms with the hairy hands at the end of them. Plus — he must be fifty!"

"He's a fine-looking man."

My gallbladder shook I laughed so hard. "Well, his beauty must be the kind that's magnified by liquor!"

10

"He's tolerable," she said. "Not all men are tolerable, but you could tolerate Garth."

I grabbed my head. "Is that what marriage is, Mother? Tolerating somebody?"

She looked at me like I was a kook. "Well, it has a lot to do with it! If you don't get sick looking at somebody, you're halfway there in tolerating them."

I couldn't even respond to that. She started to hunch down and I waved my hand in the air at her. "Don't get down here. I'll have a world of a time getting you back up. I'll finish these. You just commence to worrying about which sad, lonely buck I need to hook my horns into." And when she leaned her bent, tiny frame over her cane and looked out over the garden, I knew she was doing just that!

Mother was my closest friend. We spent our time working in the garden, canning, cooking, and baking together, and we'd talk about Pop until we were both giggling like girls. We loved sitting down at the table and eating a slice of pound cake with a cup of coffee while we listened to Maxine Harrison read the news on the radio station out of Greenville. We'd shake our heads over the obituaries and talk about the poor, old widow who was left behind, or make a high-pitched noise in our throats on hearing about the birth of a new baby. Mother didn't wear a watch; she didn't need one — she just knew when it was coffee-and-cake time. It didn't matter where we were or what we were doing — if we were stooped over in the garden, Mother would say, "Coffee and cake time," and we would stop our work and sit down to listen to Maxine. I always knew when Mother was thinking she needed a rest with a glass of sweet tea, and she could sense when I needed to pick up a book and hide out on the back porch. I've always been too impatient with myself and others, my expectations of them too high, but Mother just loved people, plain and true, warts and all. Her hope was always cell deep and child simple.

My six brothers are all married with children. By the time I was born (when Mother was forty-two — a miracle anywhere), my oldest brother, Henry, was already settled down with two children. Shoot, at my age Mother had had six of her seven children. Whenever I looked at her and Pop I could hear time speeding by me. Tick: *There's a man!* Tock: *Better grab him!* Tick: *Time's running out!* Tock: *Too late.*

Morgan Hill, Tennessee, is just seventy miles north of Knoxville, but it's as far from the city as it is the ocean, in my opinion.

It's not big enough to be a city or even a town; we're a community — the Morgan Hill community. We've got Walker's Store, which my brother Henry owns, the Langley School Building, the church, and that's it (not exactly a hotbed for available suitors), but I can't imagine living anywhere else. These hills and farmland are home.

Pop served in Africa during the Great War, and while there, he held a piece of ivory in his hand, claiming it to be the prettiest thing he'd ever seen. He brought it home with him and laid it on the chest of drawers in his and Mother's bedroom. Mother held that piece of ivory the night I was born. I didn't come easy. "You about ripped me sideways to Christmas," Mother said. When Mother grasped for the sheets, her friend Nola threw the ivory into her hand to give her something to hold on to. She and Pop named me Sarah Ivorie. I claimed Ivorie as my first name during my second year in school when another girl, a pinched-face, puckered-lip thug was also named Sarah. She was so sour that her cheeks turned red as a plum when she got mad. I told my mother that from there on out I would no longer share the name Sarah with that brutish blob of a girl but would answer only to Ivorie. "Pretty name for a pretty girl,"

Mother said. Imagine the heartbreak when years later that pretty name wasn't attracting a husband.

In the early years, when I was right out of high school, the people in Morgan Hill still held out hope for me: *Which young man do you have your eye on? Have you seen the way that Carl Winters makes over you? Before you know it, you're going to have three or four proposals.* But when I hit twenty-four and was still living at home, it threw the whole community into crisis mode. A distress signal spread throughout it: *Awkward Walker girl doomed to manlessness.* Gasp! I went from resident old maid to queen of the downtrodden parade. There I was, sitting high on my float and just waving and blowing kisses to the sorriest lineup of the lonely and cripple-hearted I've ever seen. The phone rang off the hook. *Have you met my nephew, Lenny? He's the man with dropsy over in Midway. Have you ever met my uncle Lew? His wife died two years ago and he's got a house full of good chil'ren. Have you met Harold over at the Co-op in Morristown? He's that real nice man that works there with the eye patch. Real funny. Nice head of hair.*

For the longest time Ed Popper would visit on Sunday afternoon, bringing three oranges with him. We didn't get oranges too

14

often in Morgan Hill so Ed would pick them up each week when he drove into Knoxville to visit an ailing aunt. Ed was five years older than me with a head as big as a hippopotamus and a face almost as ugly. His stomach rolled over his belt like a sack of cornmeal and his feet always looked freakishly tiny and too narrow to hold up all that weight. We'd sit out on the front porch — Mother, Pop, me, and Ed Popper — and we'd share those oranges and talk about the weather or who died, who was getting ready to die, or who we thought already died, and as I watched orange juice drip down Ed's massive face, I wondered why I couldn't die.

Mother was thrilled with Ed's attention. He grew — these were her words — *some of the prettiest tobacco in Greene County.* Well slide a ring on my finger so I can be Mrs. Pretty Tobacco! Ed visited every Sunday for months and sat with his manure-caked shoes pointed to opposite corners of the porch. All I had to do was take one look at those nasty shoes and my stomach would knot up. I have no idea why he came back as long as he did because I never gave him any reason to believe I wasn't anything other than completely bored. I was as comfortable with him as a frog is in a bottle.

One Sunday, Ed brought a watermelon to

us and I took it from him, marching it inside the well house, where I set it on the floor and then closed the door on it. Ed swayed from foot to foot like an overweight pendulum for a while as Mother groped for something to say, her mouth gaping like a carp. Ed resigned himself to leaving, and Mother rose to her feet. She said, "You didn't offer Ed Popper one slice of his watermelon, and now he'll never long to come here again." If I had known that's what it would take to stop Ed Popper's longing, I would have thrown his fruit in the well house months earlier.

Two years ago, in 1948, when I was twenty-eight and we buried Pop after eighty-two years of living in Morgan Hill, the community gave up on me. Polly Jarvis married Ed Popper, making her Polly Popper, a ridiculous name for a grown woman, and that marriage ended the community's hope to marry me off. People started referring to me as *that poor old thing.* I heard them whispering at church or when I was shopping in Henry's store. "Ivorie just sits down there and takes care of her mother. That poor, old thing, I guess she'll never marry." I laughed out loud at a church picnic when I overheard two women, a cabbage-round-faced one and a skinny, ropy-armed one,

16

mumbling about my plight over a plate of fried chicken. "That poor old thing has never been with a man," Ropy Arms whispered.

"Well, ain't that her good fortune!" Cabbage Face said.

Mother heard people talking, too, and this old-maid business worried her something awful. "Mother, I am happy," I said time and again. "I love my job at the school and I enjoy coming home and working in the garden and spending time with you." She'd look at me with those aging eyes and tree-like wrinkles that branched out from them and try to smile and there we'd stand: me trying to convince her that I was really okay and her not believing a word of it.

Time to time she'd get real quiet and glance up into the hills, the sun landing bright on her face, and say, "Don't live with regret, Ivorie. It's an awful thing."

For the longest time I thought she meant the regret of me not having a man, but one day something struck me on the top part of my brain and I said, "Mother, what regrets do you have?"

Law, she was quiet! A beetle made more noise breathing than she did. She stared up into the hills and finally said, "I have one and it plagues me terrible."

There was something in her voice that I'd never heard, or rather, something *not* in it that I wanted to hear. Her eyes and her mind were someplace I couldn't go. "What is it, Mother?" She didn't answer. "Mother?" That's how we lived out what ended up being the last of her days.

I knew she was tired and grieving. I knew her body was frail and knobbed with bone. What I didn't know was that her heart was weakening and breaking down. I woke up one morning and put the coffee and sausages on like I'd done every morning for years. Like clockwork I would hear the padding of her feet across the wide-planked floors, but that morning the silence stretched from one room to the next and all I heard was the deafening tick, tick, tick of the clock hanging on the kitchen wall. The fire stopped burning and stars fell from the sky. I buried her six months ago, in January, a month before my thirtieth birthday, and on some mornings that time feels long as a mountain's shadow but short as a day. The void she left blows through the house, and sometimes the emptiness chokes me. Death sure can work you over.

The house is quiet now and settled in sadness. On the most silent of nights, when the dark is cold and still, I swear I can hear her shuffling down the hall toward me with the tap, tap, tap of her cane, but when I turn to look, I know it's just me wishing she was here. There's always some maddening noise of emptiness here — the breeze against the windows, the rustle of trees, a creak in the floor or from the roof settling.

Each night I wander the rooms and walk to the table with three legs that sits in the corner of Pop's bedroom and pull the chain on the lamp with the too-heavy white base. The amber globe colors the room in a dull shade of yellow. This furniture is practical, sturdy, like Pop himself, and while I don't particularly like it, it's too sentimental to sell. I reach for the dust rag I keep on the trunk at the end of the bed and polish the knobs on the iron bed that were always too much work to keep shiny. I move to Mother's room with the pretty eyelet curtains in the window and the cherry chest of drawers with the tall paw-footed legs that held her Bible on top. I haven't moved it since she died. I walk to the half-made quilt that lies in the rocking chair by the window. What will happen to it now? Who would take the care that Mother did with each square? What about that whining kitchen door she always complained about? What of the tractor tire that Pop said was bent or the dress without arms that lay on the cedar chest at the end of Mother's bed? Who would finish all this unfinished business and what would be the point?

When I'm busy during the day I don't mind the thoughts or the quiet, but never does the house seem as silent — so much like granite — as when I clunk around the empty rooms at night, when even the hushing noise the breeze makes sounds like a branch of iron against the windows. These rooms hold too many memories — too much laughter and anger and tears and outrageous moments happened here. Some people's lives are imprinted into a home like handprints. Seven children left their imprint here: Grady's robust laugh, James's disappointment, Lyle's gift of mercy, Howard's dry and ironic humor, Caleb's flash of anger, my spirit for fun, and Henry's commonsense way of meeting the day. Seven children were born here and two people left the world here. When Pop lay withering, the smell of his illness clung to the curtains and towels, and when I took a breath it felt as if the house was consuming me. The morning that Mother died, the house didn't feel like death — smells of coffee and sausage saturated the rooms and seeped into the sheets, making her death so jarring to me. All the imprints of life are here, but loneliness is as thick as mud inside these walls.

School let out the second week of May and besides the two weeks at the end of the year and the two weeks prior to the beginning of the year, when I either tie up loose ends or begin my secretarial work in the office and organizing the school library, I get the whole summer off. It's just me and my garden to harvest, berries to pick, Gertie to milk, and this old house to keep running. These first six months of 1950 have gone by as slow as molasses in January; I can't imagine what the rest of summer is going to feel like.

The screen door groans as I open it and I sit out on the back porch, looking out over the garden. Sally runs to me, pushing her shaggy, blond head under my hand. She looks up at me with sorrowful, brown eyes. She misses Mother, too. We are a pitiful twosome but surely things will get better. Or worse. I never know.

THE BOY

The water took him every night. It pulled him down past the slippery vines and gliding fish into the muddy depths below, where the muck and the murk all but shut out the sun. He sank farther, his arms spread and his mouth and eyes open, into the dark waters where nothing stirred, into the still, hazy world of deepness. But before the darkness blinded him, her hand reached in and grabbed his, pulling him up like a bubble rising to the surface and out into the light, where he sucked for air in great, gasping breaths. That was the dream. Each night he'd awake drenched with sweat and clawing for breath, like a man pulled from the sea.

When he awakens tonight, his heart is banging against his ribs and he pulls his knees into his chest, hoping the man can't hear it. Bang, bang, bang! The sound is so loud that the boy covers his ears. When his breathing slows, he lifts his head, watching the man; he is asleep on the cot on the other side of the shack. His pot gut stands as tall as the hills they live in and it hides his face. The boy leans over on his pallet to see the man and notices that his mouth is open and sucking air like a sleeping animal. The boy straightens his pallet on the floor and lies down.

"What are you doing, boy?" The boy lies still and closes his eyes. Moments later he hears the man roll over and begin to snore.

Before the sun rises, the boy slips by the man and pushes open the door. The oaks meet high above him and make the woods as dark as dusk in the early morning. Chickens scatter when he steps off the porch of the shack. He pulls the straps of his overalls over his shoulders and begins to run through the trees and onto the well-worn path. He smells bacon and knows it is wafting out of the stovepipe from the cabin that sits at the edge of the trees. He remembers one time when she took him to that cabin. He was in her arms and a blur of faces surrounded him, one pressing something to his forehead, while another put something under his nose. When he awoke, he was back in the shack and she was stroking his arm. "You'll be better soon," she said, kissing his head.

Two days prior to the nighttime visit to the cabin, he had awakened sick and vomited in the shack. She wasn't there, but out on the hillside pulling up wild onions. The man awoke and slipped on the mess, screaming at the boy to clean it up. He snatched the boy up by his drawers, rubbing his face in the slippery bile. "Clean this slop up!" he screamed, sliding the boy's face through it.

The boy tried to rise to his knees.

The man latched on to his arm and heaved him through the door. "Clean that puke up, you worthless sack of shit!"

The boy's head felt like it was loose on his neck and there was a roar in his chest.

The man picked him up and shoved him headfirst into the rain barrel, the boy's head banging the bottom. His throat and lungs filled as he tried to push up with his hands. The man's voice was muffled through the water. "Clean it up! Clean that shit up!"

The boy's head was smashed again and again on the bottom. Whack. Whack. He sucked in another gulp of water, and fragments of light dimmed with each thud. The light faded and his lungs stopped flapping as he felt himself suspended, bobbing, floating in the barrel.

The air hit his chest like a brick through a window. He strained to see her through the fuzz. She was crying and broken into a thousand pieces. The man lay next to them, the frying pan next to his bleeding head. "You'll be okay. You'll be okay," she murmured, rocking him. "I've got you. He won't hurt you."

As his mind fills with images of her, a new day dawns in the woods. Sunlight reaches like fingers through the trees, and in the same breath the boy feels warmth and then shadow on his back as he runs down the hill, planting his feet first this way and then that to steady his steps. When the cabin is in view at the bottom of the hill, the smell of bacon is stronger and the boy runs faster. It's been three days since he's eaten. The man had made rabbit stew, but the animal was a puny thing, no bigger than a mole, really, and the man shared only a couple of bites.

He runs under the tree with the colored bottles dangling at the end of each limb. "They think evil spirits live in the trees," she had told him. "And on the way out of the tree the spirit gets trapped inside the bottle." She ran her hand through his hair. "Do you believe that?"

He squinted up at her that day and

shrugged.

She tapped one of the pretty green bottles. "Evil's not inside a bottle," she said. "It's too big for that."

The bottles jangle as he lifts his hand above him, ringing them like bells as he runs to the stump and leans against it, panting. He doesn't know how long it has taken him to get here, but the sun has made him sweat. He brushes his arm over his forehead and turns in all directions. Nothing is here. He looks on the ground and inside the hollowed-out tree, but there is no food today. The pot isn't here.

Days after she was buried, he ran as fast as he could and stumbled upon a black pot sitting on this, the biggest stump. He lifted the lid of the pot and discovered two biscuits with sausage in the middle of them. He clutched the pot to his chest and spun on his heels like a trapped felon, but there was no one after him; no one was looking. The boy shoved those biscuits into his mouth and left the pot as he had found it. The pot was there every second or third day and inside he found a fried chicken leg with corn bread and a slice of melon or a pork chop with fat yeast rolls and corn on the cob. He never knew where the food came from but envisioned an angel leaving the pot and then hovering above the treetops to watch him eat. When he was finished he would squint up through the trees flickering light down on him and nod.

This was, in her words, their secret place together. She would tell him stories here and they'd play hide-and-go-seek among these mighty oaks and the big, dead pines that stood around the stump. "How much do I love you?" she asked, every time.

He'd point to the sky and she'd grin.

"To the stars and back. That's right! How much do you love me?"

He looked at a tree. "To that tree and back? That's no more than five feet away!"

He shrieked when she crouched down as if to chase him. He ran out into the dazzling brightness of the hillside and fell, laughing.

She jumped on top of him and held him down. "How much do you love me?"

He giggled and pointed to the sky, holding up two fingers.

"To the stars and back two times?" she asked, hugging him tight. "That's more like it." They sat and looked out over the houses of Morgan Hill in the distance below. "Someday, we'll get out of these hills and live someplace like that."

He looked over at her face; she was sad,

thinking.

"Don't you listen to him. There are good people who live down there."

He watched her face; she was looking beyond Morgan Hill.

She picked up his hand and put it in her lap. "Someday, we'll get out." She kissed his hand and pulled him to her. "I promise."

He slumps down against the stump and listens as a train passes below. He stands and runs out of the trees onto the hillside overlooking Morgan Hill. Clackety, clackety, clack, the train shakes along the rails and he sits on the hill, watching it. Three children run after the train, a white boy and girl and another boy the color of the coffee the man drank each morning. The boy strains to hear what they're saying, but it doesn't matter. They're laughing and carrying on, so he can only imagine that they're happy about the sight of the train, or the way the sun makes them feel after so many days of rain, or maybe because their mothers have promised them a piece of chocolate cake when their chores are through. They keep running behind the train, and the boy stands to his feet, moving toward them. In his mind he can hear the man yelling at him to stay put on the hillside, but her voice shouts over his and urges him to keep running. An hour passes or maybe more before he makes it to the jagged bottom. He grasps the rocky ledge and shimmies his way down onto the grass of the valley. The last time he was this far from the shack he was with her and she was picking buttercups and daisies and sticking them out of the pockets on her dress, the one with the faded blue flowers on it.

He crosses the valley and stops at the creek, watching the water ripple over the protruding rocks. The dream plays out in his mind and he stumbles backward, held fast to the ground as his heart blares like a siren in his ears. He looks to his left and notices that the creek narrows farther down the valley. He runs alongside it and spots a cluster of rocks sticking up from the water, dry and brown as buns. His heart leaps like a horse let out of its stall and he crosses to the other side. He doesn't know what to do now; he feels like a bird freed from its snare but with nowhere to fly. The track rails gleam in the sun, and he reaches down to touch them; they are hot and smooth and he steps on top, teetering as he walks. He stays on the rail closest to the bank and sees the roofs of houses that face the hills where he lives. If anyone is home they won't be able to see him on the track below. He races along the bank and stops at a set of stairs dug out of the earth that leads up the bank. He steps onto the earthen bottom stair and cranes his neck to peek over the top of the embankment. A plain, white house sits in front of him with sheets hanging out to dry. They flap toward him in the breeze like curtains on a windy day, and he leaps up onto the bank and runs behind the sheets into a patch of tomatoes.

He crouches low and listens for any sound. Something wet pushes against his arm and he jumps, turning on it. A dog's yellow body sways with each wag of her tail, and she pushes his arm again, nuzzling her head under his hand. He pets her head and she licks his face, making him smile. A tomato dangles in front of him and he pulls it from the vine, pushing it to his mouth. Red juice drips down his chin, and the dog busies herself cleaning it. A row of onions is next to the tomatoes and the boy pulls one from the ground and peels off the first muddied layer, revealing the slick white head. He gnaws into it and shoves the rest in his mouth. He notices cucumbers on their vines and steps over a row of beans to get to them. His pockets bulge with the cucumber, two more onions, and a handful of peas. The boy looks over his shoulder to make sure no one has seen him and grabs another tomato before dashing down the side of the bank. The dog runs to the top of the embankment and barks, watching him on the rails below.

IVORIE

I throw open the back door, waving my way through the sheets on the line. Sally's down on her front legs with her hind end up in the air, barking. "Sally! Hush that yapping!" She turns to look at me and sniffs my hand before looking back to the tracks to bark some more. "Nothing's there," I say, taking a sheet off the line and folding it. She barks again, and I kick my leg toward her and then grab my back. "Now look what you did! You made me put a hitch in my back." She rubs against my leg and I ignore her. "No point in trying to make up. What's done is done." I fold another sheet and put it in the basket. I head to the house and notice something in the garden. I set the basket down on the steps and walk to my tomato vines. One is broken and dangling like a puppet from the weight of the tomatoes. "Did you do this?" I ask Sally. She lies down and wags her tail. "It's funny how this wasn't like this two hours ago when I was out here working, but the minute I turn my back one of my best-producing vines gets broken." I pick the two drooping tomatoes and snap off the limb, tossing it aside. Sally nudges her head under my hand and I smooth out the yellow fur, brushing away bits of grass and weeds. "You and your making up." I hold on to the tomatoes and pick up the basket of sheets. "Stay out of my garden!"

I hear tires on the gravel driveway and follow the porch around to the front of the house, setting the basket of sheets on one of the cane-backed chairs. I groan when I see the car but throw my hand up in a wave. Davis Carpenter works at the bank in Greenville and he's as bland as the brown suit he's wearing. His face is nice in an aw-shucks kind of way, his eyes are small and gray, and his dishwater-pale hair stands up on his head like a wave. He saunters when he walks and I don't like that. If he's here on business, then he should walk like it. "How are you doing this morning, Miss Walker?" His voice sounds like a rusty gate hinge.

"Fine, Mr. Carpenter. How are you?"

He walks to the porch and smiles into the sun. "It's a beautiful day."

"It is at that," I say, and we stand there

33

looking at each other, wondering who will be the next to say something mind-shattering. I don't know much about Davis, except his father was given to drinking too much and one rainy night the drunken fool climbed on top of the roof to fix a leak and fell to his death. They pulled his body inside the home and drops of water from the ceiling splattered around his feet. Somebody finally put a pot under the drip while they waited for the men to come take him to the funeral home. Davis has a wife somewhere in Greenville and five children, who are probably being raised to be bankers and who have never stepped foot in a crop of tobacco.

"I got another call from Mr. Lewis in Knoxville," Davis says, forging ahead. "And he's ready to move ahead with that service station." He keeps smiling and looks at one of the chairs on the porch, hoping I'll ask him to sit. "All he's waiting on is for somebody to sell him the land."

Mother and Pop told me a few years ago that they were giving me thirty acres of land they owned out at the crossroads. After years of my taking care of them, they wanted me to settle down and raise my family on it. If you drive into Morgan Hill out of Greenville or are coming from Morristown you drive right through the middle of those acres. A man in Knoxville, some Mr. Abel Lewis, with some big something-or-other construction company, wants to buy ten acres of the land and plop what he's calling a service station on it. But I know full well it's a truck stop, plain and simple — a big fancy thing with rows of gas pumps for tractor-trailers and a restaurant and bathrooms with lots of toilets. He says it will be called The Big Q. I don't even know what that means. What sort of name is that? He claims there isn't another service station for 120 miles, and the crossroads sit right off the highway, so Mother and Pop's land is the ideal spot for The Big Q. Mr. Lewis has asked Davis and the bank to handle all the financing and such. That land has been in our family for fifty years. Pop and Mother would never have allowed such a thing to be built on that beautiful acreage.

"I'm not interested in selling," I say, smiling as wide as Davis is. I even raise my eyebrows to make my face look extra bright. "Even if I was, I wouldn't sell it so something called The Big Q could be built. That's an absurd name."

"*Q* is for *quick,* Miss Walker." I look at him. "The word *quick* starts with *Q.*"

"I know that."

He clears his throat, readying it for the big explanation. He's grinning like a cat. "It's short for 'The Big Quick.' "

I bore my eyes into his. "The Big Quick, Mr. Carpenter? That sounds indecent and I hate it even more."

He's really sweating now and that smile is getting thin. "All he needs is ten acres, Miss Walker. That leaves you twenty acres to keep."

"I'm aware of the simple math. I'm not interested in selling." Davis's smile turns into a fixed, straight line across his face.

"Miss Walker. I urge you to think about this because this deal would offer you a great deal of money."

I cross my arms. Water beads have lined up on his upper lip but he doesn't brush them away. "How much today?"

"One hundred an acre."

I whistle and throw my head back. "One hundred dollars an acre. Well, where do I sign?"

"Is that sarcasm, Miss Walker? Because I'm never sure."

I step toward him. "Yes, it's sarcasm, Mr. Carpenter. You know and I know that if you were dealing with my pop or my brothers, your client, Mr. Big Q, would be offering three times that. My answer is still no."

He stands there gawking at me with his wet lip and small eyes and looks at his shoes. His shoes! "Are we done, Miss Walker, because I never . . ."

"We are most assuredly done, Mr. Carpenter."

Several days later I get up before sunrise and slip on one of the dresses Mother made me from the flour sacks. When I was younger I worked in overalls but discovered somewhere along the way that dresses are cooler. I open the screen door, the one with the loud, complaining creak that Mother fussed about so much, and head to the barn to milk the cow. I wish I could sleep later but when you've lived with old people your whole life you take on their schedule as natural as breathing. Since Mother and Pop died I've been taking most of the milk to my brother Henry to sell at the store. One person does not need a cow but we've had Gertie so long that I can't see getting rid of her. I make a few extra dollars a week selling the milk and the extra eggs from the chickens, so it works out fine. By the time I finish milking each morning and eat a bowl of cereal or a few sausage biscuits, the sun's starting to rise and I head to the garden.

I spent most of my childhood working

with my brothers, planting and cutting tobacco, cleaning out stalls in the barn, milking cows, and pulling weeds in the garden. Even now the muscles in my arms and thighs are rounded and firm from the heavy work. When we were tiny, I'd fall into bed with my two youngest brothers, our wiry bodies tangled together like the clematis vines that grew on the fence, exhausted from the day's work.

I hoe and weed and pick Japanese beetles off the tomato plants before picking a peck of peas and gathering the cucumbers. I'll make some pickles before the kitchen gets too hot. Sally runs alongside the garden's edge and lies down in the grass. "You *better* stay there," I tell her. "You come over here and break down my tomato vines again and it's out you go." Mother said I talked to the dog too much, but there's always something in those large, deep eyes that ask, "How's your day? Where're you going? What are you doing now?" and I have to answer her.

Heat leaks down my back, and I pull a handkerchief out of my pocket and wipe my neck. "You want some pickles, Sally?" She wags her tail and I pat her hard and firm on the side. "If I'd asked if you wanted arsenic you would have gotten just as excited." Without looking at my watch, I know it's coffee-and-cake time, and the memories of walking to the house with Mother at this time feel like a bruise behind my ribs. Sally runs alongside me, and I set the basket of cucumbers on the porch. I wash my hands in the kitchen sink, and since it's too hot for coffee and I don't have any cake, I pour a glass of iced tea before turning on the radio. Maxine Harrison is giving the hog report, which will be followed by the obituaries. The day after Mother died, I stood in the kitchen and listened as Maxine read the words I had written about Mother's death, words I thought would not strike me hard because I am not easily given over to emotion. I listened, waiting for Maxine to say Mother's name, and as soon as she said Regina Latham Walker, the air was sucked clean out of my lungs and I crumpled onto the table. Mother's life was reduced to five hundred words on a plain, white sheet of paper, and in moments Maxine had moved on to the next notice.

I grab Mother's apron, the one made from the sugar sack with the large pocket in the front, and reach for a knife out of the drawer. My slop bucket is on the porch, and I sit in one of the ladder-backed chairs, pulling the bucket between my legs and letting the cucumber peels drop into it. They pile in there together like slippery green fish. Sally sticks her head inside the bucket and I push her away with the back of my hand. I listen as Maxine reads the last of the obituaries, a man from Greenville who died at sixty-six, and I think about all the sad-hearted people who are just wandering around today, wondering what to do with themselves. Maybe they were making pickles they didn't need.

I eat crackers with peanut butter on them for dinner, along with a bowl full of blackberries I picked on the other side of the railroad tracks. Mother would disapprove. "Crackers don't make a dinner," she'd say. "You need something to strengthen you." She always said I needed something to strengthen me. I must have come across to her as fragile as a daisy in the wind because she was always plying me with food. "Put some lemon in that tea," she'd say. "It'll strengthen you." Today she would look at my bowl of berries and say, "Pour some cream over those blackberries. It'll strengthen you." I sip my tea and grimace. When the war was over, Mother and I celebrated the end of rationing with sugary cakes and pies and tea so sweet it set your teeth on edge when you drank it. I've got too much sugar in it this time but no one but me is here to complain.

After dinner, I leave my plate at the side of the sink and set the eight pints of pickles I made into the peck basket. I open the door to the well house and set them right next to the remaining four quarts from last year. There's no need to can in quart sizes anymore. I reach for two quarts to take to Henry and Loretta before straightening the rows of tomatoes, beans, pork, relish, and fish. The fish was Pop's idea. I hold a quart of it in my hand and wonder again what in the world I'm going to do with canned fish. Three quarts of it join the pickles for Henry and Loretta. I fluff the dainty, white curtains with the sunflowers on them and pull them open at the window before closing the door behind me.

The grass is long, so I walk to the barn for the push mower. The blades whir round and round and I watch as slender, green grass shoots out from the silvery whirling edge and onto my legs and shoes. It doesn't take long to mow, about an hour by the time I walk around the house and trim up around the trees. The sweat streams down my chest and back. My face is wet and I wipe it but by the time I rub the handkerchief across my neck my face is wet again. I push the handkerchief deep into my eyes to stop the flow of tears. I shove the handkerchief into my dress pocket and push the mower with all my might, determined to wear myself out. I push it back and forth with all the strength and power I have and my heart throbs like a robin with a broken wing, beating its one good wing to get off the ground. I scream into those spinning blades but I may as well be shouting into a windstorm. I sit in the backyard, exhausted, hot, and sopping wet. Sally sits down next to me, looking out over the tracks.

At eight thirty I put down the book I'm reading and get ready for bed. I brush my teeth and rinse my face and take a drink of water with lemon in it to strengthen me before I lift the covers. I sleep in the same iron bed I slept in as a girl but use Mother's faded blue-and-yellow–checkered quilt. For as long as I can remember it covered her bed but I pull it up under my chin every night now.

As I drift, I hear Sally start to bark and I groan. "Don't make me get out of bed," I say to no one. She barks again but then is done with it. Even if she hadn't stopped, I'm too tired to get up anyway.

THE BOY

The dog stops barking when the boy runs to her side in the garden and pats her head. She licks his hand and he leans his head onto hers, squeezing her neck. She follows the boy to a row where he plucks a small, round tomato from the vine. He sits on the ground and eats it while the dog licks the juice from his hand. He strains to see but the moon is behind a cloud. The boy crawls to the cucumbers and feels for one; the vines have been picked clean. The dog nudges her nose into his backside and he tumbles forward into the dirt. The dog leaps onto his head and the boy swats her muzzle. She jumps back and forth and lets out a playful yelp. He puts his finger to his lips and strokes her neck. He heads for the onions and pulls up three before picking two handfuls of peas that he shoves into his pockets.

He lies down between the rows of peas

and looks up, watching clouds slip past the moon. The wind whispers and shakes the top of the oak tree next to the garden. Lightning bugs flicker above him and he reaches out a finger to touch one. He closes his eyes and lets the wind sneak over him while crickets tick softly in the grass. The dog lies down near the top of his head and he reaches his arms up, letting them drape over her. He knows he should be making the trek back to the shack but somewhere — in the silence in his brain or the emptiness in his stomach — he realizes the liquor won't give the man up until morning, so he rests his head into the dog's side and smiles, eating one of the onions.

He remembers how she used to love onions. She would fry them with squash and zucchini and set them on a plate with a thick piece of corn bread. She'd talk to him while they ate together and tell him about her mother and father and living in Florida as a girl. "Florida's way down here," she said, using the skillet of corn bread as a map. She ran her finger along the edge of the corn bread. "And the ocean is right here. Someday I'll take you there. Would you like that?"

The boy nodded and took another bite of the squash and onions.

44

"Maybe we'll find Mama and Daddy." She got quiet and ate the rest of her meal in silence. That was her way sometimes. The man was never quiet. His mouth flapped off its hinges and when he was sipping the white lightning there was no shutting him up.

After a day of swilling the lightning and before the man could get his hands on the boy, she'd run with him deep into the woods, to their secret place, and tell him about swimming in the ocean or of a flying boy named Peter Pan who refused to grow up and played with Indians, mermaids, and fairies. The boy would touch her swollen eye or bloody mouth and she'd make like they didn't hurt.

"Right as rain," she'd say, blood cracking around her lips.

He searched her eyes one day, the great fear of who he was clamping down hard in his chest.

Her eyes started to water and she worked hard at a smile, holding his face in her hands. "You're not like him." She wrapped her arms around him and tapped his chest. "You've got the light of the world right here." When it was dark, she carried him back to the shack and lay down next to him on the floor, whispering his name as he fell asleep.

The dog shakes and the boy bolts upright, startled. The sun slants on the hills and he reaches for another tomato before running toward the embankment. A heaping bucket of blackberries catches his eye and he runs to the porch, crouching low as he scoops out two handfuls and opens his pockets. He is careful as he jumps down the bank to the tracks. The dog barks but the boy runs away, waving and pulling out a blackberry to eat. He is breathless as he runs to the creek, stopping at the sight of a girl older than him with a plain face and short brown hair.

"Hey," she says. "Who are you?"

He steps over the dry rocks in the creek to cross to the other side and turns to look back at her.

"What's your name?" she asks.

He watches her from across the creek.

"Mama says it's rude not to answer somebody when they talk to you unless it's a stranger who's going to hit you over the head." She throws a rock into the creek. "I'm a stranger but I'm not planning to hit you over the head. So, what's your name?"

He turns and heads to the rocky ledge, stopping at the base of it. He can hear the girl behind him yelling at him about being

46

rude and something about taking a bath.

He pulls a few blackberries from his pocket and eats them, rubbing his hands on his overalls but the purple stain sinks farther into the tiny circles on his fingertips. Holding the tomato in one hand, he shimmies up the rocky ledge and onto the hillside and stops at the sound of a whistle in the distance. He waits for the freight train to pass; it's the closest thing to a parade he's ever seen, with those tiny gray-and-rust-colored cars all lined up together and moving below him like a dream. The whistle blows again and he waves like a man flagging down a plane in the desert. Both arms flap crisscross over his head and a look of rapture shines on his face as the cars clack their way through Morgan Hill. He watches till the train's out of sight, then he turns back to the hillside.

It will take him most of the morning to make his way to the shack, so he begins to run, holding the tomato first in one hand and then the other. Every step stirs up a little life on the hill — a swarm of bugs or a rabbit racing for cover. He reaches the edge of the woods and stops. The trees are still and cool this morning, holding their secrets among them. A scent of breakfast reaches him on the western breeze and he knows the cabin on the edge of the woods is bristling with morning. He takes off fast this time, the roots and limbs tearing at his bare feet, and his heart leaps like a fawn in high grass but he doesn't stop. When he sees the stump, he glances for the pot and keeps moving when he sees it's not there. Up, up, up he climbs and runs, panting as he goes. The shack is quiet as he approaches. Hushed and cautious, he creeps onto the planks of the porch and peers through the dirty glass. The great, mounding stomach moves up and down, just inside the window.

He fetches the wood and starts the fire before grabbing hold of the earthen door's heavy ring. He pulls with all his might and opens the cellar, stepping down into the darkened pit. The morning light is enough for him to see the hanging slab of pork and he cuts off a thick slice, grabbing three potatoes on his way out. He lowers the door flat onto the ground again and throws the pork into a skillet over the fire. It sizzles and pops, and he takes the cork out of the jug and pours water into a pot, filling the metal basket with black coffee grounds. He lowers the basket into the pot and puts it over the fire. The skillet swims with hot, splattering grease and he lines the bottom with sliced potatoes, covering them with salt. He sits and watches the grease bubble over the potatoes, noiseless in his work. He stands to flip the potatoes when the shack door opens. He busies himself with fetching a pewter mug and a plate.

The man watches, pulling the straps of the overalls over his shoulders. "Where were you, boy?"

The boy doesn't answer but fills the plate with the meat and potatoes.

The man doesn't move. "I said where were you?"

The boy waves his arm toward the trees.

"Out here?" the man asks, moving toward the fire.

The boy nods, handing him the plate.

The man grabs his arm and the plate shakes at the end of it. "You come to me tonight, you hear?"

The boy doesn't respond.

"You only bleed a little. That should stop." He takes the plate of food and the boy pours coffee into the heavy cup, handing it to him. The man sits on the cane-bottomed chair and lets the grease drip down his chin.

The boy looks out into the woods and the man eyes him.

"You be back here by nightfall or I'll make sure you bleed real good."

The boy's heart throbs in his throat and

he turns to run. The man yells into the trees but his voice is drowned out by the sound of her voice in his mind telling him to run and never stop.

He races to the fallen trees and crawls on his belly through the narrow opening in the hillside. She had found this cave for him. Inside, he sits up and the sound of his breath echoes around him. He feels something warm and looks down; his pants are soaked. He scrambles out of his overalls and two blackberries fall out of the pocket into the yellow puddle.

IVORIE

I reach for the bucket of blackberries on the back porch and stop when I see several on the stairs. Two more are on the stone walkway leading to the embankment. I pick up the bucket and notice it's not topped off as it was the day before when I picked the berries. Sally runs from around the house and wags her tail good morning. "Did you eat these?" I ask her. She yelps at me to come play and I pick up the stray berries, putting them back in the bucket. "What has gotten into you?" She circles me and I groan out loud when I look into the garden. I put the bucket down hard on the grass and march into my cucumber patch. "What happened out here?" Two vines are smashed down and broken in several places, another tomato vine is snapped clean off, and pea pods are strewn across the ground. Anger fills my chest and I stomp my foot. "All this work for nothing!" Sally lies on the grass and I look at her. "I know it's not you, Sally Dog. I've never known you to open pea pods before." I storm out of the garden to the barn.

I swing open the feed-room door to look for Pop's animal traps. The room is full of old wagon wheels, rusty hoes, frayed ropes, rotting fence pieces, and stray machinery parts that I'll never figure out what they belong to in my lifetime. I pick up some contraption that looks like shackles from a slaving ship and put it back down. A rusty, maniacal-looking trap clangs when I pick it up and I set it back down on the shelf. The chickens scatter out of my way as I hurry to the truck. I hear the rumble of an engine behind me and turn to see Pete Fletcher pulling up to the house. I squint, looking into the passenger-side window. "Morning, Pete!"

He closes his door and steps around to the back of the truck. "Morning, Ivorie. I'm headed to Wade's house. He's got a sick tractor. Thought I'd stop by and check on you." Pete's been working on cars, trucks, and tractors for as long as I can remember around here. When our preacher of thirty years retired, the congregation asked Pete if he'd step in till another preacher came. Three years later, Pete is still bringing a

Sunday message the best he knows how to the Morgan Hill Baptist Church. He's the first to say he's not a preacher and that's the truth, but he's got heart and I suppose that's why nobody at the church has moved too quick in finding a replacement for him. "You doing all right? I've missed seeing you on Sundays." I tried going to church after Mother died but could take only so many sorrowful, hound-dog looks and lopsided comments about peace on the other side. I felt suffocated and swallowed up and I haven't stepped foot in the church in six months. And, if the truth be told, I've been more than a little mad at the Lord for not doing more to keep Mother here.

"I'll be back someday, Pete," I say, propping my hand over my eyes to block the sun. "Mother would be all over me, wouldn't she?"

He laughs and kicks the gravel with the toe of his work boot. "I suspect she would but that's what mothers do." He looks at me and I know he wishes he could say something else, but Pete's never been good with words, so we both look tongue-tied at the barn before I launch us into something new altogether.

"Something's tearing up my garden," I

say, pointing in the general direction of the crime.

Pete walks with me. " 'Coon?"

"I don't know. The vines are broken, peas are shelled, and the cucumbers pulled clean off."

Pete squats down and surveys the damage. "Well, I'll be," he says. "We had something in our garden a few years back and we never could trap it or see it. We never had any idea what it was. Finally, the kids called it a *jumabu*."

"What's a jumabu?"

"It's not anything," he says, lifting his cap to scratch his head. "Just a made-up name the kids came up with for something that's not there."

"Oh, it's there," I say, picking up a handful of the pea shells and throwing them. "And come hell or high water, I'm going to catch it."

I walk Pete back to his truck and he climbs inside, fumbling for the keys in a clumsy, word-groping way before he talks to the steering wheel. "Looking forward to having you back in church when you're ready, Ivorie."

"Thank you, Pete," I say, meaning it. I wave as he backs up and turns around and I slide into my truck.

Sally runs down the driveway after me and then jumps into the truck bed before I turn onto the road and head to Walker's, Henry's store. Henry is the only one of my brothers left in these parts; all the others married and scattered across Tennessee, Kentucky, and Alabama for work. Jerry Cleats is pumping gas into his truck when I pull into a space at Walker's. Jerry's wife, LouAnn, sits in the truck, waiting, and I holler out to her but she doesn't wave. Maybe she doesn't hear me or maybe her mind is off someplace safe and cool where the colors are golden and words are pure. "Your hair looks real pretty, LouAnn," I say, taking another stab at reaching her. Her mouth turns up in a weak, barely there smile. When you've been called a dog your whole life it's hard to believe you're a duck, let alone a swan. She waves as Jerry pulls away and I close the truck door. Sally jumps out of the truck bed and runs onto the porch of the store, sniffing for peanuts or bits of sausage from somebody's biscuit.

My brother Henry has owned this store longer than I can remember. He and his first wife, Edith, ran it together until she died, when I was twelve. He married Loretta when I was seventeen; his oldest son was nineteen at the time and already had a baby up on his shoulders. Old and young men come to Henry's every day to smoke their pipes or roll their cigarettes and drink Loretta's strong-enough-to-float-iron coffee she keeps on the stove in the wintertime or an Orange Crush or Co-Cola from the soda pop machine in the summer, while they talk about their crops, hog reports, the weather that needs to change, or their women who won't. Some of them have been loafing here at the store for so many years that the chairs on the front porch hold the shape of their bony or bulbous butts. Mother always said that women don't have the time to loaf around the store like men do because women literally *do not have* the time. Nothing in this world rushes me back to childhood quicker than walking through the door at Henry's and breathing in the smells of bologna, cheese, onions, chicken feed, great giant pickles, coffee, and huge jars of candy on the countertop.

I nod at Clayton, Gabbie, and Haze, three old codgers who have been loafing here longer than I've been alive. George Coley steps out of the store holding a brown sack of groceries as I reach for the door. George is only two years older than me but his wife died nine years ago, when she was twenty-four, creating awful pressure on the community to bring George and me together in marital harmony. Mother mentioned him a couple of times but he lives, works, and goes to church in Cortland so I rarely see him. He's a fine-enough-looking man in a sensible way with a full head of short-cropped brown hair and skin as brown as biscuits. The gossip has always been that George has a woman somewhere, but nobody's ever seen her. I guess people can't fathom that the poor man just might want to be alone in his grief a while longer before marrying again, so they made up some invisible woman for him.

The last time I saw George was three weeks ago at the community dance at the schoolhouse. I stood with Henry and Loretta, and he talked with a handful of farmers across the gymnasium. Out of pity or great boredom, Holt Oxman asked me to dance. Everybody calls Holt *Ox* (though he isn't the size of an ox but rather slight and slim wristed) except me. I think Ox is a buffoonish name. He's close to fifty and owns a dairy farm at the end of the county road. Women don't bother with much make-up in Morgan Hill, but his wife, Avis, paints herself something terrible in the face, giving the impression she's always embarrassed or is, at the very least, sick with fever. Avis is a round-hipped, discontented woman with bow-tie lips, blond hair the texture of straw, and a firecracker laugh. She has a way of looking at everybody as if she's chewing on lemons. She's as full of hot air as one of those excursion balloons and, on most days, is probably a fine mother to their three children but not a very good wife. They make an oddball pairing: the farmer and the hot-air balloon.

Poor Holt probably knew his wife wouldn't dance with him so he offered his hand to the resident old maid. Holt had been helping me plow the garden since Pop died. He was always ready to help Mother and me any way he could.

"George Coley seems like a good man," Holt said.

"I suppose," I said, pretending not to notice George watching us dance.

"I believe he might be thinking the same thing about you," Holt said, grinning at me.

I felt myself getting hot and rolled my eyes. "Good Lord, Holt! Don't tell me you're taking over where Mother left off."

He laughed and twirled me around the floor. I saw George eyeing us but he never cut in or asked for a dance. Before I knew it, it was time to leave and that was that.

"Hey, Ivorie," George says. The shock of

pleasure that the sound of my name makes when it passes through his lips stops me. He looks at me, and when he smiles, my stomach twitches.

I'm aware of my mess of hair and push on it with the palms of my hands, pulling it into a tighter ponytail. "Mornin', George. What have you been up to?"

"Farming. Mending my fence." He smiles and my stomach trembles again. Lord have mercy! What is wrong with me? I've always thought George was as thrilling as oatmeal; yet here I stand with a knot in my stomach. Something about him is changed today, or am I the one who's changed? "I've been meaning to swing by your place. I've got blueberries coming in and I thought maybe you'd like them."

I feel some of the old coots on the porch looking at and listening to us. "I'd like them, George. Thank you." I can't put on a show for the lazy bones sitting here any longer and slide past George. "I'll be seeing you, George."

The screen door screeches as I enter and Henry's face opens in a grin. Tiny lines in the shape of a bird's foot crinkle in the center of his brows and several strands of his thinning hair stand on top of his head like sprouts. "Well, there's my sister, Sarah

Ivorie, on this bright, spring morning."
Henry is the only family member who still
calls me Sarah and I let him get away with
it.

Holt and Avis Oxman are ringing out at
the counter. "Morning, Holt," I say. "Hi,
Avis. How are you doing?"

"Fine," she says. Avis says *fine* the way
some people might say *fungus* or *cause of
death.*

"Henry," I say, grabbing a loaf of white
bread from the shelf. "Something is tearing
apart my garden."

"Maybe it's Sally."

"It's not Sally," I say, from the refrigerated case. I reach in and grab a package of
bacon, throwing it onto the counter. "But
she is acting weird. She's barking her fool
head off lately."

"Well, that is weird," he says. "A barking
dog." Loretta cackles as she wraps a pound
of cheese in white paper for Avis.

I ignore him. "Pea pods are strewn out
everywhere. This morning my berries were
lining the path to the tracks." I pick up a
loaf of bread and walk to the counter, opening up the jar of red jawbreakers. I pull one
out and pop it into my mouth.

"Sounds like 'coons," Holt says. "They
get into my bull feed and tear through my

60

barn something fierce."

"I need a trap," I say.

Henry rings up my items and puts them in a brown sack. "Is this what you're living on? Bread, bacon, and jawbreakers?" I give him my best bothered look and sigh, waiting. "Pop's got all sorts of traps out there."

My eyes pop out at him. "From 1862! I can't tell which way is up on those things. Do you have one I can borrow?"

"Live or killing?"

I hand him some money. "I don't want to love on it, Henry."

The cash register drawer dings open and Henry hands me my change. "I'll bring it out to you this afternoon."

"I need it now," I say, grabbing the sack.

He leans on the counter and scratches his head. "Now what animal do you know that goes foraging through a garden in the middle of the day?"

I pick up the sack and move the jaw-breaker to the other side of my mouth. "Fine. I'll be home making blackberry jelly. You all want some?" I don't give Henry or Loretta time to answer. "I'll make you some. I've got some pickles and fish for you, too." I look at Holt and Avis. "You want some?"

Avis pinches her brows together like she's trying to figure out what I said. "I'd love some pickles," Holt says, and Avis rolls her eyes. "I've got a few traps, too, if you need them."

"I might," I say, swinging open the door.

Loretta reaches under the counter and hands something to me. Her fox-colored hair is cropped short and rings her head in small waves. "I forgot. A woman traveling through left this here with me and I thought you'd like it." It's the *Redbook* magazine. "It's got an article in there about Vivien Leigh I thought you'd like to read." Henry's laugh sounds like a car engine sputtering. "Or are you still mad at her?" Loretta asks.

I've seen one picture show in my life. When *Gone with the Wind* came to the Greenville moving-picture house in '39, I went with a car full of girlfriends and waited in line for thirty minutes to get inside the building. As soon as Scarlett opened her mouth I felt a roaring in my head like carpenter bees buzzing. "We don't sound like that," I hissed to anybody in my row who would listen.

"It takes place in Atlanta," BeBe Land said.

"Well, I don't know anybody from Atlanta who talks like that!" I hissed back.

"Who do you know from Atlanta?" she asked, keeping her voice low.

I didn't know anybody from Atlanta. "Just hush up," I said. I was so aggravated by that dripping southern accent that I swore off moving pictures and Miss Vivien Leigh from that time forward.

I snatch the magazine from Loretta. "I don't have anything against Vivien Leigh or her kind. But if she does another movie set in the South I hope they put somebody else in it who knows how we talk."

Henry shakes his head. "An eleven-year grudge against an innocent woman. Woe to the rest of us who are guilty of not talking good on a daily basis."

Loretta cackles again and I give Henry a final, searing look. "Don't forget to bring me that trap."

A cross breeze blows through the kitchen as I squeeze the warm berries in cheesecloth; the dark purple juice laps over my fingers and into the pot. The clock ticks as loud as a bomb behind me and I brush beads of sweat off my forehead with my arm. I bear down on the cheesecloth and squeeze the blackberry juice into the pot till my arms shake. Drip, drip, drip. Tock, tock, tock. Why in the world did Pop buy such a deafening clock? Moisture dribbles down the side of my face and I put down the bulging cheesecloth and rinse my hands, grabbing the towel. I push it into my face and the clock drums away behind me, pounding in my head.

I reach for the sugar and scoop it into the pot, stirring it into the dark purply blue liquid. While the juice heats, I open the *Redbook* magazine on the counter, stirring with one hand and flipping pages with the other. We don't get magazines in Morgan Hill; if we get the notion to read about Miss Vivien Leigh or how to make a roast, we have to drive into Greenville to buy a magazine such as this. Staring out at me is a woman wearing a turned-up smile, her teeth lined up pretty and straight like fence posts. The neck of her dress stands up in a white ruffly wave, the skirt flares out, and the sleeves slide just below the elbow, accenting her thin wrists and slender fingers. She's holding a refrigerator door open and has her high-heeled foot turned at an angle. I wonder if she knows how to cook anything she pulls out of that Frigidaire or if she keeps smiling like that when the clock on the wall behind her sounds like it's about to explode. Tick, tick, tick. I wonder what it's like there in her Frigidaire world. Tock, tock, tock. Silence like a cloud surrounds this place except for that clock! I use the dish towel to sop up the sweat racing down my cheek. The juice begins to boil and I keep stirring, keep thinking about happy Refrigerator Lady and her Frigidaire world.

I didn't think this much when Mother and Pop were here but now the day stretches out in front of me like the Tennessee River itself. Even when Pop was dying the house still hummed with life and expectation, but I've resigned myself to a rhythm of lonesomeness and gloom. There's something beneath my skin that annoys and troubles me. Tick, tick, tick. I swipe my forehead with the dish towel. Tock, tock, tock. Mother's presence always generated a sense of calm and well-being that I lack on my own. Even Refrigerator Lady has more calm than I do. I see it right there in her bright eyes and toothy smile. Tick, tick — I fling myself at the clock like a hawk swooping down on a chick and yank it off the wall, throwing it out the door.

I shove my hands into my dress pockets and sit on the porch, resting my head against the house. My mind wanders to George Coley and cooking gravy and biscuits for him. I'm wearing Refrigerator Lady's dress and my Frigidaire is sparkling and neat as a pin, like hers. Although it's morning, George's breath is sweet, like honeysuckle, and he smells like soap and shaving cream. We kiss in front of the open Frigidaire and the thought of it creates some sort of quivering sensation that circulates through my body. "Great Lordy day! What am I doing?" I say aloud. I guess when Mother and Pop were here I was too busy to poke around my insides and now that they're gone I'm afraid to — too dark and scary. It's far too easy to tote around a pocketbook of virtues when people are around but the truth always claws its way out in silence. This business of quiet and aloneness is working me through and through. "The mind can be an awful thing, Sally." She licks her paw and ignores me.

When Henry gets here I'm sitting on the porch shelling peas and the jelly jars are lined up pretty as can be across the kitchen counter, the jelly sparkling like wine. He reaches for the trap out of his truck bed and lets it dangle at his side as he makes his way through the yard, eyeing the clock.

"Confounded thing wouldn't stop ticking," I say, watching him.

His whiskers make a scratching sound when he touches them. "Yeah, a clock ought not to do that." He sets the trap in the grass and peers in through the screen door, whistling through his teeth. "How many pints of jelly do you have in there?"

"Sixteen," I say with the serenity of Refrigerator Lady. "I picked some more berries this afternoon."

He sits down and looks at me. "It's hotter than blue blazes out here." I nod. "It must be close to ninety. What does that make it in the kitchen?"

"Two hundred and ten."

He runs his shirtsleeve over his face. "What in the world are you doing running that stove in the heat of the day?"

I throw a handful of peas into the pot and glance over at him. "The berries were ready. It needed to be done." He stands and leans against the porch railing. "Davis was here again."

"Is he offering any more money?"

I shake my head. "Same old song and dance. Hundred dollars an acre."

"What'd you tell him?"

"I'm not interested in selling Mother and Pop's land."

He crosses his arms and makes a popping noise with his mouth that annoys me. "It's no longer Mother and Pop's land." I look at him. "It's your land to do with what you want. You took care of them all your life. They gave it to you years ago. It's yours. If you sell it . . ." I open my mouth and he throws up his hand. "Before you get riled up, let me finish. If you sell it you could use that money and get something smaller." My voice catches high in my throat but I can't speak. I just sit with my mouth flopping wide like a catfish on a sandy bank. "We've talked about this before . . ."

I won't let him finish. "And there's no need to talk about it again, Henry. Mother and Pop would never want that land to —"

He interrupts me. "Mother and Pop are not here! This place is too much for you." I shake my head. "You're clanging around down here in a three-bedroom house and bumping into shadows every which way you turn." He points to the clock. "And now you're beating up clocks."

"It didn't work right," I say, shelling the last of the peas and stepping inside the kitchen.

"That's right," he says, following me. "It ticks."

"Too loud," I say, putting several pints of jelly into a brown sack.

"It never was loud before."

I hand him the sack of jelly and fill another one with the pickles and fish I had brought in from the well house. "What about that trap?"

Henry sighs and pushes open the screen door. It moans and Henry stops to look at it. "I can fix this."

"I don't want it fixed," I say, banging it shut behind me.

He shakes his head; I can tell he's holding his tongue as he picks up the trap. "I'm going to set this thing but you stay away from it. It'll clamp down so hard it'll cripple you. You call me when you trap something and I'll come out for it." I nod and follow him out to the garden. He looks around. "Where do you want it?" I point to my tomatoes and Henry moves to them, scanning the ground. "You found these peas like this?"

"This morning," I say. "And the cucumber vines were broken and ruined."

He leans down and picks up some pea shells. "I can't figure out what sort of animal would shell a pea!" he says, holding the broken pods in his hand.

THE BOY

He rests against the embankment of the woman's house, watching heavy, silver clouds glide across the sky, and waits for the sun to drop below the trees on the hillside. He peers over the top, looking for the dog, but can't see her. In the escaping light he races up the bank to the garden's edge. He picks two tomatoes and feels the warm, familiar nose press into his hand. He smiles at the dog and leans his head on hers, seeing something strange and shiny on the ground. Stepping closer, he holds the dog back. She crouches down to play and the boy leaps out of the garden, waving her toward him. He sits on the grass, holding the dog's neck. Insects buzz softly around him. The dog leans down on her front legs and burrows her nose under his leg, urging him up. She leaps toward the garden and the boy lunges for her. She runs into the garden and something like grapes lodge in the boy's throat. He bangs his hands together to get her attention and runs under the oak tree, searching the ground. Reaching above him, he pulls a dead branch from the tree and runs for the garden, lunging the branch into the metal teeth of the thing. He bears down and the snapping sound makes him flinch. He picks up the metal jaws and flings them over the side of the embankment before he races down the earthen stairs.

The dog follows and the boy shoos her away, pointing up the bank. She runs after him and he grabs the fur on her neck, turning her toward the house. She lifts a paw and bats it in the air. The boy walks toward the house and urges her to go up the embankment. She barks and the boy sits on the ground, pressing his finger to his lips. The dog barks again and the boy pats his thighs. She runs to him and pushes her head under his chin. He leans back onto the bank and she lies down, resting her head in his lap. The trees are thick and still and covered in pitch on the hillside. The man is up there waiting. Rain as warm as bathwater begins to fall and the boy lifts his face.

"Sally!" The dog jerks her head up and the boy holds his breath. "Sally!" She bounds up the embankment. "Don't you have the sense to get in out of the rain? Get up here on the porch."

The boy creeps up the stairs and holds on to the vines that trail down like waterfalls over the bank. A woman sits on the stairs of the porch, petting the dog's head. She has long brown hair and a face like his mother used to have, soft and pretty. "I thought you knew when to come in from the rain. What were you doing down on those tracks? You know I've told you those trains will smash you flat as a penny. Then what would I do?" She pounds the dog's side. "Huh? What would I do without Sally Dog?" The dog rests her head in the woman's lap and the woman begins to hum. The humming turns into a song, one the boy has never heard before, and he presses closer to the top of the embankment to hear. Her voice is as clean and pure as the water that's splashing on his shoulders.

He hugs himself tighter to the stairs, listening; he is cocooned and unseen here and something slips an inch or so beneath his skin. As he watches, a sadness like the sun flickering out at the end of the day settles over him. Without knowing, the woman and the dog exclude him, making his heart sore at the sight of them, aching as if that streak of lightning above him has entered his chest and is burning it up.

He lowers his foot to the ground and moves like a shadow down the tracks, slick with rain. Clouds cover the moon and the boy keeps his feet on the tracks, careful as he steps. He reaches the creek and stops. Hard drops of rain slap the top of the water and the boy's heart pitches up to his throat. He searches with his toes for the protruding rocks but he can't find them. He looks up toward the black veil of trees on the hillside. Somewhere up in there the man is drinking. If the boy strains his ear, he thinks he can hear the man yelling for him. The water moves in front of him and the boy backs away, falling to the ground when he nearly trips over something soft. The dog's nose burrows under his hand and the boy smiles, hugging the shaggy neck. A streak of lightning slices the sky and the dog shakes herself down to her tail. The boy sits on the muddy creek bank, listening as the water rushes by him. He waits. He has to cross it; the man is looking for him. If he doesn't go home . . . He waits. If he doesn't go home . . . The dog licks the rain and tears from the boy's face and he stands to his feet, sticking his foot out again. He steps along the water's edge with an awkward, sideways walk, searching for the rocks with his toe, his heart bamming hard inside his chest. The water will take him and if it doesn't, the man will. He steps closer to the edge.

The dog barks and the boy turns to her, waving her away, but she barks again, a yelp that cuts through the rain and the racing creek. She backs away and barks longer and higher and the boy steps toward her, holding her mouth closed. She growls and backs away, yelping louder when the boy inches toward the water. She runs to him and pushes her head under his hand, barking. He reaches for her ears and she whines, stepping back and waiting. He looks up at the black hillside, then steps toward the dog.

She runs down the tracks and up the embankment. The boy follows and watches as she leaps onto the darkened porch and shakes. The boy races up the earthen stairs and creeps onto the porch like a tired animal looking for a spot to bed down. A swing hangs in front of the windows, so he moves away from it, curling up at the end of the porch where the dog lies beside him. As the rain cascades off the porch roof, he rests his hand on the dog's side and closes his eyes.

He awakens when the dog shakes. The sun is rising, red and full of fire. He jumps to his feet; light is scattering over the hillside. He leaps down the bank and raises his hand for the dog to stay. She lifts her nose and watches him, sniffing the air for secrets.

The earth is loose on the hillside, squishing between his toes as he runs. Shadows scatter through the woods as he races under the colored bottles and up the slope. He is breathless and wet when he reaches the shack but it's quiet. With the silence of the moon he moves to his work but the skillet isn't on the porch. He searches the ground and around the shack, then sneaks to the window, looking inside. The skillet is on the table. He looks to the cot and watches the man's belly rise with each breath. He lifts the wooden latch and pushes the door, holding his breath as he enters. The air is hot and humid, filled with alcohol. He reaches for the skillet and a hand clamps over his small arm.

"I told you to come to me last night."

A shot like electricity seizes the boy's nerves and his stomach lurches, but he is still.

"I waited." He pulls the boy close, and that bald, pink head leans down to his ear.

The sickening odor of liquor on the man's breath fills the boy's nostrils and a foul taste sticks in his throat like a bone.

"I'm still waitin'."

The skillet clangs like out-of-tune thunder when it falls to the floor and then stops.

IVORIE

I watch pinhead-size bubbles of grease sizzle and splatter as I move three pieces of sausage around in the skillet. This cast iron pan used to be full when I made breakfast for Mother and Pop and me. Sally comes to the kitchen door and presses her nose to the screen. "That was some rainstorm we had last night, Sally. Did you stay dry?" She wags her tail and her whole body sways back and forth. I check the biscuits in the oven, touching one with my finger, and look at Sally. "All I've got this morning is a few biscuits. You ate all the leftovers yesterday." Sally's been eating scraps for the three years we've had her, but there haven't been many in the last six months. Mother would throw her head back and groan at the notion of fixing a dog biscuits for breakfast today. I set the sausages on a plate and brown a little flour in the skillet before adding some milk. Nobody else in Morgan Hill would bother making such a paltry skillet of gravy. I break open two biscuits and steam rises like mist over the hillside in the early morning. I throw two pieces of sausage onto my plate and cover everything with gravy before tossing the remaining sausage, six biscuits, and the rest of the gravy into Sally's bowl. She sits and waits with big, anxious eyes as I open the door and set the bowl on the porch. She bumps my hand like she always does and looks up at me. "You're welcome," I say.

I eat in silence. I'm not in the mood to listen to Maxine telling me about the obituaries or hog reports. People die and pigs get sold. That's just how it is. I finish my breakfast and jump out of my chair. "I forgot all about the trap, Sally!" I run out onto the porch and around to the back stairs, leaping down them. "Stay with me," I yell to Sally when she gets too close to the garden. She runs to my side, and I sneak to the edge (I'm not sure why, the animal would be dead and you can't be at all surprised in that state), looking for the trap. "What in the —" I step into the row of tomatoes and spin around. I run up and down each row as Sally watches from the side, wagging her tail. "What is going on here?" I say, frustration spreading over my chest. I hear a horn and look up to see a truck pulling up the driveway.

Holt Oxman tosses up his hand and calls to me as he closes the truck door. He's wearing pants the color of a brown bag and a blue work shirt. "What'd you trap?"

"Nothing," I say.

He walks to the edge of the garden and rubs Sally on top of her head. Sprouts of gray pepper his sideburns and tiny lines branch out from his eyes when he squints but you'd think living with Avis would have aged him like Methuselah. He is a fine-looking man. His hair is sandy brown with sprinkles of salt and is thick as molasses and he always smells of tobacco. "Did you bait it real good?"

I laugh. "Henry did but it's not here. The trap's gone."

Holt's eyes bug and he plants a fist on his hip. "Then it's not an animal you've got out here."

"Couldn't it have just dragged it off somewhere?"

Holt steps into the garden and looks around. "Well, the trap would have had to clamp down and there'd be blood somewhere." Something uneasy fills my belly. "I brought out a couple of traps in case Henry couldn't find his but I don't think you have

79

a trapping problem anymore."

"Who in the world would come out here and steal from my garden?"

Holt shrugs. "Maybe somebody jumped off the train." He looks toward the barn. "Anything else missing?"

I try to think but the thought of someone jumping off the train has my mind in a jumble. "Nothing." I follow Holt to his truck and he lifts two traps from the bed, carrying them to the porch.

"I can set these for you," he says in an offhanded way that is afforded to spinsters and widows.

We stand there looking at each other in an awkward-making way — the handsome farmer and the spinster woman. It'd be a fine book if it weren't true. "I need to work out there today and Sally runs the rows. I'll set them after supper when I know she won't be in the garden."

"All right, Ivorie." Something always told me that Holt was like one of those Egyptian tombs that was once full of treasure till somebody named Avis came in and robbed it blind. He waves and walks toward the truck.

"Holt," I say, remembering the pickles and jelly. I run into the well house and come out with two pints of each. "I hope Avis enjoys these," I say, knowing full well that Avis enjoys very little of anything.

Sleep comes hard that night. At midnight I turn on my side and look out the window; the dark is paler now than when I went to bed, as if the wind blew some of the black off it. The clouds are low and spongy. I keep my ear tuned to the jumabu in the garden, envisioning it coming inside the house, where it first eats the chocolate cake and then opens the Frigidaire, snarling and growling as it sucks down my pickles and jelly and jam. I put on the light and pick up the *Redbook* magazine, flipping through the article about Vivien Leigh and her next movie based on a Tennessee Williams play. *Another southern drawl and probably another movie award,* I think. I snap the pages and see Refrigerator Lady smiling out at me. Was her jumabu in that refrigerator? I think about George Coley and him protecting me from whatever was outside my door. The hollyhocks tap against the bedroom window and I picture the jumabu coming into the house because it's hungry . . . but not for food. For the first time in years, I walk to the doors and lock them.

After I do the milking in the morning, I

pour the milk into a silver canister and get the can from last night's milking out of the Frigidaire. Henry and Loretta count on my six gallons of milk every day because it's what they sell with sandwiches during dinner break. When school's in session lots of kids tumble down the hill to Henry's and line up for a bologna or ham sandwich with a slice of cheese and a cup of cold milk. I gather the eggs into a basket and am putting everything in the front seat of the truck when I hear an engine roaring up the driveway.

George Coley's blue truck pulls next to me and he grins. I don't even bother with my hair. It looks like a rat's nest, and I know it. "Hey, Ivorie! Milking done?" He strolls around the front of his truck and slips his hands into the pockets of his jeans. George is narrow chested, strong legged, and solemn, the complete opposite of his father, who is a cumbersome yet jovial man. George's mother, Pearl, has been the cafeteria lady at the school ever since I was a kid. She's too loud for my taste and all wind; thankfully, George seems nothing like her.

"Headed to Henry's with it now," I say.

Sally pushes her head under George's hand and he kneels down to give her a good rub on the belly. "It's going to be a pretty day," he says. Sally's nearly comatose with all the rubbing and patting.

Holy cow! I feel so gawky. What in the world does he want? I look up into the sun and squinch my face up in pain from the glare. "Yeah, it looks real pretty." Bright sun dots glide past my eyes when I try to focus on George.

"I love pretty days," he says, thumping on Sally's belly.

"I do, too," I say with conviction. This is painful to the core. I gave up trying to talk to single men when, years earlier, I told Lloyd Parker I felt *fine as frog hair.* There's no way back from something that idiotic.

He stands, finally, and pats his truck. He's into patting things this morning. He opens the passenger door and pulls out a few quart baskets of blueberries. "It's still a little early but more of these will be coming in."

I take them from him and set them on the passenger seat of my truck. "Thank you, George. I'll be able to make a cobbler with these."

"I'll have more for jam and jelly, if you want them."

I look at the berries instead of him. "I would. I would." Why did I say that twice?

George clears his throat and commences to patting Sally again. "Ivorie, if you're ever inclined or have the notion . . ." He rubs at a spot on Sally's back and drifts away for a second. "Well, it'd be up to you, but I thought maybe I could call . . ." He's back at that spot again and my brain can't think of a word to say that will come out right. What I want to tell him is, *No, don't do this. I don't think I'm ready!* "I'm just saying, well, I'd like to call on you." So, it's finally happened. We've come down to this: two washed-up thirty-somethings who have no other choice but to fall into each other. George scratches Sally behind her ears before walking to his truck's door.

"I appreciate that, George," I say, feeling small ponds where my armpits used to be.

His tires kick up gravel on his way out of the driveway and I lean my head on my truck. Part of me didn't want him to broach the topic of calling on me, but the other part, the quivering part, desperately wanted him to say it. *I appreciate that, George? I appreciate that?!* I yank open the door and slide behind the wheel, disgusted with my bumbling self.

On my way to Henry's I turn into the drive for Joe and Fran Cannon. Fran's first husband died three years ago, leaving her with two kids and one on the way. They were as splintered a family as I've ever seen and poor as church mice — they didn't have a pot to pee in or a window to throw it out of. I honk at Jane in the garden and look for John and Milo. The face the color of milk chocolate pops out of the corn and waves at me. Milo's family died in a house fire the year Fran lost her husband, and that black boy kept Fran and her kids from cracking apart altogether. People thought Fran was either courageous or crazy for taking Milo in, most leaning toward crazy. Joe Cannon fought in the war and I guess he thought marrying a woman with a house full of kids was safe in comparison. Before Joe came along, Fran's house wasn't even hooked to electricity and she didn't have running water. He changed all that when he married her.

Twelve-year-old Jane walks to my truck and Sally jumps out of the back, running after Fred, Milo's three-legged dog. Sally catches him lickety-split and pins him to the ground. "Hey, Miss Walker," Jane says. She's far from pretty: her teeth are uneven, her hair is a victim of Fran's haircuts, and freckles are splattered across her nose, but her face shines like fresh, dewy hope. There's nothing truer than a face, and Jane's is as true as faces come.

"Morning, Jane," I say, getting out of the

truck. "Where's everybody at?"

"Daddy and John are out working the tobacco, Milo's in the garden, and Mama's in the house with Will Henry and the baby." Loretta helped bring Will Henry into the world two and a half years ago, while Henry paced the floor with the kids. That baby turned every which way except straight inside Fran but finally decided to come out. "Are you driving down to Henry's?"

I walk with her to the house. "Got the milk in the truck."

"Tell him I said hello."

I stand on the porch and laugh. "You'll be seeing him before the morning's out." Henry was more of a father to Jane and John than their no-good dead daddy, Lonnie, ever was, and I don't think a day goes by that she doesn't run down the tracks to see him. He calls her Pretty Girl, and although that's about as accurate as calling me Buxom Girl, I know Henry means it.

I'm talking as I open the screen door. "Fran, are you home?"

She walks into the kitchen with the baby on her hip. Lonnie Gable was an explosive man devoted to doing everything contrary to what a married man should do and he just about wore Fran down to bones and nerves. His dying was the best thing that

86

ever happened to her, and I'm not sorry to say that. Fran's always been one of those standing-off-to-the-side, no-fuss kind of girls who's never worked for or realized her simple beauty. Lonnie nearly beat the beauty off her, but his efforts didn't last. Joe Cannon brought color and sound back to her corner of the world. "Morning, Ivorie," she says, putting Paul down. Will Henry throws himself into my legs and I pretend to fall into the wall. Paul toddles to the kitchen table and reaches up for a biscuit left in the pan from breakfast. "Are you hungry?"

"No, but I'll take a cup of coffee," I say, pulling out a chair. The boys open the screen door and let it close with a sharp snap. I watch as Paul gives Will Henry a bite of his biscuit.

"What's on your mind, Ivorie?" Fran asks, pouring coffee into my cup.

"Why should there be something on my mind?"

She smiles and pours herself a cup of black coffee, turning her good ear toward me. Fran is deaf in one ear from a childhood fever and she keeps her head turned with that good ear aimed at whoever's talking. "Because you never drop by my house in the morning. There are always berries to pick and make into jam or cakes to bake to be given away or . . ."

I fling my hand in the air to stop her. "That reminds me. Do you need any blackberry jelly?"

She laughs and shakes her head. "Lord have mercy, Ivorie! No one in Morgan Hill needs any blackberry jelly." She sips the coffee and nibbles on a biscuit, only because it's there. "How're you doing this week?"

I roll my eyes and sigh. "I stay busy. I beat all the rugs this week. I can't remember the last time I did that."

"Last week," she says.

I shrug. "They needed it again."

"Sure."

"I made more blackberry jelly and I've got some blueberries for cobbler. The cucumbers are coming in, so I'll be making more pickles. I'm cleaning out the barn stalls today."

"The stalls that don't have any animals?" Fran asks.

"They still need cleaning."

"Sure."

"And I'm having thoughts about men that I've never had before."

Coffee sprays out of Fran's mouth and she jumps for a towel, laughing. "What in the . . ." She can't get the words out. I watch as she holds the table and shakes down to her toes, cackling like a hen who's laid an egg. She straightens up and looks at me, tears pooling in the corners of her eyes.

I set my coffee down with a thud. "Well, if I'd known I could be this funny I'd have joined up with one of those traveling sideshows a long time ago."

She sits and fans herself with the dish towel. "Shew," she says, dabbing her eyes. "I'm sorry. It's just that I've never heard you say anything *close* to off-color, Ivorie." She howls again and I roll my eyes, waiting for her reaction to pass. For a moment I regret stopping by but then laugh at her. "How in the world did this come about?" she says, trying hard to compose herself.

I look out at Will Henry and Paul. "Too much time on my hands, I guess." I hold the coffee cup between my hands and talk into the dark liquid. "George Coley came by this morning and said he'd like to call on me."

She stands to get me more coffee. "George Coley! What'd you say to him?"

"I said, 'I appreciate that.' "

Fran pours coffee into my cup and then sits. " 'I appreciate that'? Like he'd just loaded a sack of groceries for you?" I nod and she starts laughing again.

"I shouldn't have even come by here this morning!"

She swats at me with the dish towel. "Sit down. Sit down. You're not going anywhere." I slouch in the chair and look at her. "You always called George mush or grits or . . ."

"Oatmeal," I say.

She runs her finger here and there on the table, making a figure eight in front of her. "You'd make pretty babies together."

My head snaps up so fast it puts a kink in my neck. "You've got us making babies together? All he did was say he wanted to call on me. I'm too old to have babies."

"Your mother was forty-two when you were born."

"Oh hush up, Fran!" She grins and keeps tracking that figure eight. "All this time I've never given George a passing thought but now my mind is off somewhere thinking about . . ." I sigh into the cup and shake my head.

"Thinking of a man is normal, Ivorie," she says. "It makes you realize you're just bone-sad and lonely without your family. One day you're happy and busy with your mother and then she's gone, blown out like a match flame. And the next day you're making cake and jelly for the entire community."

I watch the boys chase each other on the porch and something like a rushing wind sweeps across my ribs. "I feel like I'm losing my mind on some days, Fran."

She sighs and watches the boys. "Well, I have those days, and this house is full of people."

I laugh and stand to my feet, putting the cup by the sink. "I need to get that milk to Henry." I open the screen door and look at her. "By any chance, has Jane or the boys been in my garden?"

"I have a hard enough time keeping them in our garden. I can't think why'd they get in yours. Why?"

Will Henry grabs my leg and looks up at me. "Something's getting into my vegetables. I'll figure it out." I lean down and kiss Will Henry's cotton-topped head and kiss my finger and then place it on Paul's nose before walking to the truck.

Two days later, after I deliver milk to Henry's, George Coley is waiting at my house when Sally and I pull up the driveway. I feel an odd catch in my chest. I sure am glad to see him standing there in the sun. "Morning, Ivorie," he says, lifting something out of the bed of his truck.

Sally runs to him and George hands a peck basket of blueberries to me. "Picked these this morning."

I take the basket from him and look down at the dark, almost purple berries. "These are beautiful, George. Just as pretty as can be. Thank you!" He smiles and I nod toward the house. "Can I get you a cup of coffee?"

"I'd appreciate that," he says. I pause, looking at him. He grins and I feel the hairs on the back of my neck stand at attention.

George sits on the porch with Sally as I warm the coffee from this morning. I want to ask about his wife. I never really knew her, what with them living out in Cortland and going to church there. I want to know what she was like and what he misses most about her. "Would you like a piece of pound cake? I know it's early but Mother always needed something to eat with coffee. I made it yesterday."

"That'd be fine," he says, leaning over to pet Sally. I watch him through the screen door and wonder what he's thinking.

I take his coffee and pound cake to the porch and go back inside for mine, wondering which chair to sit in when I get back to the porch. I decide to take the one across from him so neither one of us has to work up a sweat craning our necks to see each other while talking. "I'll work up those blueberries today," I say. "I'll make up some jelly and get some out to you. That is, if I have any left after making another cobbler and blueberry pancakes."

"Cobbler's my downfall," George says, sipping his coffee. "I could eat a whole pan of it."

"I made a hog of myself the other day when you dropped off those berries. I made up a small cobbler and ate every bite myself. I'm real glad nobody was around to see that."

He smiles and takes a bite of cake, making smacking noises in his mouth. "Lord have mercy! This is good. You are some kind of good cook, Ivorie!"

"Mother taught me. She was a much better cook than me." I feel his eyes on me and I look down at my cake and poke at it with my fork like something unidentified has been found.

"She was a good woman," he says.

I don't want to talk about Mother. I can't sit here with drippy eyes in front of George Coley, so I think of something else to change the subject. "How is your mother and pop doing?"

"They're fine. Getting up in age but still putting out tobacco. Mama's still slinging potatoes in the cafeteria."

I hope he'll say more so the conversation won't sputter to a standstill, but he doesn't and I start poking at my cake again. "I should have washed up some of those blueberries for the top of the cake." I jump up from my seat. "What was I thinking?"

"No, no! I'm fine." He takes the final bite of cake and sets his plate down on the empty chair beside him. "I need to get back home and get busy. I just wanted to get those berries to you before they turned bad." He stands up, and we both stand there looking at each other, wondering what to do or say. It's as if we're both wearing ill-fitting shoes and have been alone too long to know. He's close enough for me to smell his skin; it has a sweaty, new-mown-grass scent, and I notice the hard look of his chest under his shirt. I feel a tremor in the lining of my stomach when he smiles and I look out toward his truck.

"Thank you again for the berries." I walk him along the stone path to the driveway and he nods, slipping behind the wheel of his truck. He waves out the window as he drives away and I look down at Sally. "That wasn't so bad. Could have been worse." And I hope George will come back.

■ ■ ■ ■

The next day I fry up a few pork chops and potatoes for supper, along with the first of the beans out of the garden, and slice some tomatoes. I whip up a small cobbler and pour some sugar on top of it for extra sweetening. When I notice George's truck pulling up the drive I make a mad dash to the bathroom to wash the sweat off my face and pull my hair back into a neat ponytail. My dress is dirty from working in the garden but there isn't time to change. I fumble for a tube of lipstick out of my pocketbook and slide some color onto my lips before George gets to the door. "What in the world are you doing here?" I ask, stepping out onto the porch. He's wearing his work clothes and boots and my stomach feels like it's tipping over when I look at him. I want to wrap my arms around him in the worst kind of way.

"More berries," he says, grinning.

"I've already made a run of jam with the first batch and have a cobbler in the oven. Have you had supper?"

"No," he says, and the sheerest smile crosses his face.

I feel those low tremors again and open

the kitchen door. "Well, come on in. I've got plenty!"

George is a hearty eater and he doesn't fall short on compliments: "Law! These are good chops!"; "There's nothing like new potatoes in beans and these are some of the best!"; "Lord have mercy, these are good tomatoes!"; "Who taught you to make cobbler like this?" He doesn't help with the dishes but I don't know a man who helps in any kitchen in Morgan Hill! Sally gnaws on the pork chop bones till they're naked and clean and I give her what's left of the potatoes, putting the leftover chops and beans in the Frigidaire, opening it with my foot turned just so like Refrigerator Lady, hoping George will notice.

We sit together on the porch and he reminds me again of how good his supper was. "I can't thank you enough, Ivorie. That was some good eating."

"I'm glad you liked it." I wonder how long people have to make small talk before they kiss. It's been several years since a man kissed me; I don't even know if I remember how. As he talks, I watch his lips and imagine them on mine, his hands cradling my head. Did I like George or did I just like the thought of companionship? If truth be told, we haven't had any conversations deeper than food at this point.

"You're a fine woman, Ivorie," he says, reaching out and touching my knee. A current runs up my leg and sets my chest on fire and I realize I like him . . . or maybe I'm hopelessly desperate.

"I never knew your wife, George." He leans back in his chair and I'm not sure if I should have brought her up or not. "I think I saw her at a community dance once, but I didn't know her."

He looks up at the ceiling of the porch. It's funny how we lay memories out like quilting squares, arranging them by color and feel, seeing which ones look best next to another and which ones we need to toss altogether. That's what George was doing, looking up at that ceiling, seeing which memories he wanted to remember right now. "June was honest. Serious. Hard worker." It sounds like he's filling out an application for a job. "She died when she was seven months pregnant." That's the final quilting patch he wants to lay down and he stops talking.

"I'm sorry for you, George. I shouldn't have asked."

He stops staring at the ceiling and looks at me. His eyes are smoky blue and sad. "If I keep coming here, then you have every right to ask."

My skin tingles at the thought of his coming here, of us being a couple, and I rub my hand up and down my arm, hoping he won't notice the breakout of goose bumps.

Day's end is getting gray and fuzzy, and George stands. I want him to stay longer so we can talk of the weather or crops or anything beyond food but he reaches his hand for mine. "Could you walk me to my truck?" His hand feels rough in mine, and I'm disappointed when, as I get to my feet, he lets go. We walk together down the stone path, and I feel his hand fall ever so light on the small of my back. My heart is going crazy and I swear it's loud enough for him to hear. When we get to his truck he looks at me and I know he wants to kiss me. I can see it. "Thank you, again, Ivorie." His eyes lock onto mine and I sense him moving closer. "Night," he says, reaching for the door handle.

He slides inside and I sigh. "Thank *you* for the berries. Oh! I forgot to give you some jam."

"Bring it to me," he says, smiling. "It'll be a good excuse to see you again." He backs up and turns around, and I watch him drive away like I'm some love-struck teenager.

■ ■ ■ ■

When outside is heavy with the song of katydids I make my way through the rooms as I always do, noticing Pop's rifle propped up in the corner behind his sitting chair, the one with the faded blue upholstery and straight back. I pick up the rifle and hold it in my hands before cutting off the bedroom light. I walk to the front room and cut the lights off in there and head to the kitchen, pulling the string on the light above the table. I creep out the kitchen door and notice Sally isn't on the porch, which is a good thing. She'd make too much of a fuss about my being out here. I tiptoe around the length of the porch and settle into a cane-backed chair, waiting, not moving, barely breathing. I feel oddly out of place on my own porch and notice that the man in the moon is peering down at me, between hazy clouds, wondering what I'm doing.

Time passes way too slow when you're waiting for the unknown, and I fade to the hum of crickets, sleep first folding down my eyelids and then the corners of my mind. I am standing hip deep in the creek, talking to George about blueberries, when a branch falls to the water with a giant splash. The sound in my head startles me and I jump awake, realizing it's a snapping noise I'm hearing, the snapping of my vegetable vines. My breath comes in short spurts and a bird or something like it flutters high in my chest. I listen for movement and stand to my feet, reaching above me. I pull the string on the porch light and aim the rifle into the garden. "One move and I'm squeezing this trigger," I say, into the dark. Sally comes bounding out of the shadows, wagging her tail. I hold the rifle steady and my stomach churns with fear and dread. "Come out of there!"

The sound of rustling comes from the garden and Sally bolts back down the stairs toward it. I step forward, straining to see in the dim light of the porch the small, solemn face.

THE BOY

She lowers the rifle and looks at him with confusion and wonder. "Have you been eating my vegetables?" she asks, in that honey-dissolving voice. She looks like she's grinning or relieved or her mind is swirling with thoughts.

He doesn't answer and the dog circles his legs.

She lowers the rifle. "I see you've met Sally."

He doesn't look at the dog but keeps his eyes on her.

"What's your name?" He has a dark, hollow-eyed stare as she looks at the rifle. "This? It's not even loaded. But if you had been a two-hundred-pound man that jumped off the train I'd want you to have *believed* it was loaded. For a few days I was thinking you were a train-jumping man, but you're not. You're a little boy. What are you? Six? Seven?" She lays the rifle across one of the chairs and stands on the top step, smiling at him. "Where do you live? Looks like you've got some blond hair under all that dirt." The dog runs to the woman and rubs her head into her legs. She leans down and pats the dog's side. "You must live somewhere close-by to visit my garden so often."

The dog runs to the boy and pushes her head under his hand but he doesn't move.

"Well, come on in," she says. "Are you hungry?"

He needs to breathe but remains tombstone still.

She puts her foot on the next step and leans against the porch post, white like teeth in the moonlight. "I've got some pork chops and green beans in the house. I gave Sally the rest of the fried potatoes but if you want some I'll make some more." The dog pushes her head under his hand again, and the woman smiles, bigger this time. "Sally's telling you to eat because when you eat . . . that means she eats." She watches him. "Surely you're hungry?"

He nods.

She cocks her head toward the house. "Come on around to the kitchen."

He follows her onto the porch and Sally marches between them, leading him.

The screen door creaks as it opens and

the woman holds it open for him. "I'll put the light on once we get inside," she says.

His legs are marble slabs and won't move.

"All right, I'll put the light on *first* and *then* you come in." She pulls the chain and light bounces off the peach-colored walls.

He peeks through the screen and takes in the table and chairs and big white box that sets up against the wall, a picture of a man over a supper plate praying, shelves on the wall that hold blue-and-white–patterned plates, jars of jelly on the counter, a red-and-white calendar on the wall with a picture of a cow at the top, and what looks like an enormous yellow cake under a glass dome sitting on the table next to a milk bottle filled with flowers.

She pushes the door open for him. "Come on in."

He steps inside and she puts her hand under her nose.

She steps to the sink and washes her hands, burying her nose into her shoulder. She turns to him and her mouth forms into the shape of a question; she looks at him for an eternity with that question on her lips but says, "Let's go out on the porch. It's cooler there." She opens the door and the boy follows. "Why don't you sit down here and I'll fix you some potatoes and warm up those chops. Okay?"

That honey voice drips in his ears and sounds so sweet it makes his eyes pool. He sits and Sally places both front paws on his lap.

The woman opens the door again and steps inside, then sticks her head back out, looking at him. "I'm Ivorie, by the way." She waits for him to tell her his name but when he doesn't she lets the door close with a hard, quick snap. She talks loud while she works. "I don't want your mama and pop worrying about you, so I'll cook fast, okay?" She waits a beat for any reaction. "Do they know you wander about in the middle of the night? What time is it anyway? Eleven o'clock!"

He can hear the potatoes sizzle as she slides them into the hot grease.

"I thought eleven o'clock only happened one time a day." She moves to the large white box that sets against the wall and opens it. "The chops are right here in the ice box."

He leans over, putting his face up against the door's screen.

She loosens waxed paper from around two thick pork chops and puts them on a plate before pulling a plate-covered bowl from the icy box. She spoons a few green beans into a small pot and puts them on the stove.

The smell of heaven wafts through the screen and the boy closes his eyes, sitting on his hands to keep still.

"The chops will be cold but they'll still be good," Ivorie says.

He can hear her moving the potatoes around in the skillet and he bends over to take another peek. She is sprinkling salt onto them and stirring the beans. His stomach gurgles and he bounces his legs up and down. She pulls on the handle of the big, white box and pulls out a pitcher filled with milk. He watches as she pours it into a tall glass with red cherries on it and carries it to the door. He sits tall in his chair and looks up at the milk when she steps onto the porch.

"I thought you might be thirsty," she says, as he takes the milk and gulps it. She watches as he empties the glass and hands it back to her. "Would you like more?"

A sorrowful look crosses her face and he wishes he hadn't drunk all the milk.

"I have plenty if you'd like more."

He doesn't say anything and she holds the glass in a fumbly, wishing-for-something-to-say way. "I'll get you some more." The door snaps closed and he watches her pour another glass up to the top cherry and move to the stove. She turns the potatoes a final time and scoops them onto the plate with the pork chops, spooning the green beans on last. She reaches for a fork and the milk and talks as she walks to the door. "This is the first time I've ever served supper at eleven o'clock at night," she says, pushing the door open with her hip.

She hands the plate of food to the boy and he grabs a pork chop with one hand and lowers the plate to just under his chin with the other. He tears at the chop with his teeth, jerking his head to loosen the meat from the bone.

"Don't make yourself sick," she says, watching him. "Where is your mama and pop?"

He pierces as many potatoes as his fork can hold and shoves them into his mouth, scooping a great mound of beans in as well.

"Slow down before you choke," she says.

He moves quicker and chews faster. The dog watches and waits and casts a glance at the woman and then the boy, wondering and hoping if there'll be anything left. The boy rips apart the next chop and pushes in another loaded fork full of potatoes and beans.

"Are you lost?" Ivorie asks, leaning close to him.

He can smell something like flowers on her.

"I know everybody in Morgan Hill. Is your family wandering through?"

He finishes the pork chop and gulps the milk, letting it drip over his mouth and chin.

"Would you like some cake?" He nods and she wanders into the kitchen and back out again as easy as a dream. "It's not too big," she says. "I don't want you to get sick."

He picks it up with his hands and devours it in two bites. Her face is shocked or surprised or sickened; he doesn't know. He stands, hands the plate to her, and bolts off the porch.

He ran off the porch like sparks away from a blazing fire. "Hey," I yell into the night. Sally chases him, and I stand holding a plate that was emptied faster than Sally herself could do and I shake my head. "So that's my jumabu!" Sally doesn't chase him for long and runs back to the porch, remembering the pork chop bones. "Here," I say, throwing them out on the lawn. The lingering smell of the boy fills my nose and I walk into the kitchen to escape it. It smelled as if he'd rolled in manure and urine and then bathed in slop. I set the plate on the counter and walk back to the door, looking out. "Where'd he go?" I ask Sally. She gnaws at a bone and lifts her hind end in an effort to get up but decides against it. I walk on the porch to the back of the house and pull the string to cut off the light, looking out through the shadows. "You can come back anytime," I yell across the yard and down the embankment. "I always have food." I don't know if he hears or even why I have just done such a crazy thing, and I open the back door and walk inside.

The next morning I milk Gertie extra early and set out for Henry's. The morning crowd is there loading up on chicken feed and gossip. I say my hellos to Clayton, Haze, and Gabbie on the porch. "Morning, Ivorie," Loretta says, behind the counter.

Jane Cannon is working with Henry and Loretta today, and she runs to give me a clumsy hug. "Hey, Miss Walker. You want me to make you a sausage biscuit?"

"No thanks, Jane. I already ate." Her face hangs in disappointment. I catch a glimpse of Pete Fletcher in the store and I smile. "I caught my jumabu," I say, setting the milk canister and basket of eggs on the counter.

Dolly Wade, a speckle-cheeked woman with pear-shaped legs and the face of a child, looks at me over the meat counter. Dolly's mind never developed above an eight-year-old's and she still lives with her parents, who hold her hands in church. "You caught a what?" she says, in a voice high enough to reroute birds.

"A jumabu," I say, to Loretta, Henry, Jane, Dolly, Pete, and anybody else who's listening.

"You know my daddy caught one of them years ago," Dolly says, taking a pound of cheese from Henry. "And it cut him real bad." She pauses, remembering the horror. "And you know he went crazy after that. Plum out of his mind." She wanders deep into the store and the rest of us smile.

"I still don't understand what you caught," Henry says.

Pete laughs and walks to the front of the store beside me. "It's a word my younguns made up, Henry. What'd you get, Ivorie?"

"A little boy," I say, putting the canister of milk into the refrigerated case and grabbing an empty canister for my next milking. "No older than six or seven, I guess. Blond hair so dirty it's gray, and blue eyes as big as a barn owl's. Showed up at eleven o'clock last night."

Pete's face flattens. "A boy? Who is he?"

"Never told me his name. I couldn't get a word out of him."

"You've never seen him before?" Loretta asks.

"Never. But he's been eating out of my garden for two weeks or more. I asked about his folks, if he was traveling through, if he was staying with somebody here. Nothing."

My aunt and Mother's sister, Dottie Ferguson, is eavesdropping. She's a stout

110

woman with an ample bosom and fuzzy white hair. We've always called her Hot Dot because she's so cantankerous she could start an argument in an empty house. How she and Mother came out of the same womb is beyond me. "You mean you fed some kid you don't even know? A kid who was stealing from you?"

"Because he had to. He's a hungry little thing."

"Stealing's stealing," Hot Dot says, her face getting red and frumpled. "You don't look at a thief and say, 'Come on in. I've got more good stuff in here.' "

I feel my neck tightening and ignore her. Henry grunts and crosses his arms. He wipes imaginary dust from the cash register and leans against it. "Could it have been that Lark boy from over on the hill?"

"Them people don't live up there anymore," Jerry Cleats says. "They left years ago." He sounds angry about it but Jerry always sounds angry, mostly with his wife, LouAnn, who is a constant disappointment to him. I guess he figures smacking her around will make her less disappointing. I've never liked him and don't intend to start making conversation with him today.

"I thought *all* those people who lived up in those hills either died out or moved on,"

I say to Henry.

"Even if they were up there nobody would wander down those hills in the black of night," Loretta says.

"Nobody's up there," Jerry says again, rolling a cigarette between his stained fingers.

"I saw a grubby little boy at the creek a few weeks ago," Jane says. "He was a scrawny little thing and ugly as a frog. Dirty, too. A worm crawling out of the earth is cleaner than he was."

"Did you talk to him?" I ask.

"Tried to. He turned tail and ran toward the hills, though. I guess he remembered how ugly he was and how hard that would be on me, looking at him."

"Jane," Henry says, gesturing with his hand as if to say *that's enough.* "Do Clyde and Esther have any grandchildren visiting them from Bristol?"

"Don't know," Loretta says. "But surely they'd know if a grandbaby was out running around at eleven at night."

Clayton Dunn had moved off the front porch when he heard Hot Dot get all hot and bothered and has been standing behind Pete with his hands in his overalls pockets ever since. I've known Clayton my whole life and couldn't tell you what he does for a living. Word is, he doesn't buy anything with a handle because it could mean work. He's fiftyish and balding and has six kids. His clothes never hide the curves or rolls of his body. He believes in showing them exactly as they are, letting himself protrude from his overalls at every side. "What am I hearing in here?"

"Nothing, Clay," I say.

"Are you feeding some daggum kid out of them hills?"

I wave my hand in the air. "It's no big deal, Clay."

He steps forward as if he's just been called as the star witness at a murder trial. "No big deal? Do you know those people up there? Me and Bobby used to drive a team of horses up there to haul down timber. Them people got their own ways. Every one of them is dangerous as hell. They'll cut your throat like that." He snaps his fat fingers and Henry stops him.

"All right, Clay. Secret message received."

Clayton and Jerry both give me a look that says I'm crazy for not heeding Clayton's words, and I grab a bag of sugar and a jar of peanut butter. "I'll let you know what I find out," I say to Henry, putting the groceries on the counter to pay. "I told him he could come back."

"Be careful," Pete says. "You could be inviting the devil himself in."

The sun is rolling fast up into the sky and the air is thick enough to poke my finger through when I get into the garden at eight to pick the beans that are ready for canning. A river of sweat runs off my nose and down my neck as I fill the basket and thoughts of the boy roll in my mind. I stop my work and step to the embankment, looking across to the hills. They are lush and green, shimmering with light. "There's no way that boy is coming down from those hills," I say to Sally. I look down at her and fold one of her ears in my hand, rubbing it. "We're not supposed to have secrets between us, you know." She cocks her head and I bend down, looking her in the eyes. "You should have told me what was going on out here." Something shines at the bottom of the bank and I stand to get a better look. I walk down the stairs and wade through the weeds, reaching for a branch. I pull at it and lift the trap Henry had set. Sally scurries to my side and I hold the trap up by the branch. "See! Like this! You should have told me all about this." She wags her tail as if she's done something magnificent when I hear a voice near the house.

"Miss Walker? Are you back here?"

I carry the trap up the stairs and sigh when I see Davis Carpenter back for another visit. This time he has a narrow-chested man with him who's as pale as milk. He smiles and his tall teeth put a strain on his upper lip. His long face is topped with white woolly eyebrows. "Mr. Carpenter, how are you?" I ask, tossing the trap to the side. I pull a handkerchief from my pocket and sop up the water off my face.

"I'm doing fine," he says, smiling in that slick-salesman way of his. "I'd like you to meet Frank Nutt. He's the manager of our fine bank." If Mother were here, once Mr. Nutt had left I would refer to him as The Nutt, or Nutt Cake, or Nutt Job, and she would scold me for not being kind to him behind his back. But then she'd put her head down and laugh into her chest or turn to the dishes and giggle into them.

"Awful nice to meet you, Miss Walker," Frank Nutt says, extending his hand and pumping on mine long enough for water to shoot out of my mouth. "This is a real beautiful place you have here."

"Thank you, Mr. Nutt," I say.

The sun bears down and Davis loosens his tie. "I just thought you'd like to meet Frank in case he could answer any questions you might have," he says, smiling through the sweat and the sun and the heat of what will be another failed visit with me.

"Questions about what?" I ask, moving back to the row of beans I had been picking.

"About the ten acres we've talked about," Davis says, using his hand as a sunshade for his face. He's still smiling. I'm smiling, too. We smile so much at each other that we should both be on overseas peace committees.

I pick the beans without looking up. "Oh, I don't have any questions about that."

A pause big enough to drive a team of horses through it separates us before The Nutt steps toward the garden. "I understand your apprehension, Miss Walker," he says. "Nobody wants to see something come to your community that's not in the best interest of the people here, and I give you my personal assurance that this will be a fine business and something for the folks of Morgan Hill to be proud of." He smiles and ignores the streams of water on either side of his face racing down to the thatch of white hair beneath his open collar.

"I appreciate you personally standing behind it, Mr. Nutt."

He presses on. "Why, folks traveling on

the highway will be able to pull off and fill up their cars and maybe take a drive through this beautiful area and see firsthand what a fine community this is." I throw beans into the basket and out of the corner of my eye I can see Davis and The Nutt looking at each other. "Miss Walker, I want you to personally know that no one is trying to take advantage of you or your situation. We are all sorry for your loss."

A slow, throbbing headache pecks away at the back of my eyes and my dress clings to the moisture on my back when I look up at them. "How much today?"

"Why, one hundred dollars an acre," The Nutt says, as if he's thrown wide open the window to my good fortune.

I wipe the back of my neck and smile at them. We're all three smiling now. We could be a singing trio we're smiling so much. "Thank you both for coming. Would either of you like some blackberry jelly or jam? I have both."

Large, wet drops trickle off Davis's nose and he swipes at them with his hand. "Miss Walker, this is a very —"

"Jelly or jam, Mr. Carpenter?"

The air goes out of his smile and we stand dripping and drooping and looking at each other in that gangling way we always do.

"Are we done, Miss Walker? Because I'm never really . . ."

"Yes, Mr. Carpenter. We are done," I say in a tone that says *once and for all.*

Making the jam and canning the beans takes up most of the afternoon, and when the beans are done I line them up on the kitchen counter and wipe the moisture off the top of each pint. Pint. How pitiful and small. Reduced in size and volume. I pour a glass of iced tea and sit on the porch for a rest, hoping for a cool breeze, but there isn't one. The air is sleepy with heat, sitting thick on my skin, and Sally sticks her tongue out, panting as if she'd just pulled someone out of the creek.

My eyes close despite my will and a warm breeze covers me as my brain takes me here and there through fog and haze. A cold pool on my leg rouses me and I jump to my feet, wiping tea from my dress with my hands.

"Look what I did, Sally!" I walk into the house, talking to myself. "Falling asleep in the middle of the day like I'm a queen of leisure." I change my dress and open the Frigidaire, reaching for two chicken legs. For some reason, I reach for six more legs and close the door. I roll them in flour and salt and pepper and put them on to fry, checking the beans I cooked earlier in the day. Tiny white potatoes poke their heads out between the beans and I pop one into my mouth. "Mmm. George's right. Nothing like it, Sally." I whip up a skillet of corn bread and reach for the peanut butter to make a batch of cookies while the chicken fries. I haven't made cookies in a year or more and keep tasting the dough to see if I have enough sugar, vanilla, and salt. I use the remaining blueberries to make another pan of cobbler; I'll put blueberries *and* blackberries in this one. I'll do the milking, clean up, and wait.

I put on a pair of blue jeans with a green button-down shirt and brush my hair, keeping it down. I use rose-colored lipstick and busy myself in the kitchen until I hear tires on the gravel. I smile when I recognize George's truck and walk out on the porch to greet him. He carries a fresh peck of blueberries onto the porch and stops, looking at me. "You are some kind of pretty," he says, making my face feel hot.

"Have you had supper?" I'm smiling and can't help it.

I feel his hand brush against my back as we enter the kitchen and I just want to turn and bury my nose in his neck and take a big whiff. He watches me pour him some tea and he smiles when I set the food on the table. "I don't think I've ever seen your hair down like that."

I touch it and sit down. "If I'm done working for the day I let it down," I say, knowing full well I usually keep it pulled back so it doesn't drive me out of my mind.

"How was your day?" I ask, and I feel weak with stupidity. It sounded like something an old, married woman would ask.

"Well," he says, shoveling a fork full of beans and potatoes into his mouth. "It was a fine day except I have an awful problem."

"What is it?"

He puts down his fork and looks at me. "I can't keep my mind off of you and I'm having an awful time doing my work." Something jump-starts in my chest and all my cells are firing at the same time. I feel flushed and can't look at him. "You are blushing, Ivorie Walker."

The heat spreads down my arms and my stomach pitches this way and that. I jump up and manage to keep my legs under me. "Would you like more tea?"

"I would," he says, laughing. As I pour the tea, he looks up at me. "Do you have any trouble getting your work done?"

It feels like an ocean of sweat is on my upper lip and I brush it away when I turn to put the pitcher of tea on the counter. "Maybe." He's smiling and I point my finger at him. "Stop that smiling."

He laughs and rests back against the chair. "Why can't I smile? Don't you think it's interesting that we're both having trouble getting our work done?" I can't look at him; I'm afraid my heart will explode and make an awful mess. He leans toward me and the laughter stops. "Isn't that interesting, Ivorie?" He lifts his hand to my face and draws me toward him. It feels like my stomach wants to empty as he kisses me and my breath speeds up. I feel the muscles in his back beneath my hands and never want him to stop. He looks at me and grins. "What have we been doing all these years?" I can't answer because he kisses me again and I feel like I'm floating. I have no idea how long we're like this, but when he looks at me again we realize our food is cold and the glasses are slippery with moisture. He laughs, squeezing my hand. "I won't get a lick of work done tomorrow."

George kisses me beside his truck before he leaves and Sally and I watch him go. "Doesn't kiss like oatmeal," I say to Sally.

I make an extra plate of food and set it inside the Frigidaire to keep till later, just in case the boy decides to come again but he doesn't. I lie down in bed and think about him before the memory of George kissing me scrambles my brain and I'm left dizzy with the thought of him. I think he's right: I won't get a lick of work done tomorrow, either.

For five straight days George has shown up before suppertime, and I'm prepared with a full meal, clean, brushed hair, and even a hint of rouge on my cheeks. We take walks with Sally down to the creek and sit and neck like we are in high school. Today, he holds my hand while I balance on the rocks jutting up from the creek bed. "One small push is all it'd take to give you a good soaking," he says, pretending to push my arm.

"Don't do it, George Coley! Things would end very badly for you." I jump from rock to rock and hold tighter to his hand.

As I expected, he uses his other hand to push me off-balance, and I pull him in with me, screaming as I go. He hollers out but it's too late: he's soaked up to his waist. Sally jumps in after us and barks her fool head off as George dunks me. I scream, coming up out of the water, and try to force him under, pulling with all my might. "You can't do it, Miss Walker," he says, standing firm in the water. "I'm so strong you'll never pull me under." I try to buckle his legs from under him and he pushes me away. "Say it. Say, 'George, you're so strong.' " I laugh and he holds my face in his hands. "Say it, Miss Walker. Say, 'George, you're so strong.' "

I make my breath all airy like Scarlett O'Hara. "Why Mr. Coley! I do declare, you are so very strong."

He leans in like he's going to kiss me and rocks me backward into the water. I slam into his legs and finally knock him off-balance, holding him under. He picks me up out of the water, holding me like a child, and yells like Tarzan himself, plopping me down at the edge of the creek. He's still in the water as his gaze settles on me. "What's that you were saying? Who's strong and mighty, Miss Walker?"

I lean down to kiss him. "You are, Mr. Coley." Every time my lips touch George's, something sloshes around inside me and I wonder if this feeling will ever stop. The air is spiked with the smell of honeysuckle, and there are only low-hanging trees, frothy clouds, a few blackberry brambles, a sleeping dog, warm creek water, and us. I smile at the thought. Just . . . us.

After George has left tonight, I turn the

radio on and sit out on the porch, listening as the lids continue to seal on the beans I canned earlier in the day. *Pop* . . . there goes one. I smile to myself and close my eyes. *Pop* . . . there goes another one. I love that sound and lean my head against the wall, sighing with the satisfaction of a job well done, and think of George. *Pop.* George is kissing me. *Pop.* Sally barks and I open my eyes.

The boy's hand is resting on Sally's head.

In this light I can see that Jane was right: a worm crawling through the earth is cleaner than him. His overalls are beyond redemption. "You're back! I was wondering where you've been. Are you hungry? Would you like something to eat?"

He nods.

"All right, but we really need to know more about each other. I told you I'm Ivorie. Who are you?" It's unnerving how still he can stand. "Are you one of Clyde and Esther's grandbabies?"

He's as active as a dead man but finally shakes his head.

"Are you anybody's grandbaby here in Morgan Hill?"

He doesn't take his eyes off of me and shakes his head again.

I lean in closer. "Do you live up in those

hills?" I ask, gesturing toward them.

He doesn't move and his stillness is excruciating.

"It's okay if you do. I just always like to know where my visitors come from. I used to climb those hills when I was a little girl around your age. Then I got old and hill climbing wasn't all that exciting anymore."

He moves his hand around Sally's head and she nudges him with her nose.

"It sure is pretty up there, though. Isn't it?"

He bobs his head.

"Do you live way up?"

He moves his head up and down again.

"Let me get your supper." I walk into the kitchen and warm up some chicken, potatoes, and beans from a few days before.

He's playing with Sally when I bring the plate out to him. I notice something bulging on his chest, beneath his overalls, and point to it. "What do you have in there?" He lets down a strap on the overalls and I see a book strapped to his chest with a piece of rope. He pulls out the book and hands it to me as he sits on the porch, gobbling on a chicken leg. "A Bible?" The cover is old and cracked and the corner of most pages is torn away. I turn to the front and read a name: Ruth. He doesn't pay attention and pops one potato after another into his mouth. "Is Ruth your mama?"

He dips his head and picks up the corn bread, shoving it under his nose.

"Is she up in those hills worried about you?"

He reaches for the Bible.

I give it to him and he takes great effort to put it back in place under the rope. "Is your mother here in Morgan Hill?"

He grunts as he eats and I stand to go inside for a glass of milk. I look at the back of him through the screen door — his arms trail down like vines and the blades of his shoulders rise up long and thin like bird wings. I push open the screen door and ask my question again, holding the milk: "Is your mama here in Morgan Hill somewhere?" His silence is maddening. I sit on a chair and lean close, handing him the milk. "Where is she?"

He throws a chicken bone to Sally and picks up another one to tear into.

"Where is your mother?"

He uses the chicken leg to point upward.

I think I know. "Where?"

He points upward again and grunts while chewing.

"Is she in heaven?" He nods, and a little bit of my throat slips down to my stomach.

"My mother's there, too."

He doesn't look at me but throws another bone to Sally.

"Is your pop with your mother?"

He doesn't respond.

I look back toward the hills. "Is he up there?"

He shrugs.

I sit back, watching him. "Does that mean yes?" He shrugs in such a way that I know he wants to be left alone to eat. I walk inside and pick up the phone, dialing Fran's number. Something had to be done about the condition of the boy's clothes, and the only logical solution was to set fire to them. I scoop some cobbler into a bowl before reaching for some of the peanut butter cookies I made earlier in the week.

On the porch he hands me his plate and takes the cookies, pushing one under his nose and sniffing it. In a few minutes Jane, John, and Milo run from around the back of the house. They can run down the tracks and get to my house in no time.

"Here you go," Jane says, holding a pair of overalls at arm's length. "Hey, that's the boy I told you about!"

The boy doesn't look up.

"What smells like feet and poop?" John says, whiffing the air.

Jane smacks his head. "Hush up! What are you, an ignoramus?"

"What'd I say?" John says, nursing the side of his head. "Miss Walker, something has died at your house."

Jane smacks him again. "Hush up, ya dumbbell."

I gesture for both of them to calm down, and I notice that Milo and the boy are looking at each other with a steady stare, each trying to size the other one up. "What's your name?" Jane asks, her voice breaking the silence like a bugle.

The boy doesn't answer.

"I'm Jane and this here is John and Milo."

He looks at the cobbler in the bowl and the cookies on the side of his plate and decides on a cookie, pushing it whole into his mouth. Then he digs into the cobbler and inhales all of it in four bites.

"Why don't he say anything, Miss Walker?"

I fold the overalls over my arm and smile at her. "It's all right, Jane. We're just taking our time getting to know each other."

"I know he needs a bath," John says. Jane whacks his arm and he howls, holding on to it. "What'd you do that for?"

"Hush up before I clobber you good," she says, hissing at him.

"We live that way," Milo says, leaning his head as if pushing it through the house. "We got a houseful of kids, but you could come over if you want to someday."

"You better take a bath first or Mama won't let you in," John says, moving away from Jane.

She runs after him and twists his arm between her hands. "I am going to beat the snot out of you," she says, wrestling him to the ground.

"You all better be getting home," I say. "Your mama's ready to get you into bed, I'm sure." John and Jane line up next to Milo to take one final look at the boy.

"Well, bye, Miss Walker. Bye, boy," Jane says. "Don't say anything hateful," she whispers hot and loud into John's ear.

"Can I have one of your cookies?" he asks the boy.

"Don't ask somebody you don't know for food," Jane says, throwing her arms in the air. "You are the biggest dumbbell I know. Can't you ever say anything smart?"

"It's all right," I say, jumping to my feet. "I made plenty." I run inside and come back out with a cookie for each of them. "You don't even have to tell your mama." The boy and Milo stare at each other again, and Milo lifts his hand in a wave as he, John, and Jane run around the house to the tracks. "They are some kind of a mess! One day I'll tell you all about them." I hold up the overalls in front of the boy. "They gave you this pair of overalls. Do you want to put them on?"

He shakes his head.

"You can have them."

He's emphatic. No!

I set them on my lap. "If you keep coming back here, then we really need to get you cleaned up and get a new pair of overalls on you."

The food and milk are gone and he sits stiff as a horseshoe.

"Okay?"

He dips his head.

"Do you want to put them on now?"

He shakes his head and we listen to the humming silence of nightfall.

"Can I give you some cookies to take with you?"

He shrinks down into the chair.

"They'd be my gift," I say, moving to the door to put some in a brown paper sack for him. He shakes his head again but I step inside the kitchen, pulling open the drawer for a small, used sack. I put six cookies inside it and hand it to him. "For later tonight or tomorrow morning."

He won't take it.

I put the sack in his lap. "You just tell your daddy that Miss Walker and Sally in Morgan Hill gave them to you."

He snatches up the sack and disappears off the porch.

THE BOY

He sinks through deep upon deep of darkness. He drops down, heavy as a stone, his arms opening wide over his head like a great fan. Broken bits of sun ripple on top of the water like puzzle pieces and he watches as the sky drains of blue. He sinks into the fuzzy waters where he is blind, mute, and deaf, the world closing off above him. It is quiet here and he feels the pull of the water dragging him deeper and deeper. He lets it take him but when the hand clasps around his he jerks like a fish on a line. Up he goes through the murk and silence where he can see her hair. He fights to stay but she keeps pulling, her voice muffled and full of water. He rises closer to the surface when he's shaken awake.

"Where'd you get these?" The man is holding the sack of cookies.

His sour breath stings the boy's nose and he can see the bloodred threads in the man's eyes. The boy points wildly.

"Where out there?" the man asks, pulling the boy to his feet. He shoves the boy out the door of the shack and the boy falls off the porch. The man's foot lands in his ribs and he crumples to the ground. "Did you go down into town?"

The boy shakes his head and points down the hillside.

"Where?"

The man's voice booms like thunder and the boy points again down the hillside.

"The cabin down yonder?"

The boy agrees, lying.

The man pulls him to his feet. "Didn't I tell you to stay away from them?" Tears stream down the boy's face and the man slaps him hard. "The next time you do something like this I'll kick your scrawny ass into next week, you hear me?"

The boy nods.

"You are a worthless sack of shit. I should shoot you and be done with it." The man fingers the straps on the boy's overalls, letting one side fall. "Get on in there," he says, looking at the shack. A warm stream runs down the boy's leg and onto the man's foot, making him jump. "Look what you did!" He backhands the boy and the boy's heart thrashes about when he falls. "I'm hungry anyway," the man says. "Get over there and fix my breakfast."

The boy moves to his work but turns back for the sack of cookies on the ground. He picks them up and hands them to the man. In the earthen cellar the boy digs out the small corner of ground she dug up years earlier and removes a teabag-size sack wrapped in waxed paper and brown cloth. He pinches the white powder between his fingers and puts it in the palm of his hand, working quickly with his other hand to put the bag back into the ground.

"He'll sleep with this," she had said to him one night. The boy noticed the blood on her face and how she wiped it away so he couldn't see. "He'll sleep so you can rest easy. Do you hear me?"

The white powder is nearly gone now. He grabs some meat and walks up out of the earth, letting the powder fall into the coffee cup before he gathers eggs from under the chickens. When the coffee boils, he pours it on top of the powder and hands the cup to the man.

The man smiles, revealing teeth as brown as a December leaf. "Good cookies," he says, dipping one into the coffee.

The boy is slow making breakfast.

"What's taking so long?" the man booms.

The boy points to the fire.

"I've told you to start that early in the mornings."

The boy fills the coffee cup again and turns back to his work. He takes a stick to the bacon and flips it over. Two birds land on a branch above the shack and sit hunched over, watching him. After filling two cups of coffee, the boy hands the plate of food to the man and watches him push the bacon into the hole in his face.

"Dry yourself up," the man says, his mouth loaded and making wretched noises. "We'll go inside when I'm through."

The boy points to the fire and the man nods. The boy moves the logs around on the fire so they won't burn down and then reaches for the skillet. He bends over the bucket of water and lifts the gourd dipper, pouring water into the skillet. He scratches at the bottom of the skillet with his hand and sets it back on the smoldering fire to heat and loosen the burned bacon scraps. He jumps when he hears the plate clang to the porch floor and looks up. The man is sprawled on the chair as if shot, his stubby hands flopping at his sides.

The boy leaps for the sack of cookies and runs with it down the hillside behind the fallen trees to the entrance of the cave. He squeezes inside and sits bent over, opening the sack and taking out the remaining cookie. He presses it under his nose and breathes it in. His blood isn't as noisy now, and in a few minutes he doesn't hear his breath, either. He keeps the cookie under his nose and remembers the dog, the woman's smile and voice, and the way she handed him the plate of food. Ivorie. Ivorie and Sally. He eats the cookie, letting the taste spread through him, and closes his eyes.

An immense pitch of pain shoots through his leg and he awakens, kicking and grasping for the rocky wall.

"You don't think I know you come here?" the man growls, pulling the boy leg first out of the cave and shaking him like prey.

The boy squints in the light, shielding his eyes.

"You get up there where you belong," the man says, pushing the boy up the hill.

The boy's blood is making a racket in his ears again as he walks to the shack; the leaves flicker with a flight of birds above him.

The man latches on to him beneath his arm and staggers into the shack, yanking down the boy's overalls.

Vinegary breath crawls up the boy's nose. He reaches back into his mind, back where the cookies smell sweet and Ivorie's voice is the sound of sunrise, and shuts his eyes.

IVORIE

The sun streams in, drizzles of yellow ribbon through my window, and I open my eyes, thinking of the boy. I look out at the hills; for some reason I can't get his scrawny little image out of my mind. Although I made chicken and dumplings and a chocolate pie, two days have come and gone without a visit from him. I put the dumplings in a bowl and set them in the Frigidaire for his next visit and darn near ate that whole pie myself. I decide to take what is left over to George this afternoon.

He lives in a small, white farmhouse he shared with his wife. I imagine when she was alive she kept flowers blooming around the house and on the porch, but now the house is quiet, like George himself. He's out working in his tobacco field but makes his way through the crop when he sees my truck. "I brought you some jam and chicken and dumplings," I yell to him. I feel out of place and gangly at his house and can hear Mother's voice in my head: *Good Lord, Ivorie! Stop that hollering and act like you've got some sense.* I am suddenly embarrassed to be here, it feels like I'm calling on him, and as George gets closer (close enough for me to see the torrents of water snaking down his face and neck), I decide to take the food to the porch and leave it there. "I'll leave it up on your porch," I say, yelling again.

"Where're you running to?" George asks. "What's so all-fired important?" He's almost to the edge of the crop.

"I wanted to get these dumplings out to you before it got too late in the day." I pick up my pace to the truck and hope to make it there before he steps foot into the yard. He hurries and grabs my arm before I can reach the driver's side door.

"Can you sit down for a while?" He lets go of my arm and takes his handkerchief out of his back pocket, drying his face. "I've got iced tea." He smiles and heads to the house. "I'm hoping you're behind me."

I smile and follow him, taking a seat on the swing under the magnolia tree behind his house. I've never felt so jittery before drinking a glass of tea. I'm as nervous as a long-tailed cat in a room full of rockers. I wonder if Refrigerator Lady ever feels all thumbs and left feet before she sips tea with a man at his house. When the screen door snaps, I look up and notice George has changed his clothes. He's wearing tan dungarees with a blue shirt and I think he's so fetching.

"You like it sweet, right?" he asks, handing the glass to me.

"Love it," I say. When he sits next to me the swing sways under his weight and I wonder how many times he sat here with his wife. "How's your tobacco coming along?"

"It's growing real good," he says, looking out on the back side of the crop. He puts his hand on the back of my neck and my insides feel squishy. "What are you hoping for, Ivorie?"

I look over at him, not sure how to respond. "You mean . . ."

His blue eyes bore through mine. "Your folks are gone. You've got a job that keeps you busy. The community has hopes. They make it obvious. But what are you hoping for?"

"I . . ." Noises are coming from my throat but they make me sound like a goat.

"Do you hope to get married someday or are you content with what you have?"

Holy cow! All pretense has been stripped

naked and everything's been laid bare out here on the swing. Had I known we'd be having this talk I would have at least washed my hair. "I don't know," I say, looking down at the tiny hairs poking out on my shin-bones. "All these years I thought I knew but maybe that's because there's never been anybody to make me think . . . I don't know."

He pushes his foot on the ground; the swing sways to the rhythm of his nodding head. "I only want to do this if we both want it. We're both getting too old to worry about what other people think. One time Hot Dot asked me if I even *liked* women." Tea spews out of my mouth and I howl, leaning on my knees.

I look over at George's face; it's draped in seriousness and I laugh harder. "I can set her mind at ease that you indeed like women," I say. He leans over and kisses me, and I rest my head on his shoulder. "If my aunt Dot saw us sitting here like this she'd have us married by morning."

"Would that be bad?" I feel nervous at the thought and he lifts my chin to look at him. "Would it?" He kisses me and my head screams, *No, it wouldn't be bad! It would be flat-out terrific!*

I don't answer but smile, feeling my heart

twisted up in my throat. I rest against his chest. "What do you like to do out here?" I know he'll say farming and mending his fences and such, but I want to know more.

"I work the tobacco and the garden and keep the barn roof patched and the fences mended."

"But when the work's done. What do you do?" He looks at me and I realize he's never thought about it before. He shrugs and pulls a knee up in his hands. "Do you listen to the shows on the radio?"

"Sometimes."

"Do you read?"

He gives me an apologylike smile. "The most I read is what's in the almanac."

I nod and look toward his tobacco. "George." I'm going out on a limb here. "Word is you have a woman somewhere."

The sides of his mouth fold down and I kick myself for venturing out on that limb so early. "I do. She lives over in Morgan Hill with Sally the dog." It's all he wants to say and I smile. "Could you stay for supper? I have chicken and dumplings."

My limbs are quick to come to life this morning. I lie in bed and think about George: sitting on his swing, eating at his table, walking through his tobacco, and kissing his lips. I throw my arm over my eyes and feel a tremor deep in my stomach as images of George race through my mind. I sit up and swing my legs off the side of the bed. We are so different. How could it ever work? Why wouldn't it work? If we were just alike we'd be stale as day-old biscuits. I head to the bathroom to wash my face and get on with the day. This morning I'll pick the ripe tomatoes and can them before the heat of the day gives me a stroke.

After I line the tomatoes up on the countertop, I pour myself a glass of iced tea and reach for the peanut butter, spreading some over a saltine cracker. I make another one and take them out to the porch, where I hope a cool breeze will find me. "You need more than that after you've been in the garden and canning in that hot kitchen all morning," Mother would have said. "You'll get weak in the legs if you don't eat more than that." I stick the last bite into my mouth when I hear tires on the driveway. I look up, hoping it's George. I stand and throw my hand up when I recognize Holt Oxman and his mud-colored truck.

"Morning, Ivorie," he says. "I was wondering if you found the critter that was tearing apart your garden."

I jump up and walk to the side of the well

house. "I sure did and I won't need these anymore," I say, holding the traps out to him as I walk.

He stoops to the ground and pulls a blade of grass, glancing up at me. "So what was it?"

I move toward the porch. "Turned out to be nothing more than a little boy."

"A boy? Who is he?"

"Nobody knows. I still don't know him. I can't get a word out of him. All I know is he came down from the hills."

Holt scratches his head and pats Sally's back. "Well, I'll be. I thought all those people were gone from up there."

I move back to my chair. "You want some tea, Holt?" He shakes his head. "I don't know what's what with him, though. He's not been back in a few days. I have figured out his mother is dead and he lives with his pop."

Holt peers up into the hills and moves around the porch post, squaring off to me. "Careful, Ivorie. If you're getting the boy here, it's just a matter of time before more of his people come. Nobody would want anything to happen to you."

"He's just a hungry little boy."

He bends down and picks up the traps and I watch him walk to his truck. "He's a lot more than that, coming down out of those hills. You can be sure of that."

Since it's still early in the day, I decide to pick some blackberries down by the creek for a cobbler for supper. The sky is a stunning blue as Sally and I make our way onto the train tracks; the sun is slanting down on the hillside and I stop to look up toward the trees, wondering why anyone would choose to live up in there. Years ago, there was a family named Anders who lived up in the hills who had eight children, each one uglier than the one before. They all had weak eyes, sloping shoulders, pendulum arms, homely upper teeth, and misshapen noses. The Anders children would trek down the hills to Henry's every month and stand there smelling like homemade hooch with their long, dull, tired faces staring at everybody in the store like we were aliens. Ugly people always look that way until you stop seeing their bulbous nose or badger teeth and you start seeing them and hear where they came from and where they're going. I got to know Reba, a girl no older than me when she'd come out of the hills to pick blackberries along the creek, and one day I realized that she wasn't ugly to me anymore. She was a fine-boned redhead with pale green eyes

145

and a crinkled brow, as if a question was always on her mind. Reba wasn't ugly at all. She was just a poor, pitiful girl who had a lazy, no-good daddy who didn't want his kids to get an education. He eventually left, dying hundreds of miles away from his children, who ended up God knows where.

I walk along the tracks and hear the sound of voices coming from the creek. Sally runs ahead, and as I get closer I recognize Jane's laugh. "Does your mama know you're here?" I ask, watching them splash in their under shorts. Sally jumps in and John screams when she does.

"She's the one who made us come," Milo says. "She said we were driving her plumb out of her mind."

I laugh and start picking the berries, reaching my hand through the brambles and thorns. "Can I help you, Miss Walker?" Jane asks.

"I never turn down good help," I say, watching her trudge out of the water.

Jane steps out of the water and hikes her underpants up before the creek takes them. She's thin and lanky and the water shines bright and slippery on her skin. "Where's that boy at?" she asks, dropping a soggy handful of berries into my basket.

"I guess he's at home," I say. "He hasn't

146

been back in a few days."

"You reckon we scared him off?" Milo asks, slapping water toward Sally.

"I don't think so. It seems to me he'd look at you three and want to be fast friends."

"Except with John," Jane says. "He'll try you. Mama says that all the time. She says, 'John, you are trying me.' I don't even know what that means, but nobody wants to be friends with John because of it."

"Jane! That ain't true nohow," John bellows from the creek.

"You don't talk good, either," Jane says. "Mama keeps telling you *ain't* is not a word."

I laugh and hold up my hands to stop them. "I don't know *why* your mama sent you down to the creek!"

"That boy sure is a sad, ugly little thing, isn't he, Miss Walker?" Jane says.

"He is sad," I say, reaching farther into the tangle of briars for some large, plump berries. "But he doesn't have a mother. She died."

"Are you still sad because you don't have a mama anymore?"

I can feel her looking at me but squat down to reach another handful of berries. "I am."

"I wonder if his mother is buried up there?" Jane asks, looking up at the hills.

147

"There's probably all sorts of skeletons and witches and monsters buried up there," John says.

"Witches?" Milo asks, stopping his splashing. "Are there witches up there?"

"No," Jane says.

"There are too," John says. Milo's eyes are the size of quarters. "But they won't hurt you none because they're all dead skeletons now."

"No witch skeletons are up there, dum-dum!" Jane says, squeezing some berries through her fingers. "There's not, is there, Miss Walker?" she says, whispering.

"No. There are no witch skeletons."

"Well, there's plenty of skeletons buried up there," John says, as if he's in the know.

I laugh and look into my basket. "Well, I've got plenty of berries for a cobbler. Tell your mama I said hey."

Jane jumps into the creek and I walk back down the tracks for home, wondering who was buried up in those hills. For that matter, what was buried at my own house? Over the years I've buried pain as easy as I've buried happiness. Sally catches up to me and I stand on the tracks and look up at the house snoring in emptiness. It's a buried life I'm living here, but when I think of George I know I'm digging my way out.

I turn the radio on while I string some beans for supper and listen to Eddy Arnold, Bob Wills, the Louvin Brothers, and others belt out one tune about heartbreak after another, and when an hour passes, I realize I can't remember one song that has been played, so I turn off the radio. I put some potatoes on to boil and make the cobbler, eating enough blackberries to turn me purple for a week. When I take the cobbler out of the oven I hear Sally bark and it sounds like she's right beside me. I set the cobbler on top of the stove and turn to look at her. She's right outside the screen door, pressed up against George's side, shaking her tail.

I feel my face spreading in a wide smile and try to catch myself before I turn all schoolgirl on him. "Come in," I say, opening the screen door.

"I have more berries for you," he says, looking out on the porch. "I left them right out yonder on that chair." He looks at the cobbler and pot of beans. "You've been busy. Are you getting company?" He kisses me and smiles. "Or are you waiting on me?"

I kiss him long and can smell the shaving cream on his skin. I pour him a glass of tea and set it at one of the chairs. "I might be getting company. I don't know, exactly."

He laughs and takes a long drink. "What kind of company is that, if you don't know if they're coming or not?"

I sit on the chair next to him and notice fresh scratches on his hands. He has farmer's hands, calloused and knicked and discolored from weeds and dirt and vegetables. Refrigerator Lady would find farmer's hands unsightly but I find them masculine and attractive. I pick one of his hands up and hold it in mine. "A little boy has been visiting me off and on for a couple of weeks now. I never know when he's coming. I don't even know if he'll be back."

George leans on the table, holding the tea at a distance in front of him. "Who's little boy is he?"

"Nobody knows. His mama died and he lives in the hills with his pop."

He throws an arm over his chair and looks at me. "You don't know anything about him?"

"Not really."

"Then why are you feeding him?"

I don't like his tone and something buzzes in my chest. I feel my face getting hot and release his hand. "Because he's hungry."

George's face softens and he rests his arms on the table. He taps my hand with his finger. "You are something, Ivorie

Walker! Not many people would feed a stranger like that. I don't know if I could do it." The heat leaves my face and I keep my hands on the table, hoping he'll touch me again. "Do you know who his pop is?"

"No. The boy doesn't talk much."

George leans back again and takes his hands with him. "So what do you know?"

I shake my head. "Not much. I'm just piecing things together."

He stands up and moves to the screen door, looking out at Sally. "I don't think this is a good idea. I mean, I think it's real nice that you're feeding that boy but you could be opening up a big can of worms if you keep opening your door to him."

The heat is rising to my face again. "What kind of worms?"

He turns to me. "You've seen people come out of those hills. We all have. Leave them to themselves, Ivorie."

I want to stand but force myself to stay in my seat. "So I turn away a hungry little boy?"

He looks out the screen door again and I want to tell him to face me. "They take care of each other. . . ." He turns to look at me. "And we take care of each other." He leans down and kisses me. "They could hurt you." His eyes are round and smoky and I shake off the anger clinging to my skin. "That's all I'm saying." He pulls me up and draws me to him. "You are a fine-looking woman. Do you know that, Miss Walker?" He's trying to make me smile and it works. He kisses me and holds my chin in his hand. "You be careful." He opens the door and says, "I'm sure I'll have a few more berries." He leaves but I don't walk him to his truck.

At eight o'clock I give up waiting and set the potatoes and beans inside the Frigidaire when Sally barks. I lift my head and see the boy standing under the porch light. "Well, where have you been?" I ask, moving toward the door. His eyes are hollow and the veins in his neck stick out like straws. There's something appalling yet beautiful about him, and I open the door, letting him inside. I hold my breath at the smell and bend down to look at him. "Sally's missed you." He turns to look at Sally on the porch and I can't get over his appearance and smell and those eyes that look right through me. "I've got some potatoes and beans. Would you like them?"

His eyes brighten a bit.

"I'll warm them up." I move to the Frigid-aire but he doesn't budge. "I was thinking that while I warmed them maybe you'd like to take a bath. Would you like that?"

He doesn't respond.

I spoon some of the potatoes and beans into a pot and put them on the stove to warm. "Have you ever taken a bath?" He doesn't answer, and I walk to the table and sit down in front of him. "Look, if you're going to keep coming here, then you really need to talk to me. Have you ever taken a bath?"

He shakes his head.

"All right, come on. I'll show you the bathtub." He follows me through the house, and I can't even imagine what George would think of me now, about to give this strange boy a bath. I lead the boy to the bathroom and point to the tub. "You've never seen one of these?"

His face is vacant.

"How do you get clean? Do you have a spigot or a rain barrel?" He's close-mouthed and I bend down to plug the tub and turn on the water. "You can take your clothes off and get in. The soap's right there."

He watches the water but doesn't move.

"Do you want me to help you?"

He can't take his eyes off the filling tub.

I point to his overalls. "Take those off and I'll help you get in the tub." He's as still as distant smoke and I point to the overalls

153

again. "Those need to come off before you get in."

He stares at me and turns around, facing the wall.

I reach for the denim straps and slip them down his arms. "Oh my Lord," I say, stepping back and stumbling over the commode. The boy doesn't move and I feel sick to my stomach. The flesh on his back is torn and crusted with blood. Words fly through my mind but I can't get them beyond my throat. I can't blink or breathe. I ease the overalls down his legs and see lash marks on the back of them. I put my hands on his arms and turn him around; he won't look at me. "Who . . ." My voice sounds hollow and lost somewhere above me. I am shaking and want to throw up but I put my hand on the bottom of the boy's chin and lift it, looking in those blue, ghost eyes. "Who did this to you?"

He doesn't even blink, looking at me.

"I need to clean you up," I say, trying to find my voice. "Can you step into the tub for me?" I take his hand and lead him to the edge of the tub.

He looks in but doesn't budge.

"Please," I say, my stomach churning. "Step in and let me clean you up."

He lifts his leg and steps into the water,

watching it from above.

"If you sit down in it I can clean your back and wash your hair."

He sits as slow as an old man and I splash the water over his legs. He doesn't catch my eye but watches the water like our men watched the enemy in the war.

I'm easy and gentle as I wash his legs and stomach and work my hands into a thick lather for his neck and face, keeping soap away from his eyes. "You can splash water onto your face now," I say.

He doesn't so much as twitch.

I use the washrag to rinse away the soap and move around to his back, where I stop working. I don't know what to do. I don't have anything to clean the wounds with except soap and whiskey and both will hurt. I decide to wash his hair first and then call Doc Langley about the open wounds on the boy's back. "Can you get the water up on your head and get your hair wet?"

He stares into the water and shakes his head.

"Can you get your head down in the water?" He can't and I look around. I remember the water pitcher and bowl we used for years to wash our faces in the morning, and I run to Pop's room to get it. I fill it up with water and pour it real slow over the boy's head.

As it drains over his face he jumps and kicks his legs, falling backward into the tub. He slides under the water, and when his head pops up, the sound of a wounded animal echoes off the tub's iron walls.

I set the pitcher on the floor and grab his hands, trying to pull him up.

He is shaking and moaning and clawing his way up and out of the tub, splashing water over the rim.

"It's okay," I say, reaching for a towel.

He is flailing his arms and his mouth is open in a soundless, unintelligible scream, and I see the crater-size hole where the roof of his mouth should be, a cleft palate that has stolen his voice.

I wrap the towel around him and sit on the commode, pulling him close to me. We are both sopping wet. "Shh, shh, shh," I say, rubbing his head. "It's okay. You're okay. I've got you."

He moans and it's the saddest, longest, and loneliest sound I've ever heard, the kind of sound that steals your breath.

"You're okay. I've got you," I whisper. "I've got you."

I don't want him to run off after supper, but he does and I stand on the back porch with a hole in my insides like I'd thrown myself on a live grenade. I had known children who had been roughed up in the name of discipline, their pops setting their hands of wicked fatherhood upon them, but never anything like this. I sit in the dark on the porch and Sally puts her head in my lap, my tears falling into the soft fur of her head.

I never close my eyes. The moon is so round and full that it looks like it's hanging right in front of the hills. I reach out as if it's setting in the palm of my hand. The boy is right there, so close, just on the other side of the moon.

The sky is the color of cinnamon when the sun comes up and I can tell by the way the clouds bulge that they are full of rain. From the back porch I watch the sun wake up over the hills and I look on them with wonder and dread and a stab of fear that makes my breathing hard. How does he live up there with all sense of hope silenced? Little boys and girls should grow up amazed at how a fish breathes or how a flower opens up to the sun and then goes to bed at night or how the wind moves. "We take care of each other," George said. "Leave them to themselves." The boy's fleshy back flashes through my mind, and I walk into the house, slamming the door.

I lift the phone to call Henry but put it back down. There's nothing he can do, and if I told him what I saw, he'd get worried for me and tell me to stay out of it. George has made his feelings known, so there's no reason to call him. I'd call Holt but Avis would be fit to be tied if he left right at milking time. I ponder calling Sheriff Dutton but I know he'd tell me those hills are out of his jurisdiction. "Then whose jurisdiction are they?" I shout to the walls. I can't think of one thing to work on, although I know there are cobwebs too high to reach that still need attention and mice nests in the barn that need to be destroyed, and there are more beans that need to be picked. I walk around the outside of the house and notice the boards on the porch that need to be replaced and the dead limbs that need to come out of the oak and see brand-new tomatoes that need to come off the vine but I can't do any of it. It's repulsive to even think about.

After a peanut butter sandwich at noon I gather some vegetables from the garden for supper. There's plenty of cobbler left from last night but I decide to make a caramel cake, too. That will take a while and keep me occupied. As the cake cools I put sugar in the skillet and stir it while it gets pretty and golden. I pull two cans of Pet Milk out of the cupboard and open them, pouring the milk into a pot along with the sugar, some butter, and vanilla. I let it all boil down real low and plop a bit of it into a bowl of cold water, forming a tiny ball between my fingers. I spread the mixture between the layers of the cake and slather the rest on top. I leave my messy pots and walk to the back porch, looking up at the hills and shouting, "I've got cake!" Sally lifts her head and I sigh, wondering what time it is now.

I manage to use up three hours before I jump into the truck. The usual suspects are at Henry's when I arrive but I don't stop to talk with them. Henry is sweeping and Loretta is moving all the candy jars off the counter and cleaning the top of it. "Henry," I say, before either of them can speak. "Can I borrow Kitty Wells?"

He stops sweeping and leans on the broom. "What do you need my mule for?"

I rest against the counter and cross my arms. "I want to plant some late corn."

He twists up his face and bends down to sweep a small dirt pile into the dustpan. "Why in the world do you want to plant late corn? You're already going to have more corn down there than you'll ever eat."

"Some of my rows aren't coming in good," I say.

"What are you going to do with all that corn?" Loretta asks.

I turn to her and smile. "I'm going to freeze most of it."

"You don't have a freezer big enough for all of it," Henry says, hanging up the broom.

"Henry!" I say, turning on him. "Are you going to let me borrow that mule or not?"

Loretta looks out the window. "Are you going to plow today? It's so late in the day and it's going to rain."

"The almanac says today is the last day to plant late corn."

"Did the almanac also say that you don't plow in the afternoon rain?" Henry asks. I look at him and he shakes his head. "Come on. Let's go get her."

Henry and Loretta live up the road, around the corner. On most days they just walk to work unless Henry lingers too long over a cup of coffee and jelly biscuit, then they drive so they can open the store at seven sharp. Henry has lived in the house for as long as I can remember, and I have nearly as many memories here as my own home. Henry opens the gate to the pasture and whistles for the mule. She turns her big, lazy head and chomps a mouthful of weeds. "Miss Kitty," Henry calls with his hands propped on each side of his mouth. "She likes to be called Miss Kitty," he says, smiling at me.

"That is the dumbest name for a mule."

"Miss Kitty Wells would be honored to know that it was her voice that inspired me when I bought this mule," he says. Henry's last mule, Roy Acuff, died around the time Mother did, and he replaced him with Kitty Wells, named after a woman he'd heard sing on *The Louisiana Hayride.*

The mule walks across the pasture toward us. "Most people name their mules something like Jake or Shadow."

He hisses at me and gestures with his hand for me to lower my voice. "Those are manly mule names. Miss Kitty is a lady."

"I am not calling that mule Miss Kitty."

He reaches out and wraps his arm around her neck. "Then you won't get any work out of her. She doesn't like 'Kitty.' It's too informal for her." I roll my eyes. He harnesses her and hands the reins to me.

"Aren't you going to saddle her?"

"What for? Can't you just walk her down the tracks?"

"I'd like to ride her so I can get home quicker." He doesn't say anything but moves to the barn for the saddle. When it's in place he helps me onto the mule's back. I'm sure I look as silly as I feel.

"Do you want some help?" Henry asks.

"No," I say, riding off. "I can do it."

The water jars of heaven tilt full over when I'm only halfway home and by the time I reach the embankment the rain is coming down sideways. I jump off the mule and pull on the reins to get her up the incline. "Come on," I say, shouting against the rain. "Get up here, you stupid mule." She's as movable as the rails on the tracks. "Come on!" I refuse to call her Miss Kitty and tug till my arms feel like they're ripping from the sockets. I sigh, long and heavy, and shout, "Come on, Miss Kitty!" She plods forward and climbs up the bank. I run her into the barn and open a stall. Sally watches from the porch, more content to be dry than running after me in this mess. When I get to the porch I slide out of my dress and wring out my hair. I fall into a chair and feel the heaviness of no sleep the night before fall like bricks on top of me. "He won't come in this," I say to Sally. I stand up and walk into the house. I am exhausted.

The bedroom is dark when I wake up, jumping like an anxious hen, and I strain to see the clock in the moonlight: three o'clock.

I'm still in my underwear and brassiere and I realize I fell into bed like this nine hours ago. George didn't come by yesterday before supper. I don't know if he's upset with me for feeding the boy, but I convince myself it was the rain that kept him away. I listen as heavy drops fall onto the roof and close my eyes, trying to sleep, but it's no use. George and the boy and the rain and the mule are all shoving at my mind. I get up and wash my face, brush my teeth, and pull back my hair. I pull on a pair of jeans and a long-sleeve shirt and walk to the kitchen, where I put on a pot of strong coffee and make a pan of biscuits, and by four o'clock I'm ready to milk Gertie. I pour the milk into pitchers and set them inside the Frigidaire.

The Thermos is at the back of the bottom cupboard where I keep the pots and I reach for it, filling it with water and some ice. I stick some handkerchiefs, a small towel, and some biscuits with ham into a knapsack and walk into Pop's room, grabbing the rifle from the corner. The shells are in the top drawer and I open it, moving his Bible out of the way to get to them. I slip two shells into the chamber, put two more in my front pocket, and grab a handful for the knapsack.

By the time I go back to the barn and find

a piece of tarp to cut so I can slip it over my head, the sun is cresting and I know it's five thirty. I throw the knapsack and rifle over my shoulder as Sally runs back and forth in front of me, barking. I lean into the stall, making sure there's a bowl of water, and call her to me. She leaps for me and I pat her sides. "You can't come with me," I say, closing the door. I can hear her barking as Kitty Wells walks out of the barn into the galloping rain. It'd take me most of the day to get to the top of those hills on foot; I'm hoping it will take me three hours or a bit more on the mule. There's no telling in this rain.

The creek is swelling when I get to it and I jump off the mule's back, looking for the best place to cross. "Come on," I yell, pulling on her. She doesn't want to cross and I slap her backside. She doesn't inch toward me and I rub the water from my eyes. "Come on, Miss Kitty. Let's go!" She takes painstaking steps across the rocks as if she's walking on hot coals and I jump onto her back when she's on land again. The rain is warm on my skin and I move my feet around in my shoes; my socks feel like mud squishing between my toes. I look up into the clouds and wonder how long this will last. There's no way to get the mule up the rocky crevice, it's too narrow, so I walk her around the base of the hill, looking for safe footing. I find a spot and dig my heels into her sides. She makes her way up the sloping side of the hill and the ground makes sucking noises beneath her hooves.

I try to lean back in the saddle and hold my legs against the mule's sides, but the unsure footing and rain on the saddle make me slide like a fish in bare hands. I fall to the ground and latch hold of the reins before the mule gets ahead of me. I stand to my feet and rest my head against her neck. She swishes her tail and I put my left foot in the stirrup and swing my right leg over her back. Thunder cracks above us and spooks her. She kicks her back legs and lunges ahead. "Whoa! Whoa!" I yell, wrapping the slick reins around my hands. The ground is sloppy and Miss Kitty pulls a hoof from the mud in slow motion. The clouds break open with a fierce, reckless downpour and I cover my eyes with one hand to see, but it's no use. I slide off the saddle and walk the mule under a tree. I let my back slide down the trunk and put my head on my knees. I watch the water puddle up around my feet and sigh. I have no plan. I don't know what I'm doing or what I'll see or who I'll meet. I am angry and frightened and disgusted and shaking. This, whatever it is that I'm doing, is out of my realm of possibilities. I wait for the storm to break and try to climb back onto Miss Kitty, but my foot slips. The tarpaulin I'm wearing over my head is no match for the rain; I'm soaked through, so I toss it aside and roll up my shirtsleeves. I try to heave myself up again and lose footing on the ground, sliding on my stomach through mud and water. I stand and sling mud off my hands, rubbing them on my pants, and march back up the hill to where Miss Kitty is standing. I pull myself up onto her back, screaming, and clack my tongue for her to move.

There's no easy or fast way up the sodden hillside for the mule, so we plod our way up one mushy step at a time. The rain is silvery gray in front of me; it doesn't look or feel like morning yet. I'd reach for Pop's pocket watch, but I'm afraid it will slip right out of my hands. We travel up, up, up, and I can't imagine how the boy ran up and down these rugged hills as much as he did. The land is uneven and steep here and then slick and rocky there. At least two and a half hours have passed by the time we get to the base of the woods. I stop the mule and look into the center of the trees; they're dark with rain and quiet as gravestones. "There's probably all sorts of skeletons and witches and monsters buried up there," John said. I look back over my shoulder and see my house in the distance. So much is buried in that house. After so many years of living with myself I have become tired of me. Is that why I'm here? Miss Kitty moves forward and steps over fallen trees and branches. I strain to look deeper into the woods but can't see anything. There is no sound save the rain; all the animals are tucked safely away in burrows or holes or hollow logs. Would the Refrigerator Lady step out of her picture-perfect world to do this? Would she get all sloppy and wet and muddy going after a boy she didn't know? What would George think if he saw me now? Miss Kitty plods farther up through the trees.

In the distance I see the rooftop of a home and feel my breath tighten. I take the rifle off my shoulder and hold it on my stomach as we near the cabin. I halt Miss Kitty some distance from the cabin and look around. The trees are filled with colored bottles to trap evil spirits, a superstition that is older than Tennessee itself. It's a decent enough cabin; the roof isn't caving in or the walls falling down. "Hey," I shout above the rain. No one comes to the door, and I look around, making sure no one is outside. "Hey!" I hold the rifle higher, unsure of who I'll be meeting here, and feel my hands shaking. The door opens and a rail-thin woman with willowy arms, large eyes, and a long nose steps onto the porch. If she's shocked to see a woman aiming a rifle at her she doesn't let on but looks at me real solemnlike, waiting. A set of eyes peers out at me through the window. "Is the boy here?" I ask above the noise of the rain, lowering the rifle.

"Are you feeding him now?" she asks. I nod. "We fed him as long as we could after his mama died but we've been bad off the last few weeks."

I glance at their cabin. They have nothing but were giving him food. The thought tears at my heart. "When did she die?"

Her face falls in on itself, looking blunt and empty. "Don't recall exactly. Over a year ago," she shouts against the rain.

"Is he here?"

She points up the hillside and I pull the reins to turn the mule. "You'll need a necklace before you go," she says, walking to the far end of the porch. She brings a necklace of chicken claws and feathers to the side of the mule and lifts it up to me. "To protect you from what's up there."

The sound of her words seizes hard in my throat, and my heart makes a sound like a gun firing in my ears. I want to ask her what's up there but I don't want to know. If I know, I might run. I shake my head and she looks at me from hollow eye sockets with dark crescent-moon circles under them. The woman lets the claws dangle at her side and she nods, keeping her eyes fixed on mine. I dig my heels into Miss Kitty's side and she climbs slowly. I hold the rifle but my hand feels loose and detached. I squeeze it harder and feel my heart banging against my ribs. What bit of sunlight there was in the woods feels like it's shrinking as the mule carries me farther up the hill. There is no way to hush my deafening blood or calm the hammering behind my lungs.

The mule climbs farther on and I spot a small shack, nothing more than a lean-to in the middle of a clump of trees. It looks forgotten and abandoned except for a few chickens. A man stands to his feet on the ramshackle porch and lifts something to his mouth. He takes a long swig and watches me approach. Something menacing and dangerous crawls through my veins. My heart is beating inside my stomach now and it's as if something closes around my ears, shutting out the rain, the mule's steps, and the knock on my ribs, and it sounds as if I'm under water. I stop the mule when I'm still a good distance away and feel my hand trembling around the rifle. A minute or an hour goes by as I face him. He's a bald-headed, pot-gutted, banty rooster type. He steps off the porch into the rain and looks at me, taking another swig from his jug. I don't know who he is and don't ask. He has hurled away his existence and come up here to stay tucked away from the world of enemies below — none who are scarier than he in this pit of hell he's created, where he beats the flesh off a little boy's back — in this secret place of horror that slithers with puke and filth and evil.

"Long time since a woman's been up here," he says. His muddy eyes are dull with poison and seeping in the corners. My throat closes and the rifle feels like lead on my shoulder. "Good God almighty," he says, his voice full of gravel. "Pointin' a rifle ain't no way to call on somebody."

"Where's the boy?" He laughs and a white flash of anger, clean and sharp as a tobacco blade, cuts through me. "I'll blow a hole in your chest if you take another step toward me." His face flattens; then he laughs and takes a step. I aim the rifle at his feet and pull the trigger. The sound ricochets off the soggy earth and wet trees and dies.

"What the hell do you want?" He's angry and drunk.

Fear pushes on my chest and I take short breaths. When the Japs bombed Pearl Harbor I was angry. When our boys came home from Germany in body bags fury flew out from every corner of my body. But rage is different. It's like a fire, flaming out and licking at things in the way. "Where's the boy?"

He sways side to side and curls his mouth up in a sick and disturbing way. "What do you want him for?"

"I want to take him." I didn't know that's why I had come, but at this moment it's clear to me.

He smiles and a fiery blaze sets aflame in my stomach. "How much?"

I grope for something to say. "Wha . . ."

He inches toward me. "Give me the rifle for him."

My mind is firing in all directions. "Give me the boy first."

He laughs and reaches for a branch on the tree to hold. "You are a fine little piece of —"

I don't let him finish. "Give me the boy!" I scream.

His eyes narrow, looking at me. "Why do you want that scrawny-assed thing?"

"Where is he?" I shout over the rain.

He makes a sweeping arc with his arm. "Back yonder."

I clack my tongue and keep the rifle aimed at the man as the mule moves toward the back of the shack. I jump down when the mule gets to the side of the shack and I can hear my breath in my ears as I look around, never turning my back on where I left the man.

My heart buckles and stops when I see small legs lying on the ground and I run the short distance to the boy. His face is in the mud, his eyes are closed and sheeted with rain, and he's still as death. Lightning flashes through my head and my legs feel numb. "God! God! Jesus!" I call out, touching him. I have no idea how I can pick him up and hold the rifle. "I need help. Lord, help me!" I put the rifle strap around my neck and lean down, putting my arms under the boy's stomach to lift him; he flops like a wet and muddy rag doll. I pull him tight to my body and shove my other arm under his legs, groaning as I stand. I slip on the leaves and muck and stagger toward the mule. "I got you. I got you." My bottom lids fill with tears and cloud my vision because I have no idea how I can get him onto the mule. The thought of the man sneaking around the corner of the shack makes anger climb hand over fist up my insides and I cry out, heaving the boy over the saddle. His face smacks against the mule's side and I hoist myself up behind him; he's hanging like a dishrag out on the line. My head is roaring as the mule moves wide around the side of the shack and I put the rifle back on my shoulder. The man has moved, and I dart my eyes from side to side looking for him. He's on the porch, aiming a gun at me.

"I don't take to nobody holding a rifle on me."

I'm not afraid. Looking at the limp little body draped in front of me, I'm ready to pull the trigger. "If I'm not out of these hills by ten o'clock, there's a posse of men who will come up here and track you down like the animals you eat. They know you're up here. They know your name, and they know what you've been doing to this boy."

He lowers the gun. "He's nothing but a sack of shit."

I hold the rifle on him. "Don't you ever look for him. Don't you ever come near him again!"

He steps off the porch. "Where's my rifle?"

I take the remaining shell out of the

chamber, putting it in my pocket. I throw the rifle far to the side and pull on the reins to turn the mule. "He's a no-good piece of shit," I hear the man yell after me. He keeps yelling and cursing as we make our descent out of the woods.

HENRY

Sarah Ivorie's ideas are like forest fires — once they take hold there's no stopping them. When Sarah was a girl she was short and solid and looked like a sturdy general with bangs. Her height never climbed above five feet four, but when she talks to you, you swear she's bigger. She grew up scrapping with six brothers and met anything — school, work, or planting tobacco — like a fight where she needed to prove something. From the time she was pint-size Sarah has been her own person, never trying on her big brothers' shoes or words. Mother always said she was too independent and maybe she was, but men always came around to call on my sister anyway. She's small boned like Mother was and has walnut-colored hair and tiny, pearly teeth. She's cute on any given day and downright pretty in the light of the sun. That's what I think, anyway. When Sarah smiles a jolt of electricity surges through Morgan Hill, and when she's mad a mighty wind sweeps over the community.

Maybe her personality did drive men off, or maybe the men here just weren't strong enough for her liking; I don't know. I never heard her complain one way or the other. She's never been somebody to wear much on her shirtsleeve, like what she's thinking about George Coley. I don't know what's happening with them but figure she'll fill me in when she's ready. There has always been, like they say, something right and true about my sister; the way right is right and true north is true. If she tells you your rooster is dipping snuff, you better look under its wing for the can.

Few things get the best of Sarah. For the last twelve years she's worked in the school office and library and has dealt with some of the dumbest kids and parents the good Lord has put on this earth. When Pop was sick, she'd go home to care for him, and he was as cantankerous an old man as you'd ever meet. Time ended up sanding off his sharp edges, but still yet, he was no picnic to live with, even then. Pop never believed in mollycoddling his kids. "You'll never amount to anything," he'd say. "You can't do that!" "You're not bright enough to graduate school." He was harder on Sarah Ivorie because he didn't know what to do with a girl. I guess he thought if he convinced her she couldn't do something that maybe she'd scrap harder to make something of herself.

He'd bellow at her, and if she was climbing a tree, throwing a fishing line into the creek, or baking a pie, she'd yell, "I'm not listening to you!" And that's just how she phrased it every time. Not, "I can't hear you," because she could hear him plain but she wasn't *listening* to him.

Though there weren't enough books in Mother and Pop's house to shake a stick at, Sarah loved to read. She must have read every book in the school library two or three times.

When she was nine, Sarah complained of a headache while she helped my wife Edith shell some peas. The headache got so bad that Edith told her to go inside and lie down on the couch. Edith finished the peas, and by the time she checked on Sarah, she was burning up with fever. Edith helped her into our bed and kept swabbing her body with cold rags. On the fourth day, I told Edith to load our two youngest kids and take them to her sister's. Sarah woke up on day five and had no idea who Mother was. Mother walked to the kitchen, wringing her hands together like rags, and asked me to fetch the doctor again.

When the doctor said yellow fever, Mother let out a low-bellied groan. Men across the states brought yellow fever home with them after the first war, but no one in Morgan Hill had suffered from it. The doctor had no idea where Sarah would have caught the virus so many years later. Sarah's skin turned yellow with jaundice, her hair stuck to the pillow like trampled weeds, and she threw blood up into a pan Mother held for her. Mother slept on the floor beside the bed and never went home for three weeks. Pop was alone to fend for himself. At the end of farming each day he'd come and stand at the end of the bed, his hands rooting around in his pockets for answers, and he'd scratch his head in search of something to say. "I know you never listen to me, but you fight harder, you hear." Pop never met my eyes when he came out of that bedroom.

When I'd come home from the store I'd sit in a chair and read to Sarah. One day she turned her head toward me and flashed open her eyes. She didn't say a word but watched me like a bug that had landed on the windowsill. It gave me the heebie-jeebies the way she kept her eyes on me, looking at me but not seeing me, but Mother said, "Keep reading, Henry. It soothes her."

On day nineteen Sarah woke up and asked why Mother was sleeping on the floor. She was all eyes and sharp bones and flat lips and Mother cradled her like a baby. Two days later Pop came to get them. Later, Sarah told me there were times when she heard Pop talking to her, heard Mother's small birdlike voice praying for her, and heard me reading and telling Mother to think about the fifty percent who do live. You look at a person a whole different way when they come close to dying in your bed.

A few years later Edith died in that same bed and Sarah sat by her side and read out loud to her each day till she was hoarse. You also tend to look at a person real different when they help your wife die in peace.

When Loretta and I walk to work a flashing thought runs through my head: *What if Sarah Ivorie wanted Miss Kitty to go up into those hills?* I call her house when we open the store at seven but she doesn't answer. I try her again a few minutes later and my thought turns into a sickening hunch. "Who in the world do you keep calling?" Loretta asks.

"Sarah," I say, watching the rain sheet on

179

the store windows. "She is crazy out of her mind."

Loretta is emptying a box of soap onto the shelves. "What are you mumbling?"

They say you go headfirst into a sandstorm and that's what I do with Loretta. "I wonder if she's gone up into the hills to see about that boy."

Her eyes simmer with blue fire like she's about to lower the boom on me. "By herself!" The box of soap lands with a hard thud on the counter. "You should have stopped her, Henry!" She pushes by me, pulling open the screen door. "This is one of the dumbest things you've ever done."

I follow her out onto the porch. "I don't know that she did, and you yourself know that I could stop the rain easier than my sister, once she gets a notion to do something."

Loretta crosses her arms and looks up into the hills. The sky rumbles like it's moving something around up there. "I'm going to her house to wait."

"If she went, she's not even to the middle of those hills let alone back home yet."

Loretta fixes her face in a knot of disgust and gives me a look that sears my eyeballs before going back to her work.

I don't know why Sarah couldn't tell me

what she was thinking. I don't know what it is that is making her climb up through those hills on the back of a mule, but I know that life is hard and awful things happen that call on us to be brave or a coward, and sometimes decisions have to be made that make us out to be wise or a fool. I don't know what Sarah Ivorie has in mind but do know my sister is no fool and is strong enough to come back from the brink of death.

At nine o'clock, and after calling Sarah's house fifty times, Loretta announces real loud to me that she's going to Sarah's to wait for her. The store has been empty all morning; the rain has kept everybody away. I throw a makeshift sign up in the window and lock the door. The wiper blades can't keep up with the rain, and Loretta aims some fiery words at me she's only used a couple of times in our marriage and I wipe the smoke off my brow, but I don't say anything back. After being married to two women I know when to keep my big trap shut.

I jump out of the truck at Sarah's and hear Sally. I run to the barn and hear her barking in one of the stalls. Her voice is raspy and she bolts from the stall when I open it, jumping like a rabbit. We run to the house, where Loretta is looking out on the hills from the back porch. "I'll make some coffee," she says in between muttering how I was a dang fool to let Sarah traipse off in those hills by herself.

When the rain comes at us sideways on the back porch we move inside the house, and Loretta dusts things that don't need to be dusted and I move things around that don't need to be moved. All the while we pace in front of the back window for any sign of Kitty Wells. At eleven thirty we see her pointy ears bobbing up the embankment and we run for the door. "Oh my Lord, Henry!" Loretta yells, running into the rain. I see the boy hanging over the mule and look at Sarah. She is haggard and pale and looks like that little yellow-fever girl.

"Call the doctor," she says, shouting at us.

Loretta runs into the house as fast as one can when you're drenched and the porch below you is sopping wet and your feet are sliding this way and that. I take the reins from Sarah, looping them over the porch railing, and run to the boy. I lift him off the mule as Sarah jumps down. "What happened to him?" I shout, following her into the house.

"I should have gone up yesterday," she

says, leading me to Pop's bed. "I should have gone up yesterday!"

I lay the boy down and Sarah disappears into the bathroom. Loretta runs into the room, helping me take off the overalls. "Doc's coming," she says. We take off the overalls and Loretta covers her mouth. "God almighty! What happened to this boy?" He is bruised red and black and the skin on his back and legs hangs in strings of pink and red flesh. Sarah throws a towel at Loretta and together they dry his naked limbs, careful as they dab the blood. I reach for the rope tied around his chest and use my pocketknife to cut through it, setting aside the book that is strapped to him.

"I should have left yesterday," Sarah says again, covering the boy with blankets. "I knew I should have gone, but I didn't."

"You didn't know anything," I say, looking at a lump on the boy's head.

"I did know, Henry!" she shouts in a water-choked voice. Her eyes are wild and big and her face is screwed up looking at me. "I knew he was in trouble, but I . . ." She is beside herself and tears and water roll over her face.

"You did do something," I say, stopping her. "Look at him! You brought him here." Her eyelids are swollen and pink and her hands are shaking. Sarah's spirit has always been as unbreakable as steel beams, but what happened in those hills has snapped it clean in half.

"One person already died in this bed," she says, falling on the floor beside the bed. "One is enough."

Loretta pats the boy's leg on top of the covers. "Doc's coming," she says, reassuring herself as much as Sarah and me.

"What happened?" I ask again.

Every part of her is withered and sagging and her voice is feeble. She looks up at me. "I looked right into the pit of hell and smelled evil, Henry. It was vile and putrid and stank like death." She reaches her hand up and puts it on the boy's head. "I never thought you could hear darkness but you can." She catches my eye, and hers are fierce and full of rattlesnake-tail anger. "Its voice slithered up and wrapped its bony fingers around my spine and sank its teeth in my ears." She leans up on her knees and lays her cheek against the boy's forehead. "And I could have pulled the trigger and never thought another thing about it."

I have never seen Sarah like this; she is totally wrecked by this boy.

Doc Langley's voice brings Sarah to her feet. "Back here," she yells, running to the bedroom door. Doc's carrying his medical bag and he throws it on the side of the bed, opening it. Doc's been doctoring in Morgan Hill for over thirty years now and he walks with his head thrust forward, as if he's always after something that is being pulled away from him.

He reaches for the boy's eyes and peels back their lids, then opens his mouth and feels around with his finger. He drapes his stethoscope around his neck and pulls the sheet off the boy, putting his hand on his neck. "What happened to him?" He lays the end of the stethoscope on the bird-bone chest and listens.

"Somebody beat the life out of him," Sarah says. Loretta runs her fingers over the boy's forehead and leans down to whisper something in his ear.

"Who is he?" Doc asks, checking the wound on the boy's head.

"I don't know," Sarah says.

"He took a blow to the head." He looks up at her. "How long has he been like this?"

"He was like this when I found him this morning."

Doc's face doesn't tell us anything. "Where'd you find him?"

"In the hills."

"Who did it?"

"His pop."

Doc pulls a bottle of something out of his bag. "I need warm water in a bowl, Loretta, and bring us some washrags." He works in silence, feeling the boy's ribs, arms, and legs as Sarah and I stand by, wanting to help but not knowing what to do. There's a fusty smell in here with the window closed against the breeze. The boy's used to open spaces, not breathing this stale air. I turn to the window and push it open.

Doc turns the boy over on his side, and his brows squeeze together in the middle, looking at the strings of flesh hanging on the boy's back. I don't have the stomach for it and move to the other side of the bed. Doc runs his hand over the boy's back and feels each rib poking up like a bony finger. "Why isn't he waking up?" I ask.

Doc sighs and touches bruises on the back of the boy's legs. "His brain is injured." He puts his hand on the boy's head. "I don't know how bad."

"When will he wake up?" Sarah asks.

Doc is quiet. "I don't know. I've never seen a patient like this." I look at the top of Doc's head and know good and well he's seen a patient like this, just as I have. Years ago, when Fred Doakes, Gabbie Doakes's older brother, was fourteen, he got kicked in the head by a horse and it knocked him out cold. That boy lay like that for five days before he finally died, but Doc doesn't mention that, so neither do I. Loretta walks gentlelike into the room so she doesn't spill the water and sets the bowl on the bedside table. Doc opens the bottle he had pulled out of his bag earlier and pours most of it into the water. "We'll need to clean these wounds," he says, looking at Loretta and Sarah.

Loretta covers two of her fingers with a rag and sticks them in the bowl, squeezing out a bit of the water before dabbing at the wounds on the boy's back. Loretta holds her mouth in a tight line and I can tell she's sick over what she sees. "Any idea how old he is?" Doc asks. I get real close to the boy's face and study it. There's something familiar in it. Maybe I have seen him at the store or maybe he has a granddaddy here and that's who he looks like.

Sarah works her hands over the boy's back. "He looks like he's six or so."

Doc studies the small frame. "Hard to say. He's underdeveloped. Malnourished. Could be older." Doc works at cleaning the wounds and keeps his voice low. "He's been sodomized." Those words are the size of a fist in my throat.

A tear slides sideways out of the corner of one of Sarah's eyes.

"Good Lord," Loretta says. "Who could do such a thing?"

"Did he ever tell you anything?" Doc asks.

Sarah shakes her head. "He can't talk. He has a cleft palate."

"Poor little lamb," Loretta says. "What's going to happen to him?"

"I'm going to raise him," Sarah says.

Ivorie

An uneasy quiet settles on the room. I don't look up at Henry because I already know what he's thinking.

"Are you sure about that, Ivorie?" Doc asks. He takes off his glasses that dig into the flesh behind his ears and runs a calloused finger along the deep crevice. Doc is short and solid, with a mound of belly stuffed into his shirt. His gray hair has taken a rest from combs and hairbrushes for years now, and his white shirt sags and hangs limp over his pants, making it look tired and done-for. "You don't know anything about this boy."

I keep cleaning the boy's wounds. "I know his mother is dead and his old man should be locked up."

"There are homes that —"

I don't let Doc finish. "The state home? Is that what you mean? Where they put all the crazies? He's not crazy, Doc." Henry still hasn't said anything and it's driving me nuts. "Go ahead and say what's on your mind, Henry. I know you're dying to."

Henry sits in the corner chair and rubs his hands together like he's trying to keep warm by a fire. "This boy has had a hard life," he says, staring into his hands. "Who knows what he was born into!" I try to listen to the rest of what Henry is saying but those few words make my mind fly off in a thousand directions. Was I helpless to undo whatever sad and awful past the boy has lived? Was his future thick with heartache and trouble because of the people or events that scarred his life before a breath of it happened? Would his past forever run after him like an angry mob? "Sarah Ivorie?" I look up at Henry. "There are people who can help this boy."

Henry's never been one to give me the what-fors but I sense it in his voice and my breath squeezes in my throat. "And I'm the one who's going to help him, Henry." Our eyes meet and Henry shrugs, his mouth pulling up a little like a string is hitched to each side.

Doc lifts a jar of salve from his bag and starts working it into the boy's wounds; it smells sweet and burnt and glistens on the strips of flesh. Loretta and I work at bandaging the wounds. "The ribs will have to heal on their own," he says. "There's no point wrapping them. They just do worse that way. I'll call Sheriff Dutton. I don't care if those hills aren't his jurisdiction. You don't do this to a child. You don't do this to an animal." He stands and puts most of his things back into the bag but hands me the salve and gauze bandages. "The sheriff will want to come out here and see the boy and talk to you." He closes the medical bag and looks down at the boy. "Do you want to leave him here or take him to my house?"

"I'd like him here," I say, and somehow, when those words fall over my tongue, I know I've moved my life in a whole new direction.

"That's what I figured," he says. "I need to go home and get some fluid for him. I'll be back." Henry walks Doc to the door and I can imagine the things they're saying to each other, but I can't think about that right now.

"Why don't you get something dry on," Loretta says. "You're soaked through. I'll sit with him."

I sit down beside the boy and feel water shooting from behind my eyes and squeeze them tight. "Am I crazy, Loretta?"

"A little," she says. I glance up at her.

"Sometimes we're called on to do crazy things."

Sheriff Dutton spends a few minutes with me, shaking his head and scratching his whiskers as I tell him all I know about the boy. He gets real quiet when we walk into Pop's bedroom and he watches the boy breathe. He makes noises at the back of his throat and thumps his thumb on the side of the gun he keeps holstered on his side. "I'll take a man up with me tomorrow," he says, as I walk him to his car. Sally stays by my side as we walk from the house. "The boy's old man might know I don't have jurisdiction up there, but he might not. We can bring him in and I'll call the men at the state office."

"Thanks, Wally," I say, wrapping my arms around me. I am still cold from being in the rain so long this morning.

He opens the driver's side door and puts his foot on the running board of the car. "Ivorie, that boy's daddy could cause a world of trouble for you."

"I don't think that man ever wanted that boy. Now he can set up there alone and waste away, his soul rotting before his flesh does."

Wally nods and gets into the car. Henry

192

left hours ago to open the store again but Loretta is still here. I look down at Sally and she wags her tail. "Do you forgive me for shutting you up in the stall?" I clap my hand on her side and she jumps back and barks, wanting to play. "I'm dog tired," I say, rubbing her ears. I look up at the house and wonder what I'm going to do when the boy opens his eyes. If he opens his eyes.

I open the door to the kitchen and suck in the smells. Loretta made vegetable soup. My stomach groans and I realize I haven't eaten since before dawn. I step into Pop's bedroom and Loretta is sitting on the side of the bed, patting the boy's leg. She's holding the Bible that was strapped to him. "The name in here is Ruth. Was that his mother?"

I nod, sitting on the other side of the bed. The book's cover is saturated and Loretta presses a washrag into it to absorb the water. "Isn't it funny that the pages are dry?" she asks. "The cover is drenched but the pages are dry as a bone." She looks up at me. "This is the only thing he has in the world, isn't it?" I nod. "It's almost as if God himself kept the pages dry so he'd always have this one thing from his mother." She flips through the pages and shakes her head. "How in the world did they stay dry if he was lying facedown in the water?"

We are quiet as Loretta works on drying the cover and I feel my bones shrinking inside my skin. I feel like I could sleep for days on end. I hear voices at the kitchen door and I stand up to see who's here. As I walk across the bedroom, Pete Fletcher's wife, Charlotte, comes stepping in soft as a cat.

"Henry told me about your troubles," Charlotte says, walking to the side of the bed to look at the boy. "Lord have mercy," she says, sitting on the side of the bed next to Loretta. "Who could do such a thing to a child?" For far too long I thought Charlotte was a stiff and stubborn woman with a mighty long stick stuck up her butt. I found out how wrong I was when I was a teenager and ugly as a mud fence but Charlotte told me how pretty I was every Sunday. I get tired of forming opinions about people because it seems I'm always wrong. "Who could do this?" she says again. Her eyes get glassy and she shakes her head, squeezing the boy's arm.

Charlotte doesn't ask about my claim to keep the boy, although I'm certain Henry told her. "He needs to wake up soon," she says, with a hammer-blow finality to her voice. "The longer he's under like that . . ."

She stops and I look up at her. "What?"

"It's not good, Ivorie. It's hard on the brain. He needs to wake up."

Fear snakes across the floor and crawls up my leg. "Why didn't Doc tell me that?"

"He knows there's nothing you can do," Loretta says. "And I'm sure he didn't want to worry you with more."

My mind runs down one rabbit trail and then another. Did I go all that way to have the boy die in my house? Can't this boy live out one day without fighting for food and breath and some small space in the world to call his own? Charlotte's words leave me empty and tired out, and although it's only four in the afternoon I'm ready for everyone to leave. Loretta and Charlotte must read my mind as they walk to the door. "You call me if you want me to sit with him while you rest," Loretta says. "The soup is ready, and I made you some corn bread."

"Call us for anything," Charlotte says. "Night or day." I nod and they disappear like ghosts, leaving me alone with the boy.

I lie down next to him and rest my hand on his sunken stomach. "Are you listening? It's Ivorie. Sally's outside the door, waiting for you to wake up and play with her. It's about driving her crazy knowing you're in here and she's out there. So, wherever you are in there, I want you to know that we're ready for you to be part of this family." I lean up on my elbow and look at his small, pale face. "You have a family now. Do you hear me?" It's a heart-wringing moment looking at him, and I watch real close to see if he's breathing. "You're going to have a bed and a bedroom and warm food in your belly every day and a dog to run down to the creek with and Jane and John and Milo to play with, and you'll have me." I get real close to his ear. "I'll read bedtime stories to you each night and from your mother's Bible. And I'll hug you when you need one and even when you don't. And I'll keep you in line, too, because you can't just run around hog wild. I have to raise you to be the young man your mama would have wanted. So, you listen to me and come on up out of there because we have a lot of things to do, and there's a whole mess of people who want to meet you." I lie back down and hold on to his hand.

If I could see inside myself I'd see everything, my liver, spleen, and guts, quaking and shaking like a leaf in a storm. "What sort of fool thing are you doing?" Pop would say. "You can't raise that boy." Mother would cast those sky-blue eyes at me and whisper, "Ivorie, it's too much on you to work *and* raise that boy. Find a husband and raise a family together." It might be a blessing that they're not here. Neither would understand; I know that. I don't understand it myself. I squeeze the little hand and close my eyes, trembling.

A knock at the kitchen door startles me and I bolt upright, swinging my legs off the side of the bed. George is on the porch and I run to open the door. "You are a sight for sore eyes," I say, throwing my arms around him. His hug is short and I feel him pulling away.

"I was at the store today," he says. "Henry told me." I loosen my arms around him. "What's happening, Ivorie?" I don't know if he's concerned for me or aggravated with me. "They say you have that boy here." He walks inside the kitchen and stands away from me.

"His old man beat the living snot out of him."

He leans against the counter and looks at me. "And you went up in those hills by yourself?" I nod. "Like a man! Good Lord! Why didn't you call me?"

I sit down and realize I'm too weary to go through this again. "There was no time. I had no idea I'd find him the way I did. You should have seen . . ."

"What woman does that sort of fool

thing?" Chaos and noise rumble inside me. "Did you read that in a book somewhere? You could have been killed!" If he's concerned, he doesn't reach for me, and I feel like a child.

I'm tired and lean on the table, holding my face in my hands. "Deal thy bread to the hungry."

"What?"

I look up at him. "Isaiah wrote the book. 'Deal thy bread to the hungry. Bring the poor that are cast out to thy house. When thou seest the naked, cover him.'"

He looks at me for the longest time, then sighs down at his chest before he walks behind me, putting his hands on my shoulders.

I lean my face over on his hand. "Would you like to see him? He's sleeping."

He pulls his hand away. "No. Not much point in seeing a sleeping boy." Something drops inside me and George seems to feel it, whatever it is, and bends down by the side of the chair, taking my hand. His eyes are wide and surprised and I want him to hold me. "You amaze me, Ivorie Walker!" He squeezes my hand harder, like he's congratulating me for winning the spelling bee. "Now what are you doing?" I search his eyes. "What are you doing with this boy?"

"I'm keeping him."

"Right. Till he's up and walking again. But then what?"

I look him in the eyes so he'll understand. "I'm keeping him, George."

He pulls his hand away and sits in the chair at the head of the table. "What? How?"

"I don't know how. All I know is I'm keeping him."

His eyes narrow and he works hard at understanding what I'm saying. "Like he's one of your own?" I nod. "I don't know how you're going to do that."

I look down at the table. "Neither do I."

Dull silence stretches out between us. "You're a single woman. Where would you get the money to . . ." His voice trails off, leaving my obvious lack of wisdom swelling in the dying syllables.

I look at him. "It can work. Don't you see that?" I desperately want him to see himself here, in this home with the boy and me, but his eyes are blank.

He stands and moves next to me. "Get some sleep."

I hope he'll lean his head down onto mine or pull me up in his arms but the screen door makes its usual groaning noise as he slips away. I am numb from George's visit as I climb into bed next to the boy. I realize the light is on in the kitchen but the room is shrinking and my body is floating down through the mattress, where exhaustion wraps around me like the wings of a great, soaring bird.

The pressure on my bladder helps me rise up out of layers of dreams. I open my eyes and realize day ended in clouds and thick darkness; I can't see a thing. I reach out and touch the boy but he hasn't moved. I pat his leg and stumble to the bathroom, putting on the light. The brightness hurts and I sit on the pot with my eyes closed. When I stand up, I squint to see my watch: one o'clock in the morning. I slept for nine hours straight and will never go back to sleep. I wonder if George is awake and thinking of me right now.

I keep the bathroom light on and walk back to the bed, where I can see the boy in the dim half-light and sit down next to him. So often, when Pop lay dying here, I would come and sit and pray, and it was as if my prayers went as far as the ceiling, where they would hang like dozing bats. Prayers for the old and dying are like that. We all know that life is ebbing away but still we pray for more days, more breaths. But what about a life that's never really even gotten started? "So much has been taken from him," I say, my voice cutting through the stillness. "Would you give him more, Lord? Would you give and give and give some more?" The IV bag that Doc hooked up on his return trip is empty, so I reach for the tape on the boy's arm and pull it off before taking the end of the needle between my thumb and index finger. I have never done something like this but I pull it straight back and slow like Doc told me. It slides right out and I feel my stomach drop a little; I wasn't cut out to be a nurse. I wrap the tubing around the IV pole and push it back beside Pop's night table.

I crawl on top of the bed and lean against the iron headboard, my hand resting on the boy's head. My thoughts flop all over the place and I'm struck by the fact that his mother never heard his voice; she never heard him call her Mama. I wonder how she died and how she ever got hitched up with the boy's father. How did they end up in the hills? Was she a pretty woman, or did he beat the beauty right off of her like Lonnie Gable nearly did with Fran? Outside the window, a fat, silver moon shines on top of the oak tree as if it's roosting there for the night, and I get out of bed and stand at the window, looking up through the branches. I look high to where the boy's mother is and hope she can see that he's safe. "Open your eyes," I say, turning back to him. I cross to the bed and sit on it. "Your mother would want you to open your eyes. I want you to open your eyes. Sally wants you to open your eyes." I sit on my knees and lean over to his ear. "Come on," I whisper. "Open your eyes." I lean back and take a deep breath. This room smells like old putty and wax. It's gray and brown, the color of old people. I vow to give it a proper cleaning and change out the old pillows when the boy wakes up. He needs a room that smells like little boy, not old man.

I run my fingers through the boy's wild, untamed hair and put a haircut on the top of the list of things to do when he opens his eyes. I'll take him into Greenville or Morristown to a barber that will treat him like a king for his first haircut. I will not buy him anything out of the Sears and Roebuck catalog, but we'll walk into a store together and I'll buy him a pair of overalls and some dungarees and a couple of shirts for play and for working in the garden and a respectable shirt for church. Maybe something in blue. I think he'd look right handsome in blue. Then I'll buy him a pair of shoes for working and playing in and another pair for church. I don't care if most of the kids in Morgan Hill wear the same shoes to church that they play in through the week. I want him to have special shoes that make him feel big. Ones that make him squish his toes around in because they're a little uncomfortable, but he'll like them anyway because they squeak when he walks and make him feel proud. After shoe shopping we'll head down the street to the ice cream shop and I'll put money on the counter for anything he wants; I won't even care if it makes him sick or if it spoils his supper.

I am not wrapping these thoughts in fairytale paper. For all I know he might be as wild as the owls that fly around the top of the barn, and he might give me fits every day of his life. But nothing is harder to live with than regrets; they come at you from every side, and I couldn't live with myself if I turned this boy away. I think of Mother and her sad eyes telling me, but not telling me about her regrets, whatever they were. And there is Pop's voice again, droning against my brain and declaring that I can't do this thing in front of me, but I work hard to shut him up.

■ ■ ■ ■

At three thirty the pounding silence is driving me nuts and I realize I am starving, remembering I haven't eaten since before dawn yesterday. In the kitchen, Loretta's soup is still sitting on the stove but I'm going to wait and eat it with the boy when he wakes up. I set the whole thing, pot and all, inside the Frigidaire. Sally presses her nose up to the screen door and I open it and sit on a porch chair. She lays her head on my lap and I scratch behind her ears. "I bet you're hungry, too, huh?" I go back inside and lift the satchel I had taken with me into the hills off one of the kitchen chairs. The sausage biscuits I had packed are still in it, and I take them out to the porch, lifting the corners of the waxed paper. I stand over Sally's bowl and the first biscuit barely touches bottom before she snatches it. "It's not much but it's a start," I say, dropping the other biscuits and sausages into the bowl.

I am watching Sally gulp her food when the thought strikes me. He has a voice. It's been locked up for years now but the boy has a voice; I've heard him grunt and groan so I know it's in there somewhere. I sit on one of the porch chairs and let the thought rumble around my brain. I don't think Greenville's big enough to have someone who could help the boy, but maybe somebody there would know somebody in Johnson City, Knoxville, or maybe as far away as Nashville. I find myself smiling and Sally pushes her head under my hand. She looks at me as if she understands the idea I'm thinking and wags her tail in agreement. *It is a fine idea,* she's saying.

I stand and open the door. "Come on." She sits, and although she understood my idea moments earlier, she looks at me now as if she can't understand a word I'm saying. "Come on," I say again. She blinks and jerks her head back to bite at something on her rump. I pat my thighs and she lies down, watching me. At least I'm putting on a good show. I take hold of the scruff of her neck and try to pull her inside but she puts on the brakes by stiffening all four legs and then lying down on her side. "It's okay," I say, pushing her from behind. "Get in the house." She turns her head to look at me and her eyes say I've lost my mind. She's like pushing a fifty-pound bag of feed with bones and flip-floppy legs but I finally get her over the threshold of the door. Mother always made it known to Sally that she had no place in the house and would scold her if she got up close to the door. Inside the kitchen she cowers up against the screen door, like she's just received the biggest beating of her life, and I shake my head. "Come on! I want you to see somebody." I move to the hallway and hope she'll follow but she just stares at me, looking sorrowful and misunderstood. "Don't make me carry you, Sally. Come here." She crouches low and crawls toward me as if in a minefield, and I walk backward through the hall, watching her. This is the most ridiculous thing I've ever seen.

I walk into Pop's bedroom and she crawls to my side. "Look," I say, pointing to the bed. She can't see a thing, cowering at my feet, and I lift her front paws and place them on the side of the bed. Mother would be beside herself watching this. Sally sniffs the boy's hand and burrows her nose under it. She looks up at me as if she gets it now and walks along the side of the bed on her back legs, sniffing the boy's arm. When she's done nosing around she sits down and looks up at him, waiting. I sit in the corner chair and wait with her.

The sun takes its sweet time waking up that morning but by quarter till six the room is glowing. Sally stands and shakes and I lean down to run my hand up her spine. When I sit back up I am shocked to see two little eyes watching us.

THE BOY

Daybreak strikes a sudden blow and the boy's eyelids spring open. He is scared and feels like he's in the middle of a gauzy dream; he can't lift his limbs to run or open his mouth to scream. He shifts his eyes and sees the top of someone's head petting a dog. As he watches, he sees it's Sally, and when the head sits up he recognizes Ivorie, who's smiling at him, but he can't smile back. He tries to move but nothing happens. He can't rise above this netted sleep.

"I knew you'd open your eyes," Ivorie says, sitting on the edge of the bed.

He watches her and feels something under his hand; Sally nuzzles her nose beneath his palm. He moves his eyes and feels something wet sliding over them.

"It's okay," Ivorie says, patting his leg. "You're in my house. I brought you down from the hills. You're safe now." She looks worn-out but her voice is like molasses in his ears.

He keeps trying to claw his way out from underneath the layers of film.

Ivorie moves closer to him and lays her hand on his arm. "You were asleep for a long time because you got hurt, but now you're here looking at me and I'm looking at you, and Sally's wondering what in the world she's doing in the house!"

The boy feels something roll down his face.

Ivorie reaches inside a drawer and pulls out a handkerchief, wiping his face. "Sally has never been inside the house before but I thought it was pretty important for her to be here, don't you?"

His eyes leak again and she is quick to dab away the wetness. Fear, confusion, doubt, and relief beat through his heart at the same time and his brain grasps for which one to feel.

"You just take your time waking up, and when you're ready I'll fix you something hot to eat. Loretta's got soup in the Frigidaire, but who eats soup for breakfast?" She stops and looks down at him. "You don't know Loretta, do you? Well, she knows you. She sat right here and patted and loved on you while you were sleeping. So did Henry. He's my brother. You'll like Henry." She throws her head back and laughs. "All kids like Henry. He's just one of those grown-ups that younguns love. He'll be tickled to death when you're able to go down to the store with him. Henry owns the store in Morgan Hill. Has ever since I can remember. He'll probably give you an ice cream sandwich or a candy bar when I'm not around but that's okay."

The boy tries to keep up but feels something holding his thoughts down. Ivorie sure is excited about something. She hasn't stopped talking since he opened his eyes.

"Doc's met you, too. So has Charlotte. She's the preacher's wife. Well, he's not really a preacher. He's a mechanic who stepped in when we needed a preacher, and he's still preaching. But he doesn't really preach. Not that fire-and-brimstone stuff you hear about. He just tells it plainlike." She throws her hand to her head and slaps her leg. "Oh, for heaven's sake! I just realized I haven't told Jane and John and Milo that you're here. Well, really there wasn't much time yesterday. We were all swarming around you like gnats on an August day. You had all of us pretty worried but look at you now! Your face is just as handsome as can be — just so fine and golden in this morning light." She runs her hand down his face and his eyes spring a leak again. Her eyes are leaking, too, and she first wipes his cheeks and then her own.

Sally puts her front legs on the bed and looks at the boy. He can tell what she's doing; her whole body is swaying. He picks up his hand and it feels like it's floating somewhere in the room. Ivorie guides it down to Sally's head and Sally licks it. A thought seizes him and he reaches for his chest, feeling around the bony terrain with wide eyes.

"Your mama's Bible is right here," Ivorie says, holding it above him. "It's a little wet but it's okay. See," she says, opening the first page. "Ruth. You can still read her name."

Ruth. His mother. He hadn't thought of her as his mother for so long, protecting her memory inside him from the man. He called her such vicious words, long after she left this world, that the boy had to keep her name safe and put away.

A voice shouts hello from somewhere far away in the house.

The boy's eyes dart to Ivorie.

"That's Henry. My brother, remember?" She runs to the door and shouts into the hallway, "Come on back!"

She wants to show her brother something and the boy wishes he could rise up so he could see it, too. The doorway fills with a man and a woman looking at him like he's one of those animals in a cage that nobody's ever seen before. The man moves to the side of the bed and is smiling like somebody just gave him a birthday present. He reaches his hand down to touch the boy, but the boy makes a hushed, strangling sound in his throat and the man steps back.

"It's all right," Ivorie says. "This is my brother."

The boy's eyes are big as the moon as he looks at her brother.

"You don't need to be afraid of Henry."

"It's all right," Henry says, looking at Ivorie. "He doesn't know us. When did he wake up?"

"Just a few minutes ago."

She's sitting on the bed again and the boy is glad to have her hand on his leg once more.

"We sure have been worried about you," the woman says.

What was her name? He can't remember, the way his mind is tottering and sliding about.

"Your eyes are just as nice as Ivorie said they were. Isn't he handsome, Henry?"

"About as handsome a little fella as I've ever seen," Henry says.

The boy watches the man and he feels something in his chest and it frightens him; he wants to run. His eyes fix on Ivorie and she squeezes his leg, letting him know that it's all right.

"You sure do look familiar," Henry says. "Have you been to the store with your mama?"

The words stumble around his brain.

"Do you have a mamaw or papaw here?"

"There is something in the eyes," the woman says, smiling at him. "He probably did come to the store at one time or another." She looks at Ivorie. "Have you all eaten?"

Ivorie shakes her head. "I've been waiting for him to wake up more. I think he's still groggy."

"Well, I can go out and get everything ready to cook, then when he's ready you can just tell me and I'll fix it right up. I'll call Doc and tell him what's what and have him come out. Henry can milk the cow this morning."

"I can?"

Ivorie laughs at her brother, and he and the woman leave the room. "You'll be seeing a lot of Henry and Loretta."

Loretta is the woman's name!

"I have six brothers, but Henry's my

favorite. Always has been. You can't tell the other five I said that, though. You'll hear Henry call me Sarah. That's my first name. Sarah Ivorie. He's always called me Sarah and I don't see him changing anytime soon." She reaches one hand down to pet Sally and keeps the other hand on his leg. "You don't need to be afraid of Henry." She pats his leg and sits on the bed next to him. "You need to help me with your name, okay?"

The boy closes his eyes. It's been so long since he's heard his name; he imagines what it will sound like coming out of Ivorie's mouth. The thought of the man screaming his name makes him jump and he tries to kick his legs.

Ivorie puts both hands on top of him. "Hey, it's okay. It's okay. I'm right here."

His heart is bucking and he's breathing heavy.

"It's okay." She's smiling and whispering something that he can't hear over the sound of his heart. "You are never going back to the hills again. Do you understand me?"

He watches her mouth and concentrates on the words.

"You're never going back up there to him again. He's never going to hurt you again. Not ever, ever, ever."

Something hot drips down the boy's face and he wills himself to wipe it away but can't. Ivorie dabs at the drips and leans over to kiss him on the forehead. His mother used to do that late at night, when it was just the two of them lying on the pallet together. The boy opens his mouth and hollow, guttural sounds come out.

"It's a lot, I know," Ivorie says, pulling the covers up onto his chest. "But sometimes the truth is hard to take in." Her face lights up in a smile again and she dabs away at the boy's eyes. "If you want, you can stay right here with me and Sally. Okay?"

He's scared and confused under the weight of the fog but something like wings are flapping inside his chest.

She picks up his hand and pats it, and Sally plops her big paws up on the bed again. "Can you tell she's anxious for you to get out of this bed?" She pat-pat-pats his hand and follows all that patting with a squeeze. "But you take your time getting up and around. There's plenty of time to play."

"Doc'll be here any minute," Loretta says on entering the room.

The boy likes her red hair; it reminds him of the squirrels in the hills. She has a warm face dotted with freckles like his mother had on her arms.

"How are you doing?" she asks, looking at him.

"We've just been talking about playing with Sally when he feels like it," Ivorie says, grinning at him.

"Well, nothing spells fun like a boy and his dog!" Loretta says, throwing her hands in the air.

He casts his eyes down on Sally. Was she his dog? That's what Loretta said just now; she said *a boy and his dog.*

"I'm knocking, Ivorie," a voice says somewhere in the house. "Well, truth is, I'm actually walking through the house." A gray-haired man sticks his old, stubbly face inside the door and takes three good paces to the side of the bed. "Welcome back, son." He takes something long out of a bag and sticks what looks like prongs inside his ears and leans down to the boy's chest, moving a flat circle around on it.

The boy's eyes widen and he jerks, trying to scramble away.

"This is Doc Langley," Ivorie says, holding him down. "He's the doctor here. He's been helping you."

The boy settles down and casts his eyes on Doc Langley.

"He can hear your heartbeat through that thing. It's okay."

The doctor takes the prongs out of his ears and sets them inside the boy's ears to hear. "Hear that?" the doctor asks. "That's your heart beating."

A loud, fast sound echoes in his ears. The doctor puts the round end on his own chest and the boy notices he has small but big-knuckled hands.

"That's my heart beating. I'll put it back on your chest again. Hear it? I can listen to somebody's heart and know how it's beating, and I can tell that yours is beating mighty fine right now." He looks up at Ivorie and nods like there's something between them. "I'm going to look inside your eyes now." He reaches for the boy but the boy makes that rasping, airy sound he makes so often.

"Doc Langley helps people get better," Ivorie says. "He wants to look in your eyes. Okay?" She holds his hand, making it all right.

The doctor lifts up one of the boy's eyelids and points a tiny light into it, making the boy blind for a second. When the doctor moves to the other eye the boy blinks his blind eye till he can see again. The doctor feels the boy's neck, making uh-huh noises behind his tongue. He looks down and the road map of wrinkles on his face smooths

217

out as he feels the top of the boy's head. He runs a rough finger over the boy's arm, cleaning it with something cold and smelly on a puffy little ball. "You did a good job taking out the needle, Ivorie." He sticks a new puffball to the boy's arm and tapes it down. "There you go," he says, the road map on his face crinkling up again. "Now I'm going to change these dressings and put more medicine on your back, all right, son?"

The boy's mind struggles to understand why he keeps calling him son.

"Is he understanding much, Ivorie?"

Ivorie moves to the other side of the bed and folds one leg under her as she sits down. "He's coming along slow but sure," she says, helping the boy roll over so the doctor can see the work that needs to be done.

He slides an old hand down the boy's back and terror pounds the boy's bones. He bucks and imagines himself lashing out and running headlong to his cave in the hillside.

"It's all right," Ivorie is saying above him. "Shh, shh, shh."

He bucks against her and feels warmth spread down his legs and up his stomach.

She holds him tight and he doesn't know how long she's been running her hand over his wet head. She just keeps saying, "Shh," and holding him like his mother did in the shack.

When the tremors in his belly stop, Loretta's voice floats through the room. "If you hold on to him I'll change the sheets."

Those words come out gray and smoky to the boy, and he grapples with what she is saying as he rides through the air and lands on Ivorie's lap.

"Thankfully, the plastic sheeting you kept on the bed for Pop Walker is still on here. It didn't soak through. I'll run and clean this plastic and get some dry sheets."

The voices of Ivorie and the doctor swirl around him but never go into his ears. The haze keeps the words out. There is a crinkly noise and then some whooshing and then another whoosh and then he's floating again, landing back on the bed. He keeps his eyes shut against the fog.

"Ivorie, I'm going to let you look about those wounds." It's the doctor's voice and he's whispering.

"He doesn't trust men," she says real low, like she's apologizing.

"He doesn't have reason to," the doctor says. Ivorie's hands feel good and warm, racing like a rabbit from one part of the boy's back to the next. "I'll leave this medicine with you. The ribs will take time.

He needs lots of deep breaths. Don't let him climb any trees or jump into the creek while they're healing." Ivorie keeps moving her fingers over his back. "Keep feeding him and make sure he gets plenty of water. Even if he shakes his head saying he doesn't want it, you make sure he gets water anyway."

"I can do that," she says, from behind the boy.

"Glad you're back, son," the doctor says and then the room is quiet.

The bed makes a slow, creaking groan from the weight of someone sitting on it. "Well, Doc has said you need food, so food it will be!" Loretta pats his arm and then taps his hand. "What would you like this morning?"

He keeps his eyes closed tight.

"Eggs? Gravy and biscuits with some sausage?"

All of it, the boy shouts inside his head.

She slaps the bed like she's just gotten an idea for a brand-new invention. "I'm making everything! And do you know what we're going to do? We're all going to bring in our plates and eat right here inside this bedroom. Mother Walker would have a fit if she were alive today, seeing this dog sitting here like she's some royal thing and all of us eating in the bedroom, but I've made up my mind and that's exactly what we're going to do!" She rises and through the slit in one eye he sees her push on her curls that spread out like red flowers on her head. "I'll be back in two shakes."

The boy opens his eyes and casts them from one side of the room to the other, rubbing his hand on the bed beneath him. The bed beneath him. His thoughts are covered with cobwebs, but the blue shine of the sky stretches down to meet him and the cool, early-morning winds reach through the window, puffing out the curtains and whispering his name.

IVORIE

Doc and I stand in the driveway and the breeze is so cool and pure it feels it's blowing straight down from Heaven, so unusual for early July. "He's confused," Doc says. He squints at me with those tiny raisin eyes. "We don't know how long his brain was shut down and it might take another day or two for it to catch up."

I think of Dolly Wade, who days earlier told me her daddy was meeting with President Truman. "Will he be like Dolly?"

Doc shakes his head and his face gets real sorrowfullike. "There's no way to know yet." He takes off his glasses and rubs an old, rough finger behind his ear. "Are you sure you're up for this, Ivorie?"

"No. But I'm doing it." He opens the door and settles behind the wheel. "Hey, Doc." I step to the truck window. "Do you know anybody who could help with his cleft palate?"

He puts his glasses back on and rests his arm out the window. "Dr. Bernard over in Greenville might know somebody but I don't even know if he's still practicing. Let me make a call or two." He shakes his head and drums his hand on the side of the door. "I don't know how that boy has lived with that palate. They cause breathing, eating, and all sorts of teeth problems. I've never seen a child this old with a cleft palate." He turns the key and the engine sputters, then roars to life. "I'll be back to check on him. Later today try to get him to walk around some and take those deep breaths. Breathing will do more good for those ribs than anything."

Henry walks out of the barn holding a basket of eggs and waves goodbye to Doc. "What'd he say?"

I hold my hand over my eyes to talk to him. "Make him eat and drink. Too early to know much. The boy threw an awful fit when Doc touched him. He clamped on to me and his knuckles were stretched white. Then he wet the bed."

Henry shakes his head and scratches at the whiskers on his jaw. "His mind is plagued." I cross my arms and look at the ground oozing up with water from all the rain. "It's like a boarded-up house." I don't look at him but watch the water squish up between my toes. The boy's mind was a bleak, boarded-up house full of all kinds of grief and sadness. I know that Henry would rather I just turned my back on this whole business. Part of me, the part deep down that's kept away from daylight, wonders if maybe he's right.

I get up to close the window in the boy's room but he grunts at me and I turn, looking at him. He shakes his head no and I leave the window open. "Look at that sky," I say, watching the sun go down. "It's the color of a bluebird's wings. Pretty, isn't it?" He nods a bit and I can tell he's coming out of it more and more. He has eaten real good today, starting with eggs and sausage and biscuits, then soup for dinner, and fried chicken with mashed potatoes, beans, cucumbers, onions, and tomatoes for supper. I also got him to walk to the bathroom but he didn't know what to do once he got in there.

"You pee right in here," I said, pointing to the toilet bowl.

He held on to the sink and looked into the porcelain bowl, his white legs as sturdy as a new fawn's.

"Step up here," I said.

He walked to the bowl and bent over to look.

"Now take your pee-pee out of your underpants and pee just like you would in the woods." He didn't move and I pulled down his drawers, stained the color of buttercups. "Now aim your pee-pee right into this water." I felt like a fool talking like that but he pulled that little thing out and made a stream right into the center of the bowl. I smiled at him and then made him wash his hands. "You do this every time you go to the bathroom," I said, helping him work the soap over his hands. I led him back to bed and he's been there ever since.

I press my head against the window screen and see Sally lying in the grass below the window. She's been out since before breakfast and won't consider coming back inside. "She's still out there," I say to the boy. Sally looks up at me and shakes her tail. "Yeah, I'm talking about you."

I sit on the side of the bed and hold a knee between my hands. "Doc and I have been wondering how old you are. Are you six?"

He shakes his head no.

"Seven?"

He doesn't respond.

"Eight?"

He shrugs and I know he's lost track of

his age somewhere; I assume sometime after his mother died. I lean in and look at him. "Do you know how long ago it was when your mother died?"

He looks at the ceiling and then closes his eyes. They're closed for so long that I wonder if he's fallen back to sleep. He opens them and shakes his head.

I change the subject. "Let's work on your name, okay?"

He gives me the same look he's given me all day and I press ahead. "I'll throw out some names and you nod if I come to your name, okay?" He nods and I look up at the ceiling as if every boy name in the history of the world is written up there. "Joseph? Tom? Charles? George?"

He gives nothing but a blank stare.

"Can you spell your name?"

No.

I try to think of all the little boys at school. "Ed? Frank? Walter? Ralph? Fred? Howard?" I go through name after name and realize that his mother could have devised any number of unusual names for him. One little boy at school is named Orie Dale, another is Brownlow, and one is called Tommy Leerex, and you have to call him Tommy Leerex because he doesn't have enough sense to answer to plain old Tommy.

Years ago we had a Ludie Bun come through school, and I still can't figure out what kind of homemade hooch his mama and pop were drunk on the night he came into this world. "Is it Ludie Bun?" His eyebrows pinch together and I laugh. "Hey! I know! Rumpelstiltskin!" His eyes bug out and I slap my leg. "Do you know that story?"

He doesn't.

I rearrange my position and sit cross-legged on the bed, telling him the story of that terrible father who lied to the king about his poor, pitiful daughter, who had legs like fenders, saying she could spin straw into gold. "Thankfully, a shriveled-up little man with a voice like a screeching bird comes along who *can* get a heap of gold out of a pile of straw!" I see a widening of happiness cross the boy's face and I forge ahead. When I get to the part about that sorrowful maiden who's now the queen guessing Rumpelstiltskin's name, he makes the sound of a tractor sputtering and I realize he's laughing. I laugh, too, and pat his leg. "Are you hungry?"

He isn't.

"Thirsty?"

He grunts at me, waving his hand in the air.

227

"You need to pee?"

He moves his head back and forth on the pillow. He pushes on my leg and waves his hand at me like he's waving away a swarm of bugs.

"Do you want another story?"

His head dips.

I settle in against the headboard and look down at him. "How about going out to the porch so Sally can hear, too?"

He swings those scrawny legs over the side of the bed and I notice he's getting stronger. I reach out my hand and he looks at it. "Come on. Grab hold so you don't fall." He slips some bony fingers into my palm and I wrap my hand around them.

As we walk through the house he stops and looks at the furniture and pictures on the walls. "That's my mom and pop," I say, pointing to a framed photo on the hallway wall. Mother is wearing a light cotton dress with big flowers on it and Pop is standing a foot or so away from her wearing a white shirt with suspenders holding up his pants. "Don't they look sad?" I ask, leaning down to see his face. "I don't know why they couldn't have smiled. You'd think they could have at least pretended to know each other. Look how far apart they are!"

He doesn't smile but looks to the next picture.

"That's me and all my brothers." We're standing in front of the house and all of us are squinting into the sun. "I'm the one with that sorry-looking bow in my hair. Look! There's Henry. He already had all his kids when this picture was taken. That's James. He was already married with two kids. Look how we're all squinting. All we had to do was move around the corner of the house and the sun wouldn't have been in our eyes like that. Gives us something to talk about now, I guess."

He looks at the next picture, an earlier version of the previous one, and my legs look like I just got off the back of the horse. My brothers and I are lined up like criminals and none of us are smiling. "Lord have mercy! What a somber bunch we are! We look like street urchins from back in the old country." I get real close to the photos. "I think I need some new pictures hanging in here."

The boy lifts his face to see some of the higher photos and he looks like a skinny mummy with all those bandages. "Let me get you something to wrap around you," I say. I move back to Pop's room and reach for a blanket out of the closet. When I turn back around the boy is behind me. He is so small and spindly legged. I lead him out to the porch and Sally wedges herself between us, wagging herself silly. The blanket swallows the boy when I wrap it around his shoulders and Sally pushes against his legs, forcing him into a chair.

"All right," I say, falling into the chair beside him. "Let me think of another story. How about The Little Red Hen?" He nods and I shake my head real dramaticlike. "Oh, she just had an awful set of lazy friends."

He pets Sally throughout the story, and when I get to the little red hen and her chicks eating a loaf of bread while the lazy cat, dog, and pig did nothing, a glimmer of a smile turns up the corners of his mouth.

"You like that one, don't you?" I lean down on my knees to tell him another one when I hear a truck in the driveway. "Good Lord, it's Avis Oxman," I say to the boy. I stand and wait for her at the edge of the porch.

"Ivorie," she says, holding a brown sack at her side. "Word is you have a sick visitor at your place." I didn't know so many people in the community had already heard about the boy. She steps to the porch and stares down at the boy. Her face is blank, almost harsh as she looks him over. Or is that pity on her brow? It's hard to tell with Avis. "Is this him?" She says it like she's about to interrogate a robbery suspect.

"It is," I say, with the casual breeze of somebody who does this sort of thing every day.

She nods, watching him. "There's some fried chicken and biscuits, potatoes, and beans in here. I didn't think you'd be doing much cooking right now." She's talking to me but looking at the boy.

I've never known Avis to be the giving kind and I hope I don't sound too surprised. "Thank you, Avis. This will make a real good supper tomorrow."

She keeps her eyes on the boy but he won't look at her. "What's his name?"

"We haven't gotten that far yet."

Her head waggles and she turns, as if in slow motion, to look at me. "It's late. I need to get on."

I sigh, grateful she's leaving because I have no idea what else Avis and I could possibly talk about. It's always so much easier to talk to Holt. "Thanks again, Avis." She looks down at the boy and I think she hopes he'll look at her. She smiles at me and leaves as abruptly as she came.

"Well, who knew?" I say, watching her go. The phone rings and the boy jumps. I pat the air in front of him. "It's just the phone. It makes that noise when somebody is calling me."

I walk inside the kitchen and set the sack of food on the table before picking up the phone. I see the boy lean over to see what I'm doing. "Hello," I say into the receiver. It's Sheriff Dutton. He didn't say it was him but he always talks like his voice has Tennessee gravel in it. I listen and smile out at the boy, watching me. When I finish I walk back onto the porch and sit down. "That was Sheriff Dutton. Do you know what a sheriff is?"

He shakes his head, watching Sally.

I wonder what he does know; what, if anything, did he learn in that godforsaken shack? "He's a man who makes sure people follow the law. Like one law is you can't take something from another person. That's called stealing. If somebody steals something then Sheriff Dutton has to step in and do something about it."

His eyes are gray-blue and lost.

"Another law says you can't kill someone else, and another law says you can't hurt anybody. Do you understand?" He doesn't move but I think he does understand. "If somebody breaks the law — if they steal something or hurt somebody — then Sheriff

Dutton finds that person and puts him in jail." Sally nudges up against my legs and I let my fingers wiggle down into her fur. "Jail is a building where people are kept who break the law really bad." I stop petting Sally and look at the boy. "The sheriff rode up into the hills with one of his men this morning and they looked all over for your pop but he wasn't there. Things are gone out of the shack and they think he's run off."

He looks out at the well house and I can see his eyes are glassing over.

"I think he's gone, too. I think he's running like a scared jack rabbit right now."

He's as unmoving as iron and doesn't even react to Sally when she shimmies her head under his hand.

I wish Sheriff Dutton would have found the boy's father and marched him, shackled, right up to the heavy bar of justice. I wish a judge in Greene County would have had no mercy and clapped that wooden gavel down in terrifying judgment. There is no justice in his running free. "He's gone," I say.

He thrashes his head so hard that the blanket falls off his shoulders.

"Yes. He's gone."

He bangs small fists on his legs.

I get down on my knees in front of him.

His skin has a tangy urine smell from wetting the bed this morning. I grab his face and hold it in my hands, forcing him to look at me. "He is gone."

His eyes are filling.

"He's running scared."

The dam unleashes and water pours down his frightened face.

"He's running as far from here as he can." I wipe his tears with my hand and lift his chin. "He's gone."

I pull his head against me and wrap my arms around him and I swear I can hear his heart slapping inside him. I wonder what endless inventory of sins has been done against him for the last several years. Would I ever know? One of those inner chills clamps down hard on me. Would his unspeakable past always keep him on the run and at arm's length from what is true and good in the world? Would his troubles ever end, or would they always plague him, growing as fast as weeds? Did whatever evil that poisoned his daddy's blood and rotted his soul clamp its vicious teeth into the boy's veins?

Sally bolts after a squirrel and follows it to a tree, where she leaps and bounces off the trunk. "She thinks she's a monkey and can climb that tree."

He glances at me, confused.

"Do you know what a monkey is?" My heart twitches, thinking about all this boy has missed. "A monkey lives in trees and they swing from one branch to another." His eyes widen and I point to the trees. "Not like these trees. Over in Africa and other countries."

He looks at me with bulging fish eyes.

"You've never seen a picture of a monkey, have you?" No, he hasn't. I file that away in the back of my mind and wipe his tears with my handkerchief.

The day is growing still and dying out and I'm ready for bed. When the boy finishes the glass of milk I brought him, I lead him into the bathroom and we stand together in front of the pot again. He takes out his pee-pee and I work at keeping my face straight.

Nothing is happening and he sighs, looking up at me.

"Just give it a second. Sometimes it takes a little bit of waiting."

When his water finally comes, he sighs real big like that was a lot of work. I show him the handle on the toilet and push it down. He steps back, watching from over by the tub. When the toilet flushes, he steps to the sink and holds the bar of soap in a clumsy ham-fisted way and I rub it back and forth in his palm to create some suds.

"Now put some more soap on your face and give it a good washing."

He tries, splashing water onto the floor and me, even on the pot.

"I need to get you a toothbrush, too, so you can start brushing your teeth. Let me see. Open up." He opens his mouth, and I don't let my face give away what I'm seeing. His teeth are a crooked, jangled mess. Half of them look like they're coming in sideways and others are pointy, like fangs.

When he lies down I check the dressings on his back and apply more salve. Just in the last two days the wounds have closed over some, and the flapping skin is healing itself to the healthy pink skin of his back. "Doc said we'll probably be taking these bandages off tomorrow so air can get to these wounds." I run my fingers around the maze of white gauze and tickle his back; his smell is strong in my nose. "I think I'll put you in the tub tomorrow, too."

He is worried, not wanting a repeat of what happened a few days ago, I'm sure.

"I'll be right there with you," I say, easing his mind. "It's just a little old tub of water." I help him lie down and pull the covers up around his neck. I reach for his Bible on Pop's night table and show it to him. "Did your mother read to you from this?"

He nods and touches the cover.

"It's still drying. It got pretty soaked. But look at the pages. All dry." The cover is cold and waterlogged and feels slimy to the touch, but I run my fingers over it, looking at him. "I never met your mama, but do you know what I know about her?"

His eyes wait.

"I know she was a good soul because she made sure you had her second-most-prized possession before she left this world. Do you know what her *most* prized possession was?"

He doesn't move.

"You."

He looks at me in sad amazement.

"And you got deep-rooted goodness from your mama. It shoots right out of your eyes."

His eyes settle on me; he's thinking, I know.

"Do you want me to read something?" He nods and I flip through the thin pages, letting them fall open to the story of young David. "Oh, here's a good one! David the giant slayer. Did your mother ever read that to you?"

He tries to smile.

I read through the account of David and Goliath, adding my own color to it, and when I finish I lean down on my knees. "Is your name David?"

No.

I flip through the pages of the Bible. "Adam? Samuel? Hezekiah?" No, no, no. "Uriah? Samson? Law! He had a mop of hair! Noah?" Nothing. "Daniel? Bartholomew? Matthew?"

He looks at me and hunches up those winglike shoulders.

"All right. We'll go over more names tomorrow." I get up and cut out the light and put my hand on his arm. "Sleep tight."

In the dark, he clamps that tiny hand down on my wrist and holds it firm.

"What's wrong?" I put the light back on and see that he's pointing next to him. "Do you want me in here tonight?" He nods and I cut the light off again, feeling my way around to the other side of the bed.

He lies so still that I have to strain to hear him breathing. He doesn't flop this way or that to get comfortable. He just lies. The night sky is nearly moonless and black, and it's so quiet I swear I can hear spiders running across the floor. I listen as he breathes and close my eyes.

"I never asked if you wanted to stay here," I say, searching his face in the moonlight. "I said you could but I never asked if that's what you want to do."

He fusses with the blanket and I help him pull it up under his chin.

"Do you want to stay here with me and Sally?"

He doesn't look at me but dips his chin.

"Well, then, it's settled."

THE BOY

His feet drop into the soft, muddy silt at the bottom and his arms tangle in the slippery reeds. He fights against them, but they're as strong as barbed wire and the harder he struggles the tighter they grip him. His thrashing stirs up the silt and it puffs up around him like brown pieces of lint, and he strains to see the top of the water. The sun sits red hot and wavy on the surface. His breath is being pushed out when an invisible hand reaches through the murk and pulls him into the sunlight.

"It's all right," the voice says, soothing him. "It's only a dream."

The light flickers in his face and he keeps his eyes shut tight. A cloth dabs along his forehead.

"Look at you. You're soaked."

He cracks open an eye and sees Ivorie dabbing his head with a washrag.

"That sure was some dream. You flopped

all over this bed. I didn't know if I'd ever get you awake." She sets the washrag on the table and pulls the covers up to his neck again. "Are you thirsty?"

He isn't and she reaches to turn out the light, but he grabs her hand. He points to the light and waves at it.

"Do you want it left on?"

He bobs his head and she settles back onto the bed, next to him. He looks at her mouth and makes little circles with his hand in front of it.

"You want me to talk? Do you want another story?"

His eyes widen and she puts that soft hand on top of his arm.

"All right then. How about one more of David the giant slayer?"

The boy is smiling beneath the bedspread and Ivorie leans in close.

"Well, I'll be dipped. I see a dimple!" She touches his cheek and acts like her finger gets stuck in a deep hole. "Would you look at that! If you have a dimple that means you're smiling underneath that bedspread." She pulls it back and says, "Aha! Just as I suspected. A great big smile and a little bitty dimple." She pats the bedspread down on his chest and runs her fingers over his face, telling him about a giant that scared the bejeepers out of an entire army and about a little boy named David who faced that giant with five smooth stones. When she finishes she says, "You better close those eyes and get some sleep. I told Jane and John and Milo that they could come see you and we are all going to need our rest for that!"

He shuts his eyes against the light and listens close to hear the story again far off in his mind.

The smells swirl up his nose and push open his eyelids. Light streams in from the windows on either side of the bedroom and he turns to see Ivorie. The bed is empty and he runs to the bathroom, standing in front of the white pot like she showed him. Two streams arc into the air and only one hits the water; the other slides down the wall and splashes in misshapen drips on the edge of the bowl. He runs down the hall, following the smells, and spots Ivorie standing at the stove. He grunts and she turns around.

"Well, good morning. I didn't hear you. I didn't think you'd ever wake up. It's eight o'clock! Did you pee?"

He nods.

"Did you flush?"

He looks at the floor.

"Did you wash?"

242

He doesn't want to tell her no but she can tell by looking at him. "Come on," she says, pushing the skillet to the back of the stove. She leads him into the bathroom and leans down, pulling on the white round roll on the wall. She wads it up and runs it along the seat. "I should have told you to be sure to lift this every time you need to pee. You see, I come in here and I take a sit-down to pee, and I do not want to sit down on this cold, wet mess late at night. So, lift this lid and that gives you a bigger target to hit. This is toilet paper," she says, holding the yellow-stained wad in front of him. "When you poop, you'll use this. Did you use newspaper or leaves up in the hills?"

He remembers the rough leaves against his backside.

She bends over and gathers more toilet paper and swipes it over the wall. "I know sometimes you're apt to get a wild stream, but you get a good grip on your pee-pee and aim it right here. Okay?"

He nods as she points to the sink.

"Wash up like I showed you last night. Rinse your face real good to get the matters out of your eyes." She's walking down the hall and talking at the same time. "Loretta cleaned your overalls and I set them on the chair in your room. Put them on and then come on out for breakfast."

He washes his hands and splashes water on his face; it drips down his neck and chest and he balls up the towel and rubs it over his face, catching the drips headed to his drawers. He lays the towel on the sink and walks to the chair in the bedroom. His overalls are lying there all straight and clean like they're laid out for a funeral. He puts them on, careful not to bend over too far because that makes a sharp pain run up inside him, and then he walks down the hall to the kitchen. He stands in the doorway and listens; another voice is talking to Ivorie.

"That's Maxine Harrison," she says, pointing to a box sitting on a shelf on the wall. "She gives the local news."

He stands in front of the table and stares up at the box.

"It's a radio," Ivorie says, turning a little knob and making the voice stop. "See, it's off. Now it's back on. That's a radio station in Greenville. They'll be playing some music here in just a few minutes." She moves to a small door on the wall and opens it, pulling plates down from a shelf. "I keep plates in this cupboard. Did your mama have cupboards?"

He shakes his head and she hands the

plates to him.

"Put each of these in front of a chair. One for you and one for me."

He takes them and does as she says while she pulls forks out of a sliding box.

"I keep silverware in this drawer, so when I ask you to get the forks you'll open this drawer, okay?" She hands them to him and nods at the plates.

He puts a fork on top of each plate and turns to her.

"All right, this cupboard," she says, tapping the one next to the plates, "holds all the cups and glasses. Here's a glass for you and a cup for me. Put those down next to the plates, and that is what we call setting the table."

Sally barks and the boy turns to the door. She is looking at him through the screen and wagging her tail fast as can be. He opens the door and gets down on his knees. She knocks him over and he makes some sort of clanging noise at the back of his throat.

"She is funny, isn't she?" Ivorie asks, setting a plate of biscuits on the table. "When you meet Sally you meet a friend for life. Come on in here and sit down."

He pushes his head into Sally's and she unleashes her tongue across his nose. He wipes his face with the back of his hand and then closes the door.

Ivorie is in the chair at the end so he takes the one next to her. She lays her hand on top of the table. "Let's say grace. Do you know what that is? That's thanking the Lord for our food and another day." Her head lowers and she talks just like God is sitting right where the boy put his behind. "Lord, thank you for bringing this boy here. Thank you for this food you've given us to eat. Thank you for another day."

His eyes are still closed when she starts scooping food onto his plate.

"Gravy and biscuits with sausage and eggs. I was raised on this."

The steam rises like smoke out of a chimney off the biscuits and he sticks his nose down close to them.

"There's plenty so don't go hog wild on me."

He puts a whole piece of sausage in his mouth and cuts into a biscuit pooled over with gravy.

"Now hold your horses. You're not a buzzard. Look at this food. There's plenty. Take part of that sausage out of your mouth and eat it regularlike." She swirls the coffee around in her cup and slurps at it as she talks. "I should have made you wash your hands again after playing with the dog, but we'll get to all these little things in due time."

She takes a bite and talks as she chews. Her hair is brown, his mother's was lighter, like straw, but it reminds him of his mother's the way she pulls it back into a tail. Her eyes are light like his mother's, and he wonders if his eyes are that light or dark like the man's. She speaks with a plain, steady voice and laughs easily. The sounds and smells are so different here. This kitchen is color and light, warm breezes and Ivorie's laugh, but it's hard to forget the sound a fist makes on flesh or the smell of alcohol after it has soured in the belly. He closes his eyes against the clatter in his head and listens to the hum of Ivorie's words.

"What's wrong?"

He feels her hand on his.

"Why are your eyes closed?"

He looks at her and knows she has that deep-rooted goodness she said his mother had.

She smiles and glances at his food. "Eat your breakfast. It'll strengthen you."

They are taking their final bites when voices through the kitchen door bring Ivorie to her feet. "It's the Cannons." She looks at him and says, "Remember Jane, John, and

Milo?" The children run onto the porch and fuss over who gets to open the door. Jane wins.

She steps inside and the doorway fills with a man and a woman and a whole passel of kids with red cheeks. "Hi!" Jane says, throwing her hand up in the air. She and John and Milo step near his chair and look at him.

He feels small and afraid with so many eyes on him and Ivorie motions to the other chairs. "Take a seat while he finishes his breakfast."

Jane and John fight over who gets to sit next to him and Jane wins when she gives John a sock to the chest with her elbow.

"Don't make your daddy whoop your butts so early in the morning," the woman holding a baby says. "Act like you've got some sense." She sets the baby on the floor and hands a pair of shoes to Ivorie. "The boys outgrew these. I thought you could use them."

"You know we can," Ivorie says, setting the shoes on the floor.

The boy stares at the baby crawling on the floor.

"This is Paul," the woman says. "And this is Will Henry and my husband, Joe. And I'm Fran."

He looks over his shoulder at Joe but he doesn't do anything except nod. The boy turns back to his food and Ivorie lifts her cup.

"Did you all want some coffee?"

"I've had too much," Joe says. "Thank you, though." He shuffles to the door and looks back at the boy. "You can come over and play anytime you want, son."

The boy notices that Joe has a small, shy smile when he talks.

"You boys get home soon so we can finish up in the tobacco."

"Have you ever worked in tobacco?" John asks.

No, he hasn't.

"Well, come on over anytime. You can do my share. I hate it." John whistles low and long between his teeth to prove his point.

"John Charles, don't make me jerk a knot in your tail," Fran says.

"When are you ever gonna talk to us?" Jane asks.

"Jane, that's rude," Fran says, picking up the baby.

"Well, he ain't said boo the whole time we've known him," John says. Fran moves fast as a mouse and thumps the back of John's head. "Ow, Mama!" John says, soothing his head. "I'm just sayin' a cat ain't got his tongue but has gone and pulled the dag-gum thing clean out of his mouth."

Milo doesn't say anything. He just watches the boy eat and stays quiet.

"I'm working on it," Ivorie says. "Doc's going to help me get him to the right people so we can get to the bottom of this not-talking business."

"What's all them bandages under your overalls?" Jane asks.

"Jane, we don't have any business asking such questions," Fran says.

"But, Mama, they're right there plain as day in front of my eyes!"

"He has some bad scratches," Ivorie says. "Doc put those on him."

"How'd you get all them scratches?" John asks.

"John!" Fran says.

John throws his hands in the air and talks loud so his mother can hear him out of her good ear. "Well, Land o' Goshen, Mama! What in Sam Hill are we supposed to say around here?" John stares at the boy and says, "Well . . . can you play with that git-tup?"

"He can't roll around on the ground or have a couple of boys jump on top of him right now but he can play like anybody else," Ivorie says.

"Well, come on before we have to leave," Jane says, scooting back from the table. She looks at her mother. "Can we play, Mama?"

Fran opens the door and holds it so the two little boys can get out. "For a while. You heard your daddy. We need to get in the tobacco."

Jane, John, and Milo are as noisy as the birds that would roost in the trees above the shack as they run through the door, and the boy looks up at Ivorie. The man's voice rattles through his head and he's afraid to move.

"Those are three fine friends," she says, watching the kids out the kitchen window. "If I were you I'd get out there and get to playing with them."

Ivorie helps lift the corner of the world he's carrying off his shoulders and he pushes back from the table. He moves to the door, looking for Sally, but she's not there; she's out chasing the kids in the yard. He opens the door and walks onto the porch. He looks up and takes a deep breath, as if he's inhaling the sky, and steps out into the sun.

IVORIE

He doesn't really play but just stands off to the side and watches Jane and the boys run around the yard and chase one another. At one point Milo comes and stands beside him. Milo doesn't say anything; he just stands there with his black bald head shining in the sun. Maybe he's pooped or tired of the game, but more likely, Milo knows what it's like to be the odd man out.

Fran and I sit on the porch watching them and my chest feels like iron bars are pressing down on it. "It's not a shy quiet that plagues him, is it, Fran?"

She shakes her head. "He's sad through and through. There's no telling when somebody made over him or spoke a decent word to him."

The boy watches Jane and John throw a stick for Sally and try to beat her to it. "What if he's like this forever? I never thought I was what people called me but I am old and set in my ways now. I don't know . . ." I stop. "Well, I just don't know."

"You'll know enough when you need to know it." I feel her watching me. "What is happening with you and George?"

I can't smile, but I try to, shaking my head. "I felt myself slipping, Fran. All these years with just Pop and Mother and then he comes along, making me think all sorts of things. We barely got started, it seems. But he's made it plain that he doesn't like the boy being here."

"Why not?"

"Too dangerous. Too stupid. I don't know."

"Maybe he'll come around to the notion," she says, trying to help.

"Maybe. Maybe not."

"And if he doesn't?"

I rest my head against the house. "I don't know."

The Cannons leave too soon but they have work to do and so do I. I can't let George occupy my mind all day. The boy sits on the porch and I have him put on the shoes Fran brought. They fit, just barely, and I kneel down to help lace them. "We'll go to Henry's later but right now we need to pick some beans. Can you help me?" I look at him and he nods. "How 'bout that name again? Is it Clayton?"

No answer.

"Vern? Denton? Mark?" His eyes are vacant. I walk to the side of the well house and pick up two peck baskets. "All right, let's go!" We walk to the garden and Sally chases the boy, trying to pull the basket from his hand. The boy likes this game and Sally plants her front paws firm in the grass and bounces her hind end up and down, tugging with all her might. She wins and the boy tumbles to the ground.

Sally follows the boy to the rows of beans and lies down in the dirt near him. "Just pick them right off and throw them in the basket," I say, demonstrating how to do it.

He picks one bean and places it in the basket.

"You can pick several at a time and just throw them in there. Boom!" I say, throwing a handful into my basket.

He picks three at a time and throws them in, looking at me.

"Perfect! Did you eat any beans in the hills?"

His chin tips.

"Did your mother have a little garden up there?"

Another tip up and down.

"Did she ever get anything from Henry's store?"

He shrugs.

His face is expressionless as he picks and I wonder what goes through his mind; what does he remember or try not to remember? "Nelson!" I say, looking up at him.

He waves his hand.

"Fine, fine. Abe? Bart? Clarence?" He shakes his head and I try my best to go through the alphabet. "Dean? Edgar? Francis?" He squinches up his face and I hold a bean in the air. "Bean!"

His eyes narrow in the sun and he looks at me like I'm crazy.

"I knew a Bean once but he was shaped more like a tater." I keep my head low, picking, and act as if this is just part of a regular conversation. "Do you remember when your mama died?"

He stops picking.

I look up at him but he won't look at me. "Do you remember?"

He nods.

"Someday you'll tell me about her, okay?" He begins to pick again and I don't say anything else.

When we've picked two pecks of beans I stand and stretch my back, making the old-woman sound Mother always made when she stood herself up. I brush the dirt off my knees, and when I turn around I see the boy sitting at the top of the embankment, looking over onto the hillside. I set the baskets of beans in the yard and sit down beside him. "Sure is pretty to look at, huh?" Sally wedges herself between us and snaps her jaws at a fly buzzing close to her head. "On some mornings the side of that hill looks gold the way the sun hits it. On other days the clouds look like they're sitting right on top of it like a hat. Sure is a lot of beauty there." He doesn't see beauty; I know that and I feel stupid for trying to make him see something that might never be there for him. I feel as empty as a hollow stump, trying to pretend with this boy.

"Let's go to Henry's store, okay?" His face is unsure but I keep talking. "He has jars of candy in there. Who knows, you might find something you like." I take the beans to the porch and get the canisters of milk for Henry out of the Frigidaire. I reach for my pocketbook I keep hung on the back of the kitchen door and walk toward the truck.

The boy's not moving.

I turn and look at him, holding my pocketbook over my eyes. "Will this be your first ride in a truck?"

His head bobs.

I hold my hand out for his. "Then come on! The train is pulling out of the station, as they say."

I open the truck door for him and he slides inside, looking small and uneasy. I turn the key, and when that clunking heap of metal roars, I feel his amazement: it bounces over the seat and knocks me right upside the head. I laugh out loud when I look in his eyes.

When Sally chases us the boy turns to see her through the back window. He puts his hand on the glass as she jumps up into the truck bed and he looks at me again with those astonished eyes. I point out to him where everybody lives on the way to Henry's, and I honk the horn whenever I see anybody working in their fields or gardens. He leans over to honk the horn and before long it sounds like the Fourth of July parade the way he keeps beeping it. The wind catches his hair and he sticks his head outside the window, opening his mouth. Sally barks and barks, watching him. He pulls his head back inside, shakes it like he's getting rid of bugs, and then pops it outside again. He puts both hands on top of the open window and pulls himself up so his torso is out in the wind.

I grab hold of his overalls and tug him

257

back inside. "You'll fall plumb out of here," I say. His overalls are catawampus and his hair sticks out like wires, making him look like a comical bird of prey, but his face is bright and satisfied.

Sally's first to get out of the truck when we get to Henry's and leads us to the front porch, where she looks and begs for her daily crumbs. I say hello to Gabbie, Haze, and Clayton on the front porch, and they stare trout-mouthed at the boy. Since they don't have the decency to say hello to him I open the screen door and Loretta throws her hands on top of her head. "Look at you," she says, walking out from behind the counter. She leans down in front of the boy and looks like she's sizing him up for a new suit. "The last time I saw you you were looking mighty puny but look at you now! Look at him, Henry!"

Henry leans on the counter and smiles over it at the boy. "Night and day," he says, reaching into a jar filled with licorice. "Would you like one?" He hands the black, sticky rope to the boy and he grips it like a fishing pole. "A lot of mamas say not to eat candy before a meal because you could spoil your dinner or supper but" — he leans over to whisper — "I don't believe that."

Five other customers are inside the store

and chatter stops midsentence when they see the boy, their faces plastered with polite going-to-visit smiles when they look at him, all except for Dolly Wade. She bounces over to him and smiles her lopsided grin that reveals a gaping hole in her teeth. "I'm Dolly. Who are you?"

He doesn't say anything.

She puts her face right in front of his. "I don't know you. I come here every single day but I don't know you. What's your name?"

"I don't know his name yet, Dolly," I say. She is shocked at this. "He doesn't talk much."

She puts her hand on top of his head and pats it up and down. "You don't have to have a name for me to like you and I do. I like you." She looks at me. "He can play at my house but not today. Today Mama and I are going to Paris, France, to eat some cake." She gives the boy another pat on the head. "Bye, little boy."

Gabbie, Haze, and Clayton stand inside the door with their hands in their pockets, looking at the boy and then at me, all of them wondering who he is and what I'm doing with him. "Is he relation of yours?" Gabbie asks. His much-too-old-for-his-age face is lined with ruts and gulleys.

"He's a friend," I say.

"Where'd your friend come from?" Haze says, squinting his eyes from the smoke off his cigarette.

"I know where he came from," Clayton says. "He's that boy from the hills you told everybody about."

Gabbie's wrinkled eyes brighten and his voice rises like a trumpet note as he says, "Law! I thought all them folks died out or left years ago!"

By now Henry's customers have formed a semicircle around us and I roll my eyes at Henry. Nosy birds. That's what they are. I put my hands on the boy's shoulders and direct him deeper into the store before they scare him to death.

He holds the licorice in front of him and walks the aisles, looking at the shelves and refrigerated cases and posters of ice cream and cheese and smiling cows. His eyes flicker with recognition as his fingers drag along the tops of cans and I wonder if his mother ever brought him here when he was younger. He stops at the potbellied stove, staring at it.

The screen door pops closed and I see Pete Fletcher looking at the boy. "Well, I'll be doggone," Pete says. "Henry said he was better."

The licorice hangs like a wilted flower in the boy's hand and he moves closer to me, hiding behind my leg.

"This is Pete Fletcher," I say.

The boy snaps his chin up to look at me.

"He's the preacher I told you about. His wife, Charlotte, was at the house the first day I brought you in on Miss Kitty."

He keeps hiding behind me and taps his chest.

"He's okay," I whisper down to the boy, trying to ease his fear. I smile, looking at Henry. "He saw Gertie in the pasture this morning, and I'm thinking about taking him to Holt's so he can see his first sheep. Then we need to get up to the school so we can find some pictures of monkeys and giraffes and such." Henry whistles through his teeth and I look in one of the aisles for a toothbrush. "He needs one of these," I say, plunking it down on the counter.

"Well, one day, when there's more time, you need to come down for the day," Henry says, ringing up the toothbrush. "Loretta and I can always use good help."

The boy doesn't respond and Loretta gives me a *bless his heart* look. He points at Pete and taps me on the leg and then his chest, and I nod at him like I understand what all that tapping means. Too many

261

dopes are just staring at the boy without much effort to talk to him or ask me jack diddly about him, so I move for the door. It's time to go.

He runs ahead of me, anxious to leave. Sally jumps into the truck bed and I head out for Holt's, the boy honking the horn again as we light out down the road.

Holt doesn't live too far from Henry's, just off Beggar's Creek Road. The white farmhouse sits at the bottom of a long gravel driveway, and the boy hangs his head out the window, watching the swirl of white dust stirred up behind us. I honk the horn as we pull up to the dairy barn and the boy and I jump out. I yell at Sally to stay in the truck and she lies down, sighing real loud like a dog's life sure is hard. Holt's cattle dot the pasture in front of us; he's got over a hundred head and some of the best milking equipment in the county. Avis looks up from the garden and waves at me. She's out working with Len, a chunky boy of nine with doughy legs and a fat middle. Len's face is always set with the expression that he just bit into something but doesn't know what it is. He sure didn't get his daddy's looks. Avis walks out of the garden and wipes her neck with a rag she pulls out of her dress pocket. Her face is mottled from being out in the heat and the skin on the fleshy part of her arms is raised with a patch of red prickles. "Hey, Ivorie," she says, keeping her eye on the boy. "Hi again," she says, looking at the boy. Len and the boy keep an eye on each other while Len chews on that invisible something in his mouth.

"He's never seen a sheep and I thought maybe he could see yours."

"That'd be fine," Avis says, her voice easing up on its usual sour-lemon sound. "Len, take 'em on back to the sheep pen."

We follow behind Len and it's all I can do not to pull his overalls out of his crack, but I figure that'd be bad-mannered at somebody else's house. "They're back there," Len says, mustering up enormous energy to point.

I lead the boy behind the barn and see two clumps of wool through the fence. I stand on the bottom rail of the fence and tap my hand next to me so the boy will climb up beside me. He does and I bend over the fence to get closer to the sheep. It smells like feed and hay and the clean scent after a rain from where the barn was rinsed out this morning after milking. "Just get on in there with them, Ivorie." I turn to see Holt behind us with his older son and smile at them. Rayburn is stubble-faced and long and lean — his father made over. The boy looks over his shoulder at them and Holt's face falls in on itself. "Is this the . . ."

I nod. "He's going to be staying with me and I discovered he's never seen a sheep before."

Rayburn moves to the gate and opens it. "Go on in. They won't hurt you," he says to the boy. The boy walks past Rayburn and steps inside the pen. "What's your name?"

"We're working on that," I say. "He doesn't talk much."

Holt sidles up next to me and leans on top of the pitchfork, holding himself at an angle. "How'd all this come about?" he whispers.

"His no-account daddy just about killed him," I say, watching the boy stick his hand deep inside the sheep's wool as Rayburn keeps it from moving. "I brought him down from the hills and he didn't wake up for two days. The old man 'bout near knocked his brain out."

Holt watches the boy and his face is as flat as I've ever seen. "What are you going to do with him?"

"Raise him."

He shakes his head and whispers while keeping his eyes down, "You can't do that, Ivorie. You don't know anything about that boy. You don't even know his name."

My heart bucks a little because I know I'm going to hear this a lot, just about as much as I heard that I was aging and pitiful and doomed to a life of being a miserable spinster. "Someday I'll know his name because I'm going to get that cleft palate of his fixed."

Holt looks down at the ground and digs the prongs of the pitchfork into it. "Cleft palate. He's just got one thing after another."

One more shovelful of crap piled onto an already mountainous pile. I know all this. "He needs a home," I say, watching the Pet Milk truck back up to Holt's barn.

The driver jumps out and waves at Holt. "Mornin', Ox!" Holt lifts his hand and I smile. The driver pulls out a long hose and begins to walk it inside the barn but stops, turning to Holt. "Saw your brother, Ox." Holt's face darkens over. I never met Holt's brother, Gray, but have long known there was no love lost between him and his family. "I hollered out for him but he didn't hear me."

Holt laughs, wiping his forehead. "Must have been somebody as ugly as him. Gray's been out California way for years."

"Well, that's what I thought," the driver

says. "I remember when he headed out. The farm here got awful quiet after that!" The man laughs and Holt works up a laugh as best he can. For years, Holt and Avis used additional hands on the farm but Avis put a stop to them years ago. Nobody knows why and is too afraid of Avis to ask. I wonder if Holt's brother had something to do with it. Between his brother and Avis, Holt's never been able to catch a break. The driver disappears into the barn and in a few moments I hear gallons and gallons of milk surging from the hoses of the bulk tank into the truck.

Holt looks to Rayburn. "Let's finish up."

Rayburn lets the sheep go and the boy stands off to the side, watching the two sheep in awkward wonder.

I can't remember the feelings of seeing my first sheep or taking my first car ride. I don't recall my first taste of licorice or my earliest memory of music coming out of the radio. I watch him and wonder if my face was like that: glowing and pink and as open as these untilled fields around us.

By the time we make it home my head is sore from thinking up names like Speck, Coop, Enis, Rowan, Jed, Wilt, and Cob. We honked and waved the whole way, and when

I pull up the driveway I know everyone in Morgan Hill is aware of the boy living with me. Word travels fast in small circles. I leave him in the yard with Sally and go inside to get dinner started.

I turn on the radio to listen to Maxine read the local news as I throw a few potatoes and green beans together in a pot with a slab of fatback and then shuck some corn before I cut up some fresh tomatoes, cucumbers, and onions. There are few obituaries today and I wonder if anyone ever knew that the boy's mother had died. Did her own mother know, wherever it is she lives, or even a friend somewhere in the world who shed a tear over her passing?

I set his dinner down and he looks at his plate, waiting for grace. Somehow, in just a few days we have escaped the darkness of the hills and settled into a routine. It's been clunky and still feels like we are wearing too-big shoes at times, but we are making a way in this house together. I don't know what tomorrow will be like but today has felt good. I say that very thing to the Lord, and then I turn up the radio so we can hear some music, and we eat.

It's been a sweltering day and the heat has intensified the boy's smell. I want to take him into Greenville tomorrow for some clothes but can't take him there smelling like the underside of a donkey's tail. I don't make a big deal of getting him into the tub — when I'm done with the evening milking I just run the water and ask him to take off his overalls. "I need to take off your bandages and give your wounds a good cleaning."

He strips down and is all knobby bones, thin limbs, and white gauze.

I take the bandages off his back and keep my face fixed tight so he can't read the lines between my eyebrows telling him the awful truth of what I see. "Jump on in."

He looks into the tub as if staring into a deep pit.

I wad up the bandages in my hand. "Go on. Sit right on down and take a good soak."

He steps in and stands with his knees bent as if the ground is unsteady beneath him.

I sit on the commode and smile at him. "Sit on down and I'll give you a washrag."

He eases himself in and the water covers his legs. He reacts and tries to pull himself up.

"It's okay," I say, handing a rag to him. "I'll turn the water off."

I sit on the floor beside the tub and rest my elbows on the porcelain edge. He doesn't move and I splash a little water onto his belly. He looks at me and I splash more water up onto his back. "I hear the king over in England takes a bath every day. I wouldn't think a king would get dirty enough to take a bath every day, would you?" I reach for the soap and run it back and forth over the washrag. "Here you go. Use this on your legs and belly and face and I'll wash your back." I lather up my hands and work them nice and easy over his back. It feels like I'm moving them over a quilt that's being made, the strings and fabric still loose and unstitched.

I watch as he attempts to work the rag over his skin and the rag seems too big and cumbersome in his small hands. "You'll get the hang of it. Can I wash your hair?" He nods and I cup some water in my hands and bring it up over his head. I should have brought in a bowl or something to help with this part.

He closes his eyes tight as the water drips down his face and he makes great puffing sounds as he tries to blow it off his mouth.

"It's just running down your face," I say, scooping up another handful before pouring some shampoo in my hand. "I'm going to use this shampoo and it'll clean your hair. I hear it's the same kind of shampoo that old king uses, too."

He keeps his hands over his face and makes a gurgling sound in his throat.

I work fast and then cup more water to rinse out the shampoo. I feel like I'm bailing out a sinking boat and act all out of breath and tired, leaning on the edge of the tub for rest. "Shew! I'm pooped." He looks at me through his fingers and I can tell he's grinning. "Is that a grin under there?" I try to move his fingers and he holds them fast in place. I splash more water on his belly.

He's making a rattling noise.

"That is a grin *and* a laugh," I say, laughing and splashing more water on him. He tries to splash me and I splash faster.

His mouth opens and closes like a baby bird's.

I laugh, watching him. "You're a good boy, you know that?"

He stops splashing and an arresting trace of sorrow settles over his face. It's a bleak, deep sadness, the kind that stomps on your lungs and lodges in your throat.

I splash his belly again and lean down over the edge of the tub to see him. Tears are rolling from his eyes and the veins are swelling in his neck. I realize what I've said and touch his knee. "You're a good boy."

His shoulders begin to tremble and a

choking sound comes from his mouth.

What despicable words and monstrous acts echo in his mind? I hope what I say will boom loud as thunder in his ears. I lean my head on his and whisper again, "You're a good boy." He shakes his head and I say, "Yes. Yes you are. You're a good boy."

His noises are louder and I put my hands under his arms and pull him up out of the water. I sit on the commode and take him onto my lap, rocking him as he sobs, long hollow wails that ring off the tub walls. "You are a good, good boy," I say over and over, holding tight to his slippery body. A cloudy mist hangs in the bathroom as I rock him, whispering the words like a song.

HENRY

People sure know how to make a fuss! I think there were five or six people at the store when Sarah Ivorie showed up with the boy one day. Before I could say Jack Robinson six more were in here grilling me like it was the Spanish Inquisition. "She don't know what she's getting herself into," Gabbie Doakes said. Gabbie's a dried-up type who could never be accused of getting himself into too much of anything, especially work. Loretta always says if he's not running his mouth he might think he's dead and call Maxine up at the radio station and list his own obituary.

"I told her to stay away from them people up there," Clayton said, putting his chubby thumbs under the straps of his overalls. "She's just bringing on trouble. I know them. I know what they can do."

"Hush up, Clay," Loretta said.

"Younguns can be a curse," Haze said,

shoving a thin, veined hand into his pocket.

"You've been batching it for fifty years, Haze," I said. "How do you know anything about kids?"

"I've seed plenty," he said, shoving a pinch of chew into his mouth, revealing tobacco-brown teeth. "I've seed all sorts come through here."

"Seeing them sure isn't the same as raising them, Haze," Loretta said. Edith had a lot more patience for wisdom dispensed through lack of experience than Loretta does. Her voice always gets tight and her back goes rigid when one of the boys spouts off, and sometimes she'll give them a look that makes my skeleton shake. She's like Mother used to be when she'd get one of her sick headaches; when that happened, we kids knew to lay low. Gabbie, Haze, and Clayton never have enough sense to lay low. "Ivorie's doing more than any of us would do, and we sit planted down at that church Sunday in and Sunday out."

Haze threw his hands in the air. "I'm just tellin' ya'll the truth. I've seed some cursed younguns come through here."

"Oh hush your yap!" Loretta said, throwing a round of cheese into the refrigerated case like it had just cussed out her mother.

I leaned in close to Loretta's ear and saw

the sweat drops on her temple. "Hold on now. You're too young to blow out your gears." I looked up at Gabbie, Haze, and Clayton, and they were all standing there with their hands in their pockets, swaying to some unheard rhythm in their heads. Margie Atwood added her two cents (the boy could be diseased) and Jerry Cleats said that most of the hill people were criminals, "thieves and murderers and such."

"Lord save my soul!" Loretta said, wiping the moisture off her forehead with the palm of her hand. "That little boy is not a criminal, Jerry." I wanted to say that how Jerry smacked his own wife around *is* criminal but didn't.

"His no-good daddy is probably a criminal," Fred Jarvis said, baring his upper teeth like a rabbit. "Ivorie doesn't know one thing about that boy's bloodline. She needs to be careful."

"Now that I think about it," Gabbie said, "that boy looks right familiar to me. I b'lieve I know his daddy."

"Then who's his daddy?" Loretta asked, balling that fist of hers on her hip.

Gabbie took off his faded blue cap and scratched his head. "Well, I don't recall right off but I know I've seen that boy."

"Maybe he comes from some of your

people," Loretta said, making sandwiches for the dinner hour.

Gabbie just about sucked his cigarette down to his lungs. "He ain't one of my people."

"You said he looks familiar," Loretta said, spreading mayonnaise on a slice of white bread. "I bet he is one of your people." Gabbie's head lunged forward and he hacked like a rat was stuck in his gizzard, and Loretta turned away to keep from laughing.

"Ivorie don't know anything about raising kids," Margie said.

"There's plenty of homes for kids like him," Fred Jarvis said. "Ivorie can't take on all that 'sponsibility."

"He might be crazy," Pearl Coley, George's mother, added. I knew Sarah would shudder, hearing her beau's own mother talk about her and the boy.

"He's not a bit crazy," Jane said. She'd come in at the dinner hour to help Loretta make sandwiches and had stood as quiet as a cloud, listening, but I've never known Jane Cannon to be cloudlike for long. "He's just a little boy who needed a good bath and something to eat and a passel of kids like John and Milo and me to play with. His mama is dead, and every kid needs a mother to pat on him and make over him and tell him to sit up straight and say his prayers and stop saying *ain't* and act like you've got some gumption. That doesn't make him crazy. It makes him a little boy."

Pearl Coley looked over at Margie Atwood with a put-on smile that said Jane needed to be pitied because she didn't understand such grave matters the way they did.

They stood together and massed themselves into a solid wall of doubt, and Loretta swept her hand in the air like she held the power to make them all disappear. That was her signal to me to say she was done with all of it. Once the sandwiches were made she slipped away into the stockroom, but there were repeated talks with different folks throughout the day. That's just how it goes when everybody has an opinion.

I lie down next to Loretta and reach for the light, cutting it off. In the half-dark room I can see her staring up at the ceiling, the same one Sarah looked up at when she was sick with fever and the same one Edith saw through eyes that struggled to stay open when she lay dying. "What's rattling through your mind over there?" I ask.

"Same thing that's rattling through yours," she says, her voice getting louder when she turns her face to me. "It's hard enough rais-

ing your own kids, let alone somebody else's
— somebody you don't even know and who
beat the snot out of his own boy!" She huffs
and leans up on her elbow. "Somebody
needs to do to him what he did to that boy."

She spews out the words, and I wipe my
face with great big motions. "I agree with
you," I say. "You don't need to spit on me."
She laughs and lies back down, throwing
her arm on top of her forehead. "That boy
has lived with the devil. To *think* what he
did to that child." She's sitting up now and
slapping the bed. "Good Lord! Who does
such a thing? How does that little boy get
over something like that? What'd that man
do to the boy's mother? How'd she die up
there?" I open my mouth to answer but she
thinks the air I take is too big and plows
ahead. "Some people would say his daddy
had a sick mind. Let me tell you that is *not*
a sick mind. That is a depraved mind. An
evil mind." She pounds the bed again and I
move my arm out of the way to protect it.
"To *do* such a thing to that boy." She lies
down in a huff and turns her back to me,
taking most of the covers with her. "I can't
even think about it. It makes me sick." She
rolls back over and bellows at me, "Don't
you have anything to say, Henry Walker?"

I laugh and pull myself up. "Every time I

take a breath you trample right over me."

I see her hand waving in the air. "Talk on then. Nobody's stopping you."

I cross my arms on my chest and study a bit on my answer. "I don't like it how folks are thinking of Sarah. First, they pitied her for being an old maid, and now they think she's batty for helping the boy."

Loretta turns on her side and tucks her hands under the side of her face. "And that George Coley is showing his tail."

"What'd George do?"

"I don't know, but he hasn't been around so I know something soured his milk." She leans up on her elbow and looks at me. "What do you think about Ivorie?"

I look at her and notice the tree branches outside the window casting shadows on the wall, like great big beasts in here with us. "Well, I'm scared for her. I am. She's alone. She'll be all the boy has."

"And he'll be all she has," Loretta says.

I try to picture Sarah Ivorie and the boy together five, even ten years from now. "True," I say. "She's as bullheaded as they come, and that is going to serve her well now with everybody looking at her like both her oars aren't in the water." My mouth tries to keep up with my mind. "She's never taken care of a child but she's taken care of people most of her adult life." I feel myself getting riled up. "What are we supposed to do with ourselves here in this world? Sit? Just sit around and wait to die? Get hemorrhoids that way." Loretta laughs and I see her hand land on top of her head.

"Ivorie sure isn't getting hemorrhoids."

"No she is not!" I think about my sister lying in her own bed and wonder what she's thinking. I figure she's scared and a little lost but I know her well enough to know she's reaching down into those places where courage and hope are melded together over a blazing fire and she's stirring the pot. I sigh and watch the beasts on the wall change shape. "I feel bad for the little fella. He's as pitiful as can be." I try to finish but Loretta trumps me again.

"He's known nothing but pain living with that . . . I'm not going to say what he is. Go on."

"Sarah's got his past to deal with, and who knows what work needs to be done in his mouth."

Loretta fluffs the covers on top of herself and looks up at the ceiling. "He never got to talk to his mother." Her voice trails off and I try to see her in the moonlight. I reach out for her hand and put mine on top of it. "She deserved to hear his voice." We're both quiet, thinking about that.

"I wish I could remember her," I say. "I'm sure she came in with the boy. I know I've seen him before."

"I know. I keep trying to recollect when she came in, but I can't. It seems we would have talked to her and asked her where she lived. We always talk to folks we don't know. I don't know why I can't place her."

"Eh, there's a fly in the ointment here but I can't put my finger on it. He just looks right familiar!"

"So we can't remember her," Loretta says. "It's probably been two years or more. Who knows when she died?" We're both quiet again, mulling that over. Some people have sadness piled right up on top of sadness. "Just because we can't remember her *or* him doesn't mean anything." She props her head up on her hand and rests her other hand on my chest. "Or maybe Gabbie was right. Maybe he knows the boy's old man or his mother or" — and she emphasizes *or* — "maybe we know the old man's brother or his daddy or mama. Maybe that's who the boy looks like, an uncle or a grandmother that we know."

"Somebody would have said something by now. The whole community knows about the boy."

She lies back down and makes a high-pitched hum in her throat that sounds like she's saying, *I don't know.* "Maybe somebody doesn't want to claim him. A granddaddy who's embarrassed or an uncle who never forgave his sister for running off and getting pregnant." She bangs her hands together. "What about that Atkins girl who got pregnant years ago? Nobody knows where she is. That could have been her up in those hills."

I turn my head on the pillow and look over at her. "That girl ended up marrying the sorry thing who got her pregnant, and they live in O-hi-a, where he works in a steel mill."

"Well, I'll be," she says, drumming her hands on top of the quilt. More humming sounds come from Loretta's throat, making it seem like she's carrying on a full conversation with herself in there. "How much will it cost to get that palate fixed?"

"I've no idea." I know what Sarah Ivorie makes, and I don't see how she can afford to pay for all the medical work the boy needs. Loretta's thinking about that, too; I can tell by how she keeps up with all that throat humming.

"Is he cursed, Henry?"

"You mean what Haze said about cursed

younguns? Lord have mercy, his mind runs as fast as a herd of turtles. He's just an old crank — you know that."

The animals on the wall look like they're about to chomp down on Loretta's head. "What about the Lord punishing children for the sins of their parents who hate him to the third and fourth generations?"

I lean up on my elbow. "What about love for a thousand generations? That's in the good book, too, you know."

She looks at me and we try to see each other in the darkness. "So which is the boy?"

"It doesn't matter what sort of hate that boy's daddy was eaten up with. All that was broken the moment Sarah went up in those hills with God Almighty filling her chest and she brought him down out of there." I can see the whites of her eyes looking up at the ceiling. "Love's in that boy's bloodline now. For a thousand generations." I lie down and turn my face up to the ceiling, too. "Not bad for a day's work."

I'm not chasing rainbows when I think of Sarah and the boy. There will be rough rows to hoe up ahead, probably more than we can imagine, but I can't even begin to figure how long it's going to take to make up a thousand generations. And to think it all started with Sarah and a gullywarsher of a rainstorm and Miss Kitty. I knew she was special but I never thought of my sorrel mule being famous for a thousand generations. That thought makes me smile in the dark.

THE BOY

He is worn-out, and once Ivorie gets salve on his back, she tucks him into bed. He points at the chair in the corner of the room and she looks at him.

"Do you want me to read to you for a while?"

He nods and lies motionless, as always; even in the world of sleep he could keep himself small and hidden and noiseless.

She picks up his mother's Bible. The cover is almost dry but is bloated and bent from the water. She opens it and begins fanning through the pages, looking for something. "My mother always said that margin writing tells you about somebody," Ivorie says. "See all this white stuff? That's called the margin of the page. I wonder if your mother wrote your name down in here somewhere?" She flips through the pages, shakes her head, and then flops the book back in her lap and starts all over again, going slower this time. She stops and turns the pages back one at a time until she draws the Bible up close to her face. "Seven thirty forty-two," she says, looking at him. "July thirtieth, nineteen forty-two. Is that your birthday?"

He can't recall.

"Is it hot when you have a birthday?"

He remembers walking over the hillside with his mother on his last birthday with her. The sun was high and blistering that day. He nods and Ivorie smiles.

"She wrote that in the Psalms by this verse: *Lo, children are a heritage of the Lord: and the fruit of the womb is his reward.*" She leans in close to the bed and looks at him. "That's who you were to her — her reward. Do you know what a reward is?"

He doesn't.

"A prize! You were your mama's prize and she marked it right here. You look like her, don't you?"

He looks at her and his eyes brighten with wonder.

"You don't look anything like your pop. Your hair and your eyes are light. Like hers, right?"

The boy smiles, hoping it's true.

She lifts up the Bible and he looks at the numbers written on the page. "She didn't write your name. I wonder why." She slaps the book on her lap. "This means you're going to be eight years old in less than three weeks. Mother and Pop never made much to-do over our birthdays in this house, save a cake, but I'm thinking about a picnic out under the trees with Henry and Loretta, the Cannons, maybe even Pete and Charlotte and Doc. Possibly George. You don't know him yet."

He draws the covers close at the mention of so many and rubs the bumpy bedspread between his thumb and fingers.

"I'll make a cake and have Henry make some ice cream, and I'll buy you a gift! I have no idea what to buy an eight-year-old boy but whatever it is, I'll wrap it in blue paper and make a bow for it."

He feels like smiling, watching her.

The final finger of light drifts into the room and moves around and away, looking this way and that for a place to rest. "You need to sleep," she says, putting her hand on his head. She reaches for the lamp and turns it off. Light from the moon spills across her face.

He watches her tiptoe out of the room and lets the thoughts of birthdays and picnics and cake piled high with frosting dash and swirl in his head.

Shafts of light poke through the window and he walks to the bathroom to pee. The white rim is down and he snaps it up midstream, causing pee to splatter onto the floor and wall. He walks through the hall to the kitchen, where Ivorie is at the stove. He claps his hands and she jumps.

"Lord have mercy!" she says. "Hair is noisier than you. Did you pee?"

His head bobs as he pulls the straps up on his overalls.

"Did you flush and wash your hands?"

He shakes his head and she points.

"Go do it right quick. Then let's get to milking and eat."

He washes quick as a raccoon and follows her out the screen door, where Sally runs her nose up under his hand. He's always happy to see that dog and bends his head down to hers, smashing his nose into her muzzle. Her fur is wet from dew and she shakes it off as they traipse to the barn.

Gertie may as well be a monster in a stall to the boy, the way he fears her size and breath and large pink-and-black nose.

"She won't hurt you," Ivorie says. "Cows want to be milked." She gestures toward the stool. "Now since you're going to be pulling on her teats, it's always polite to say good morning." She pats the cow's side and leans toward the massive head. "How you doing this morning, Gert? Okay, like I did last night. Sit on down here."

He sits on the milking stool and looks at the baggy, pink teats drooping in front of him.

"Line the bucket up and tug and squeeze, tug and squeeze. Easy as pie."

She's smiling, so it can't be that bad. He reaches for one of the teats and holds it in his hand, looking at it. He rummages through his memories and a raw, hot blade of pain stabs him. The walls of the shack are closing in and the man's voice is loud and full of venom. "Take it! Take it, dammit! Take it!" He closes his eyes and his breath strangles him, thrusting him backward off the stool. Gertie moos and shuffles her hooves.

"It's all right," Ivorie says, picking up the stool. "If you rest your head up against her side it's easier."

The boy thrashes his head and bats it against the wall. The smell of manure, urine, and hay clot in his throat and he swats at his face.

Ivorie's fingers wrap around his wrists,

pulling his hands away.

"It's all right. It's all right," she says, holding his hands.

He can hear her sigh as she sits down on the milking stool.

"Can you look at me?"

He keeps his eyes shut tight.

"Would you open your eyes?"

He does, and her eyes are tired with deep purple circles under them.

"Is this about milking?"

He doesn't respond. Not even a blink.

She puts her hand on her mouth, shaking her head. "Those wounds on your back are going to take a while to heal."

He watches her talk.

"And these memories up here will get better," she says, touching his head. "It'll take a lot of time but they will get better." She looks down at her hands and wrings them around. "I might never know what happened up in that shack, but one thing I'll always know is that it wasn't your fault." Her eyes are full of mist. "No matter what happened, it was never, ever your fault."

Her words hang between them, and he wants to reach out and shove them into his mouth, swallowing their soft sounds and warm edges.

She rubs her hands along her thighs and

shakes her head back and forth. "I want you to know that you're not like that." She looks at him with wide, round eyes of grief. "You don't have meanness all balled up inside you. You don't! I know it."

Hot liquid pools in the corners of his eyes. "He had the gates of death inside him but you're alive with light in here!"

His eyes begin to leak because it sounds like something his mother used to tell him.

Ivorie puts her hand on his chest and pats it. "He's not inside you. He's not."

Her face is set with fierce hope and anger, and he takes a breath, hoping to inhale the trail of her words lingering above him.

She turns around on the stool and wipes her face before reaching under the cow. Jets of spray ring on the side of the bucket and he watches Ivorie's muscles flex in her upper back. Squeeze, squeeze, squeeze, squeeze. The sound ricochets off the metal sides and fills the stall.

He reaches out and touches her arm, pointing.

Her face is wet and long, looking at him. "Do you want to try?" She gets up and he sits, facing the cow. "Rest your head right here on her. That supports you while you're milking."

The heat from the cow covers his head

and for some reason he feels safe against her spreading warmth. He feels for the teats and pulls on them like Ivorie showed him. He jumps when milk hits his leg and Ivorie laughs.

"You're doing it! Just aim down in the bucket." Another blast hits Ivorie and she shrieks. "In the bucket! In the bucket!"

He points a teat toward Sally and squeezes. Sally opens her mouth and lashes her tongue at the white stream. The boy feels himself smiling and hears Ivorie patting Gertie.

"Now that's the way you milk a cow!"

He has survived the monster in the stall. He has survived the monster in the woods. Milk covers the bottom of the silvery pail and Ivorie cheers.

Ivorie puts the canisters of milk inside the Frigidaire and then meets him at the truck. He climbs inside, waiting for the low rumbling underneath him that shakes his legs and tickles his back. Nothing else is like this. He pats his thighs and Sally leaps inside the cab with him. The boy hangs his head out the window and squints up into the white-blue sky. The wind pinches his nose and he holds his breath, listening to Ivorie laugh. She drives up the hill to the schoolhouse and never stops talking.

"This is where I work during the school year. Look down there and you'll see Henry's store."

He leans over so he can see past her shoulder.

"Lots of kids run down this hill at dinnertime and buy a bologna sandwich with milk at the store. Maybe someday you'll do that, too."

He looks at the redbrick building: a large, looming temple of doom.

"You'll like it here," she says.

She uses a key to open the front doors, and the pine floors look shiny and slick with the sun lighting on them. "We'll go right down the hall to the library," she says, leading him past rows of small metal doors. "Those are lockers. You'll hang your coat in one of those." She walks and talks, her shoes squeaking against the wooden floor. "The school's not big; we fit every student from first to twelfth grade in here, some grades even sit together in the same room." She stops outside a door. "This is the office, where I work. I sit right there at that desk. I help the principal part of the day and the other part I work in the library."

He doesn't know what a principal is and can't ask, so she closes the door and heads back down the hall, pulling open a door.

"This is the library." It's a small square room. "It's not much compared to other schools, I'm sure, but we do okay."

The boy stands in the middle of the aisles and looks up at the dusty shelves of books, craning his neck to see the top shelf. He's never seen a room like this in his life.

"Aha!" Ivorie says, holding a book up for him to see. "First-grade primer. This has got all the basic words in it like *the* and *and* and *he* and *she.* Surely I can help you learn how to read them, don't you think?" His eyes are vacant and she says, "All right, then!" She keeps browsing through the rows and the spines of the books make a ticking sound when he drags his fingers along them. "An encyclopedia with animals galore," she says, flipping open a book. "Here's one with a map of the world. Have you ever heard of England?"

He shakes his head.

"Well, now you have and right here is where it's at. That king I told you about lives there."

He looks down at shapes like puzzle pieces that she calls the world.

She picks up another book, and he lifts one from the shelves with the picture of a little boy on it and hands it to her. *"Homer*

Price," she says, reading it. "Let's see. It's about a boy who makes radios and has a pet skunk. Want me to read it to you?"

He knew all about skunks but very little about radios, except for how to turn the one on and off in Ivorie's kitchen. He nods and she puts it on the stack.

She closes the door and they walk down the hall to the front doors, and the boy has a sickening sensation of boys being mean to him in these hallways because he can't talk or read or even spell his name. She seems to look inside his mind and takes hold of his hand, giving it a squeeze. "We have so much to do before the start of school in September." She locks the doors behind them and they sit down on the top step, the sun hot on their shoulders. "Let's work again on your name." Sally lies in the shade of a great oak, panting, listening to them. "Harold?"

No. He has no idea how to tell her.

"Jerry? Donald? Stanley? Let me think of some of my favorite singers. Hank? Lester? Earl or Lefty?"

He cocks his head up at her and squints in the brightness.

"Not Lefty? How about Righty?"

He swats his hand in the air.

"Let me think of more of those boys on

the radio. Jimmie? Gene? Ernest? Roy?"

He half listens to her as he thumbs through the books on his lap.

"Look! That right there is a tiger — a great big, fast cat — but you can't pet a tiger. It'd bite your arm off. Look here." She flips the pages and smiles. "An elephant. Don't that beat all you've ever seen?" He flips page after page as Ivorie calls out the name of each animal. "Lion, monkey, *another* kind of monkey, and *another* kind of monkey — look at him, he grows a better beard than Henry!"

He lifts a book up in front of her face and points at a shape.

"That's a *T,*" she says. "It's one of the letters in the alphabet." She takes the book and opens it to the front, showing all the letters spread across two pages. "All of these are letters in the alphabet. *A* starts them and *Z* ends them. See?"

He watches her finger point and tries to make out all the shapes, angles, and squiggly lines of the letters.

"Every word we say or read or write is made up of these letters. One day, you'll be able to spell and read using these letters."

Something burns in his chest and he points at the letters, flapping his hands.

"Yes, you'll learn to read."

His eyes water over.

She leans down on her knees, wrapping her arms around her legs. "Did your mother read to you from her Bible?"

He nods.

"That's because she knew how to read. And you're smart just like her, and you'll be able to learn, too."

He can't believe that all those squiggles and shapes will ever make sense in his mind and he throws the book down.

"No," she says, reaching for it. "We don't treat books like that. Look at me."

He lifts his eyes because she'll just say it again if he doesn't.

"The teachers in that school have taught some powerfully dumb kids to read, so I'm plenty hopeful they can teach you, too. You hear me?" She tucks that one piece of hair, the one that always gets away from the tail in the back, behind her ear. "I think it's probably pretty hard for a caterpillar to think much of itself when it's wrapped up in the dark or a bulb when it's just laying there in the ground, but more's coming and boy is it something!" She pats his leg the way she always does and grins at him through shiny teeth. She always talks plain to him, but sometimes she says things that take the darkness and the cold and turns them into gossamer-winged butterflies and budding daisies.

She sits beside him in bed and sighs, looking out the window. "The man in the moon sure is looking fat and serious tonight, isn't he? Look how he sits there in front of the hills." He smiles and she closes her eyes, taking a deep breath. "Smell that?"

He sniffs the air.

"That is the smell that comes at the end of the day when everything's shutting up shop so Old Man Moon can do his business."

He sniffs again at the rawness in the air and she puffs up the pillow, propping it against the iron headboard. He leans into it and she points to the letters in the front of a book.

"The ABCs." She tilts her head back and opens her mouth as if waiting for something to drop in it. "Did your mama sing 'Twinkle Twinkle Little Star' to you?" She begins to sing and he smiles; the song ushers him back to the woods, to the secret spot he shared with his mother. "That's the same tune for the *ABCs.* Listen." She sings and points and then sings the *ABCs* again.

This time he tries to sing along inside his mind but there are too many letters crowding his brain.

"We'll sing that a lot," she says.

She pulls out a sheet of paper from under the stack of books on her lap and writes in big letters. *BED.* "Bed," she says. "That *e* right there is a vowel. There are five vowels: *A, E, I, O,* and *U* and sometimes we use *Y.*" She points to each vowel and says, "My name uses three vowels: *I, O,* and *E.*" She spells her name and Sally's, and he listens as the pencil makes scratching sounds over the paper.

He stares at the words on the page. They are magical and full of mystery, with the lines and dots and swirls consuming him. When every white space is filled, sadness gobbles up the boy and he taps on the book with the picture of the boy on the front.

"You want some Homer Price?" He taps it faster, and she says, "Okay, okay! Hey, is your name Homer?"

He shakes his head and she reads until, despite his will, he scuffles with his eyelids and night pulls him under.

In the morning she holds on to the back of his overalls as they drive toward the crossroads. "You are not a dog," she yells over the wind inside the truck's cab. "Get back in here."

He flops back against the seat and smiles.

"Lord have mercy! Look at your hair! It looks like a rat's nest." She laughs like a popgun going off and runs her hand over his head. She turns real slow onto 11-E and points. "See that land right there?"

He rests his chin on the open window.

"I own thirty acres of that. Somebody named Mr. Big Q wants to put up a filling station there."

He looks at her over his shoulder. Sometimes she explains what a word means, but she leaves *filling station* floating like a bubble, so he rests his chin back on the window and lets the wind blow him senseless. He sits up when Ivorie drives into Greenville. His neck feels like it's on a hinge, the way he turns it from side to side. There are way too many buildings to take in, and cars and trucks pass them as if there's a parade going on right this very day.

"That right there is the movie house," she says, driving past a white building with a big sign. "People go in there and watch a moving picture on a big screen." He doesn't understand, and she looks at the building with wide eyes. "I went there eleven years ago and saw *Gone with the Wind* with Miss Vivien Leigh and a handsome buck named Clark Gable. I haven't been back since. It might be time to bury the hatchet and get back here sometime." She pats his leg in that way she has. "With you!"

Inside the store with the dresses and pants hanging in the window and the wide plank floors, a woman with graying hair and a dull and tired face leads them to a table stacked with shirts and pants. "Shoes are over there," she says in a voice coated in turpentine.

Ivorie looks around and rests her fingers on the side of her face the way she always does when she's thinking. "I haven't been here since I bought my funeral dress for Pop." She makes a high-pitched sound and touches the clothes like she's made a grand discovery. "You'd be right handsome in blue," she says, holding a shirt under his neck. She fusses with the sleeves and stands back at arm's length, puckering her lips. "Do you like this one?"

He holds it and can smell the newness.

"This will be your Sunday go-to-meeting shirt. And these dungarees right here will be for Sunday only. No roughhousing in these." She holds up the dark pants and gets down on her knee to see how far they go down his leg. "Room for growth," she says, folding them over her arm.

She moves around the table and he follows, watching the people around him: the old man whose cane makes a thumping sound when he walks, the roly-poly woman looking at the shoes, and the pipe-thin lady who is looking at underpants like she's a spy. He eyes the shirts, pants, and socks, and hunts in his mind for the last time his mother gave him a pair of overalls. He never knew where she got anything; it simply appeared in her hands one day, and they had onions, beans or corn, soap, a skillet, overalls, or cash for coffee and bacon. It all stopped coming after she died.

He stumbles back into Ivorie when the old man bends over his cane and pushes out his teeth. They come right out of his face and dangle on the jutted pink tongue, as if he had the power to simply pull up a lung and set it on a platter or balance an eye on the end of his finger! The boy wraps his arms around Ivorie's leg and gapes at the row of teeth housed in a pink ridge. The old man rests his weight on top of the cane, cackling; his skin hangs over his bones like ancient gray paper. The teeth make a clacking sound when he slides them back into his mouth. "Made him jump," he says to Ivorie. "That was some kind of jumping!" He wheezes and rakes a calloused finger over the boy's jaw. The boy presses closer to Ivorie.

"Crazy old coot," she whispers in his ear. "His mind is as pickled as his liver. Takes all kinds," she says in a breezy way.

The Sunday shirt and dungarees, along with a pair of jeans, a green pullover shirt for everyday, and a pair of Sunday shoes in shiny black come to $7.15. The dull woman who led them to the clothes puts them in a paper sack and hands them to the boy. He holds it out in front of him like it's about to explode as they leave the store.

Ivorie stops on the sidewalk and fans herself. "There's no circulation in these blasted stores. Would you like an ice cream cone?"

The way she says it makes him want to scream, *yes, yes!*

"Have you ever had ice cream?"

No, he hasn't.

She reaches for his hand, marching him down the sidewalk. "As you pass people on the street, you always smile at them," she says, smiling at a man with an overfat belly and a pipe in his mouth. "You don't have to carry on with them but just smile to be polite and show that you've got some sense."

He tries to smile at the next woman but she doesn't look at him. He spots another woman, old and slouched, coming their way, and he looks up to grin when she opens her wrinkly mouth.

"Ivorie Walker! What are you doing here?"

"Mornin', Dot," Ivorie says, sounding none too excited. She looks at the boy. "This is my aunt, Dottie."

The old woman steps closer and examines the boy with her mouth puckered up and looking like a shrunken apple. "This that boy from the hills?"

Ivorie claps him on the back and sounds as if she's standing behind a booth at the county fair when she says, "It sure is! Isn't he handsome? Just look at him!"

The old woman makes a grunting noise and sniffs, swiping a crooked finger over the boy's forehead. "My sister saw your mother once." Ivorie's back gets stiff and she cocks her head, eyeing the old woman. "Her belly was pushing out because of you as she headed up into those hills."

The boy feels Ivorie's fingers tighten around his arm, and she looks down at him. "Look yonder in that window!" She's pulling him and pointing at a window with a picture of a huge ice cream cone hanging in it. "Go look at what I'm about to buy you."

The boy steps to the window and watches Ivorie and the old woman out of the corner of his eye.

Ivorie keeps her voice low. "What are you talking about, Dot?"

"Your mother saw a young, pregnant girl about to climb up in the hills about nine or so years ago. The girl was fit to be tied and your mama asked her who the daddy was. The girl didn't say but told her the daddy wasn't up in them hills. Your mama tried to talk the girl into staying in Morgan Hill but she wouldn't. Your mother fussed and worried about that day for the longest time. She never knew if that gal stayed up in those hills or what. She never told you?"

The boy watches Ivorie step away from the old woman.

"We need to go, Dot." She leaves the old woman on the street and grabs the boy's arm, leading him around the corner. She leans against the redbrick building and smiles at the boy. She sighs and kneels down in front of him. "The man I saw at the shack that day. Was he your pop?"

His eyes are wide and his head barely moves.

Ivorie's eyes are still; she isn't breathing. "Your mother told you he wasn't?"

He nods.

"Did she tell you who your pop was?"

He shakes his head.

Her mouth flattens as she stands and takes

his hand. "All right, then."

She walks back around the corner and through the door with the ice cream cone in the window and throws open her arms. "Ta da," she says. She leads him past varnished tables to a glass case with a poster of a child holding an ice cream cone, and he peers inside. "Ice cream," Ivorie says, her voice dripping with cream and sugar. "There's chocolate and vanilla and my favorite, butter pecan. That pink one is strawberry."

He presses his nose to the glass and tries to inhale the colors.

"One butter pecan and one . . ." She waits for him to point to his flavor. "And one strawberry." Ivorie pays a dime for each cone and leads him outside to a bench, where they sit together. "What a day this has been! You saw your first false teeth and had your first ice cream. Go ahead. Lick it." He does and she laughs, watching him. If taste is a color, this would be shimmering gold, bright gold — as if a party just gathered and was lighting torches that lit up the dark of his mouth. She doesn't fuss over his face or the drippy pink snakes that slither over his hand and down his overalls. She doesn't say a word, only laughs and says,

"That was the best dime I've ever spent in my life."

IVORIE

The boy is sleeping and I try to finish cleaning the kitchen, but my mind is buzzing. Did Mother see the boy's mother all those years ago? Was that young, pregnant girl the regret that plagued Mother in her last years with me? I couldn't imagine how it could be possible but Dot isn't able to make up such a thing. The boy's mother was beside herself in agony and my mother talked to her, on what must have been the most horrible day of her life. I sit at the table and press on the sides of my head, feeling nauseous from what Dot said — the boy's father was here in Morgan Hill. Something gnaws at my stomach when I hear tires crunching on the gravel in the driveway. I jump to look out the window and recognize George's truck. There's just a few minutes left of daylight and I wonder why he's waited so long to come by for a visit.

"I tried calling today," he says, walking up

the stone path. "Phone rang off the hook."

"I took the boy to Greenville." He doesn't say anything but I can see it annoys him that I took the boy into town.

He leans on the porch rail and crosses his arms. "How's he doing?"

He seems concerned so maybe I'm getting bent out of shape over nothing. "He's getting better."

"What'd you do in Greenville?"

"I bought him some clothes and an ice cream cone. I've never seen a happier boy eating ice cream before."

Silence is thick and loud as he looks at the well house. "I've missed you, Ivorie."

I slip my arm through his and rest my head on his shoulder. "I've been right here."

"With him."

He sounds like I've been with another man. "I've been wanting you to come by so you can meet him. You should see him, George! I took him by the schoolhouse and we got all sorts of books to help him read and learn about animals. He already knows all the vowels." His arm is stiff and I glance up at him. He's just staring at the well house.

"I don't know what to do anymore, Ivorie." He looks over at me. "I just flat out don't know what to do."

It feels like an invisible wall is in front of him. "About what?"

"The whole community is talking. My own mother is talking."

I try hard to piece it together. "About what?"

He looks inside the house. "About this. You bringing that boy here and telling folks you're going to raise him."

"I *am* going to raise him."

He puts his hands on either side of my face and looks at me. I can smell his sweat and the farm and the night air on his skin and want so much for him to kiss me and tell me he'll help me. "Ivorie. . . ." He lets go of my face and leans against the porch rail. I put my hand on his arm, hoping he'll turn back to me. "Why would you do this? Why would you ruin this?"

"Ruin what?"

He turns and pulls me to him, kissing me. I feel myself falling but put my hands on the back of his neck. "Don't do this," he says. "Don't ruin us." He kisses my face and his words hammer through my mind.

I lay my head on his chest. "How does this ruin us?"

I feel his head on top of mine. "You know," he says.

I want him to keep kissing me but some

other part, the part that surges up my spine, wants him to stop and I push away. "I *don't* know. All I know is that you somehow manage to get here late at night when you know that boy in there will be sleeping. You haven't showed up here in days because you don't want to see him."

He leans back against the porch railing and looks at me. His eyes look gray and stern in this light. "Why would I want to see him, Ivorie?"

Every cell is flinching. "Because he's a person, George!" He turns away from me and I don't bother touching him. "The other day, when you said that going to get the boy was a fool thing I'd done, did you say that because you were afraid for me or is that what you think?"

He sighs and it takes him too long to answer, so I already know what he thinks. "There are so many other people who could help him."

"Who? Who are they, George?"

His shoulders are sagging. "People who get paid to help children like him. They know what they're doing." His voice is low and even, and I'm not angry with him. He looks at me and his eyes are deep, sad. He turns away and leans his hands on the railing. "Why couldn't you just let him be? Why couldn't you just leave him where he belongs?"

"He doesn't belong up in those hills," I say to his back.

He turns on me and his eyes are blazing. He grabs my shoulders and pulls me so close I can see the pores on his skin. He looks at me and I feel the tension leave his hands. "But he doesn't belong here, either. I do. I belong here. You know that, don't you?" He kisses my forehead and looks at me. "You *do* know that, right?" I nod and he kisses me again, holding me tight.

"George, this little boy could be our beginning." I can feel him melting away and search his face. "You'd love him." I rest against his chest but his arms fall to his side.

"I really don't think I could. I'm not you."

I have to strain to hear him and reach for his hand, holding it. "You just need to meet him." I push myself against him and burrow my nose into his neck. "Give him a chance, George. Please."

"I wouldn't even know how to try. All I'd see is a stranger." He lifts my chin and looks at me. The katydids are singing in the tops of the trees but I no longer hear them. George's words have swallowed all the sound. He is solid and calm. "Who do you want, Ivorie?"

My heart stops and I pull back. "What are you saying?"

His voice sounds queer and displaced. "I can't do what you're doing. I wish I could. I know exactly what I want, Ivorie. Who do you want?" I want him to stay, but I feel sick now and I'm too tired to go through more of this. He kisses my cheek and squeezes the back of my neck before walking to his truck.

Days go by without a word from George. Common sense told me he wouldn't call but the simplistic side of me thought he would. Hoped he would. The boy is climbing his way out of himself day by day, and by the time the heavy moon raises its head I am worn-out. George's voice has been nagging me, nipping at my heels like a pesky dog and telling me the boy doesn't belong here, that I need to decide between him and the boy. I fight hard not to listen to that voice or any of the voices from folks in the community.

If somebody was a fly on these walls they'd see all I'm doing wrong, but the boy and I are doing this the best we know how. We have canned beans, made another run of pickles, put up freezer corn together, and have taken a daily trip to Henry's to say

312

hello to him and Loretta. Folks talk and offer their opinions, same as usual. Most of them think I'm walking around with a halo-lit idea in my head, but some of them figure I'm this far in and am going to see this thing through, so they keep their yaps shut. As far as I know, Hot Dot has kept quiet about the boy's father being here. It's unlike her. If she has a word of gossip, she can't sleep till everyone in Morgan Hill has gotten an earful. Maybe she's honoring my mother by not telling or maybe she took a look at the boy and thought for once in her life she should keep her big pie hole closed. I don't know.

I took the boy to Henry's one morning and Henry paid him a nickel for sweeping the floor. You would have thought the boy just danced with the angels the way he made over that nickel. Loretta got tears in her eyes but turned away before anybody else in the store saw her.

I cornered Henry at the cash register and kept my voice low. "Did Mother ever tell you about anything she regretted?"

"Like what?"

"Anything. Did she ever talk to you about anything that bothered her?"

"Pop bothered her all the time. She was always fussing about him."

"No," I say, frustrated. "I know that. Anything else?"

"What in tarnation are you talking about?" He said that too loud, and Jane Cannon looked up from her work.

"Never mind." Holt, Avis, and their boy, Len, were in the store now, along with most of the regulars like Gabbie, Haze, and Dolly. "Hey," I said, leaning against the counter to make my announcement. "I found his birthday in his mother's Bible." The boy looked up at me, and I spoke right into his eyes. "She had written July thirtieth by one of the verses and sure enough, he says he remembers his birthday being on a hot day."

"Well, isn't that fine!" Henry said, sliding his hands into his pockets. He bent his head toward the boy. "How old will you be? Six? Seven?"

"Eight," I said.

"I turned eight last week!" Dolly Wade said.

"That's the most exciting birthday of all of them!" Loretta said. "Do you remember eight, Henry?"

"Remember it? I just about think of it every day! How about you, Holt?"

Holt's mouth turned up a little on one end. "I don't really remember it, Henry. My folks didn't cotton much to birthdays and such. I reckon my brother beat the snot out of me. That's usually what happened every day." Avis shook her head and made a sound like bacon sizzling between her teeth. Holt sure had a way of bringing a lively conversation to a halt.

"Six is fine," Loretta said, saving us. "And seven is right nice, but eight is out-of-this-world good."

"I don't remember eight as being all that good," nine-year-old John said.

Jane whomped her brother on the side of the head. "You can't remember what happened five minutes ago, let alone a year ago." She jumped up on the counter and said, "Kids like birthdays almost as much as Christmas! Your birthday will be your best day ever."

The boy's eyes darted from Jane to Loretta and Henry. He listened as they inflated the eighth birthday to national holiday status and I could see his grin setting loose. "I'm planning a picnic so you all keep your day clear on July thirtieth."

Henry made an exaggerated mark in the air. "Done!"

Doc can't believe how well the wounds have healed and how much the boy has filled out. "You are filling out like a Christmas turkey,"

Doc says, listening to the boy's heart. Doc reaches inside his pocket and pulls out a piece of chewing gum, handing it to him before the boy bolts out the door to play with Jane, John, and Milo.

"I talked to Dr. Bernard in Greenville about the boy's cleft," Doc says, packing away his stethoscope. "There's a team at East Tennessee Crippled Children's Hospital who work on cleft palates."

I open the screen door for him and walk him to his car. "Where's that?"

He reaches for his handkerchief and wipes sweat off his sloping nose. "Knoxville."

My mind kicks into gear. I have never driven into Knoxville. Years ago, Bertie Smith got married there and invited Mother, Pop, and me, but we didn't go because Mother was afraid we'd get struck by a speeding taxi cab or, worse yet, robbed of the dollar and sixty-two cents the three of us were carrying between us.

"Have you been there, Ivorie?" Doc asks, slipping his handkerchief into his back pocket.

"Of course."

"It's on Laurel Avenue. Can't miss it." He reaches inside his shirt pocket and hands me a piece of paper. "Dr. Bernard said they see new patients there beginning at nine in the morning." I went through closets in my mind. I couldn't remember where Pop's map was. "It'd be a good idea to get him there soon." He stands at his car and watches the boy and the Cannon kids play hide-and-go-seek. His face is pinned up with worry.

"What's wrong, Doc?"

He shakes his head and runs his stubby fingers through that great shock of hair. "Cleft palates are not easy fixes, Ivorie. They take years sometimes, and patients are much younger than him. My guess is, by what I've seen of his palate and the damage to his teeth, it's going to take a long time." I wait for him to finish. "And a whole lot of money."

After the boy falls asleep, I strip down to my slip and wash my face in the bathroom. The light goes out as I reach for the towel, leaving me in the dark, and I flip the switch, noticing the light in the kitchen is out as well. I haven't blown a fuse since before Pop died. I walk with my leg sticking out in front of me so I don't take off my pinkie toe as I make my way through the front room. "That's what the pinkie toe is for," Henry always says. "To find furniture in the dark." I open the screen door and walk onto the back porch, where the fuse box is located behind the swing. A hand clamps firm over my mouth and pushes my face up against the house. I feel boneless and taste blood in my mouth. A man's breath is on my neck. "Get that boy out of here." Is it the man from the shack? The father? Who is it? I can't hear from the rush of blood through my ears.

I don't know if he's talking to me or to someone with him who's after the boy, and I buck like a horse, knocking my head back into his. He groans and a fist falls solid on my cheek. My knees buckle but don't take me down. I can't scream; I can't wake the boy. My blood runs like boiling water through my veins and I slam the swing into the man. He gropes at his groin and when I move to see him in the moonlight he pushes my head into the wall, covering my mouth. A trickle of blood runs over my teeth as I chomp down like a gopher into his flesh. He slaps me twice, my face thumping against the house each time. Rage and fear bubble in my stomach, and I turn to him again but he's gone, vanishing down the embankment.

I'm as sturdy as a fish propped up on its tail but stumble to the door. My legs aren't beneath me but I manage to stumble inside and lock the door, then run through the house, throwing open the door to the boy's room. He's sound asleep and I run and lock the kitchen door before falling down on the floor beside his bed, shaking. My blood is cooling but I can still hear the thump of my heart. I rest against the wall and try to breathe. What just happened? Who was it? Why? Why didn't Sally bark? Why didn't she come running? In a matter of seconds I felt like I was wandering into a strange and hidden place I'd never been before. When I took a fist to the face, something rose up from some remote place inside me and pulled back the veil from my eyes, giving me a proprietary love for this child. He wasn't just some kid I was going to feed and clothe; this little, nameless boy was mine and I wasn't about to let anyone get near him.

My bones still feel like dough as I walk to the hall closet and reach for the lantern and matches. I light it in the bathroom and look in the mirror. An inch-long cut is under my eye and it looks like cherry juice is dripping down my face. A circle on my cheek where the skin is scraped off is the color of a tomato, but I know it will be plumlike in the morning, and my lip is busted open. I feel renewed anger and confusion and splash water onto my face, then hold toilet paper against my cuts to stop the bleeding. I think about calling Henry but it's too late, and I don't want Sheriff Dutton pulling into the driveway and waking up my boy and scaring him to death. I'll call tomorrow.

I tape a bandage under my eye to stop the bleeding and lie down. I'm sure sleep won't come for hours as I wrestle with this in my mind. I lay my hand on top of my boy's chest and feel him breathe. If anybody thinks they're scaring me off, they have another think coming. They've awakened something junglelike in me, something fierce and stubborn. The moody skies outside the window will be marching toward a new day, and when it strikes I'll be rising out of this bed like a lion.

Light flickers in the room as if someone is pinching the sun and I open my eye, the good one; the other one feels like an eggplant on my face. I walk to the bathroom and take the bandage from under my eye, looking at myself. My flesh is raw and red, purple, and is that green? One side of my lip is the size of a marble and the skin on my cheekbone is still exposed and turning dark. I wonder if the Refrigerator Lady looks like this before she gets her Frigidaire makeup on. I put salve on my cheek and under my eye and apply a fresh bandage. I don't want my boy (I pause when I think that — *my* boy) to see the cut. For the first time in months I reach for some makeup and try to spruce up the good side of my face. When I finish, I look like a confused sideshow act and remove most of the makeup. I pad off to my bedroom and put on some clothes to milk Gertie and gather the eggs.

I hear Sally barking when I step into the kitchen. I open the screen door but she's not out on the front porch. I walk toward the barn and her bark grows louder and more frantic. I run and open the feed room door and a heap of flailing limbs and flashing tail knocks me down. She wasn't on the back porch last night because she was stuck in here. *Put* in here.

My boy is still sleeping when I finish milking, and I slip on a dress for the trip to Knoxville so I don't look like an old cowhand when he wakes up. I pull my hair up into a bun and try to at least look like a carnival act with good upbringing, one with class. The mirror explains that no one has ever been able to make a silk purse out of a swine's ear and I throw up my hands in surrender. I remember the blown fuse and make my to the back porch. I see a fuse ly-ing on the porch and realize the man took it out.

I'm frying sausages when he taps me on the hip. I put on my biggest smile and turn to him. "Morning!"

His hair is tangled into a feathery knot on top of his head and it sways a little when he steps back, pointing at me.

"Oh," I say, like I forgot there was an eggplant on my face. "I took a terrible fall on the porch last night. Just about knocked myself out. Fell right onto the arm of the swing and it ripped right into my eye and cut open my lip."

His face is a frozen mixture of bewilder-ment and fright.

"Looks like I went a round with Joe Louis, huh?" He has no idea what I mean and I throw my hands up and punch at the air. "The boxer."

The sound of air filters over his teeth and he makes a patting motion with his hand. I kneel down in front of him. His eyes are sad and hopeless as he reaches out to touch the bandage.

"I'm okay. It doesn't hurt," I say, lying. "I'm just clumsy. That's all."

He studies my wounds. His face is tense and I see him digging down inside himself, pulling something up. It sounds like he's saying *no, no, no,* but I can't be sure.

I take his hands and say again, "I'm fine."

He points at my face and balls his hand into a fist, slamming it into his other hand. He does it again and points at my lip.

His eyes water over and I sigh, falling into a chair at the table. "Come here."

He sits down in a chair and faces me.

I look in his face, old with sadness and awful truth. He isn't a child who has been protected from the wild but I can't tell him what happened; not yet, it's too soon. He may think I'll die and leave him, and he's already buried his mother. I pick up his hand and put it on the table, covering it with my own. "Listen. I'm okay."

He pounds his fist into his palm and I know he thinks the marks on my face look like the ones his mother received at the hand of the man at the shack. He begins to tremble and I put my hands on either side of his face, struggling down to the deeps to pull up some calming truth for him.

"I'm okay. I'm not going anywhere." This triggers a river of tears and I wipe them away with my thumbs.

He is uncertain, looking at me.

"I am fine. I'm stronger than ever!" I pull up my arms and flex to show my muscles.

He tries to smile and I stop talking. I know the well of my maternal incompetence is deep but I am determined to siphon up a calm and breathing hope for him.

He touches my eye.

It's the first time he's ever reached out to touch me, and I don't flinch at the pain. "That will be good as new in no time."

He touches my lip.

"That too."

He reaches his scrawny arms around me and gives me a clumsy hug that feels like a little piece of heaven.

I tell him to go put on his Sunday clothes while I call Henry to tell him we're headed to Knoxville.

"By yourself? You've never been to Knoxville," Henry says.

"Well, I'm going today," I say, sounding chipper.

"Do you have a map?"

"Found Pop's last night."

"From what year? Thirty-two? Drive here and I'll give you my map."

I don't want Henry to see me yet. "Good grief, Henry. It's not New York City. The map will get me into Knoxville and I'll track down the hospital from there."

I can picture him scratching his head

while leaning up against the cash register. "I'll go with you."

"You don't need to go for this visit. Maybe the next one." I hear him talking to someone in the store and I know he's distracted.

"All right, then. Call us later and tell us how it went."

I hang up and decide to make some peanut butter and jelly sandwiches, just in case we end up at the hospital for a longer spell. I throw the sandwiches and some blackberries and a jug of water into a brown sack and check over the map one more time before putting it inside my pocketbook. I grab the library books and make sure I have some lipstick.

"We are all set," I say, making my voice sound sure and strong, although my insides still feel like a rubber band, bouncing and wiggling around. The man's voice snakes through my ears but I can't make out who it belonged to; I can't hear the voice clear enough to put a face with it. My skin prickles at the thought and I lock the door while my boy loves on Sally. She runs to the truck bed, thinking she's going with us, and I close the truck gate. "Stay, Sally." She cocks her head, stricken. I lean over and whisper, "You stay and keep an eye on the place. Okay?" She lies down with her front paws crossed and watches us load into the truck cab.

My boy hangs his head out the window and I laugh, watching him. "You can't ride like that all the way to Knoxville. The wind will slap you silly." I pull out onto the road and see Pete Fletcher's truck up ahead. I cover my eye bandage and kind of look toward the boy so Pete doesn't see my face. As we pass each other, instead of throwing up my hand, which would uncover my eye, I simply honk. Pete honks and waves, and my boy turns to see the truck through the back window.

He taps his chest and points out the window.

"That was Pete," I say. "You met him."

He sits up on his knees and faces out the back window, tapping his chest and pointing.

"What's wrong? Why are you doing that?"

He makes a groaning sound and points to himself, then out the window.

He keeps pointing and poking and groaning, and I stop the truck, putting it in Park. I grab him by the arms and feel my heart bulging. "Is your name Peter?"

His head is unhinged it's nodding so fast.

I throw my hands in the air, laughing. "Peter! Oh my Lord!" I pull him into my arms and squeeze as hard as I think his ribs can take. "Why didn't I ever say Peter?" I push him away at arm's length and laugh again. "Of course your mother named you Peter. That means 'rock.' Did you know that?"

He didn't.

I lean on the steering wheel, looking at him. "Peter, the rock. That's you. Your mother wanted you to have a strong name. A name that meant something." I slap my forehead. How could I not think of Peter? "Do you have a middle name?"

He looks at me.

"Another name after Peter?"

He shakes his head and points at me, making a noise in his throat.

"Yes, I have a middle name. It's Ivorie. Sarah Ivorie."

His throat rattles and he points at me, then at himself.

"You want me to choose your middle name?" He smiles and my heart bulges at the seams a little bit more. "Well, I will study on that and choose a name that will sit proudlike next to Peter."

I put the truck into Drive and head to Knoxville with Peter.

PETER

The map is brown around the edges and yellowing in the middle parts. Ivorie holds it up on the steering wheel as she drives. "Why can't I find Laurel on this thing?" She pulls onto one road, and after craning her neck from one side of the street to the other, she turns around and goes back to the road she was on minutes earlier. "For the love of John! How do you read this crazy . . ." She sees a building with a big, round sign out front and says, "Aha! A filling station. I'll ask somebody in here." She closes the door and straightens her dress, pushing her fingers up into her hair to do something to it, and tells Peter to sit tight.

He watches as she walks to a man wearing blue coveralls and notices how the man looks at her face.

She doesn't seem to remember what she looks like and keeps her nose in the map, looking up and around like a lost swallow.

The man points first this way and then flicks his hand like he's tossing something in another direction, and Ivorie nods, heading back to the truck.

"Two blocks that way and then left and then three more blocks and then right." She puts the truck in Reverse and goes through the directions again. "Two up and left. Three more and right. Two, left. Three, right." She mumbles beneath her breath and juts her chin over the steering wheel to look up and out the window. "There it is," she says, pulling up in front of a long building. A slew of steps lead from the road up to four, small white pillars, and Peter stares at the building; he's never seen such a thing in his life. "Well, that wasn't so bad," Ivorie says, looking at herself in the rearview mirror. She spreads color on her lips and makes a smacking sound before grabbing the dinner sack and her pocketbook. "Here. Carry your books," she says, handing them to Peter.

She gets out of the truck and takes a big and long breath, saying *okay* as she lets it out. "Let's get up there." They walk up the stairs together and Ivorie stops at the sign, reading it: EAST TENNESSEE CRIPPLED CHILDREN'S HOSPITAL. She takes his hand and continues up the stairs. "That name sure is a mouthful of seriousness. They need to get them a new name right quick because you are not crippled. I bet more than half the children who come here aren't crippled." She opens the front door to a room with a shiny speckled floor.

A woman wearing glasses and a gray dress is sitting behind a desk and talking on a heavy black phone. She hangs up and her eyes fill with distress. "Oh my," she says, looking at Ivorie. "Do you need . . . ?"

Ivorie doesn't let her finish. "We're here to see the cleft-palate doctor. Our doctor told us to be here at this time." She sounds like she knows what she's doing and stands straight as Lincoln's hat, smiling, but she's using her index finger to dig into the skin around the nail on the thumb next to it.

The woman points to the stairs and says, "Dr. Culp is on the second floor and down the hall."

Peter's shoes squeak on the stairs and he wishes they'd stop making that racket when he passes a man mopping at the top of the stairs. Whatever is in that bucket makes Peter grab his nose and twist up his face, and the man smiles.

Ivorie reads as they pass several doors and stops when she says, "Dr. Gerald Culp." She looks at Peter and pushes her fingers into

330

her hair again.

He watches, wondering what she's always poking around for in there, and follows her inside a small, plain room painted white, with wooden chairs up against the wall. A couple with a small boy are sitting in three of the chairs. A woman with big eyes and a bigger nose looks up from behind a glass window with a hole in it. Her eyes lack the worry the woman's eyes had downstairs.

"Can I help you?" she asks, in a voice drenched with vinegar.

"We're here to see Dr. Culp," Ivorie says, getting her mouth real close to the hole in the window. "Doc Langley told me to be here at this time."

The woman twists a pencil between her fingers and appears to belch, or was that a hiccup? "Who is Dr. Langley?"

"Our doctor in Morgan Hill."

The woman peers over Ivorie to take a look at Peter but he studies the books in his hands, avoiding her. "What is the boy's name?"

"Peter."

The woman writes something on a piece of paper. "Name of the father?" Ivorie is quiet. The woman looks up at her. "Name of the father?"

Ivorie keeps her voice low. "I don't know."

331

The woman locks her eyes on Peter, and he looks at the floor. "Name of the mother?" Ivorie pauses. "You are his mother, correct?"

"Yes," Ivorie says. "He's my son."

Peter snaps his head upward. The word *son* lands on his skin like a white, parachuting dandelion seed and he listens for it again.

The woman scratches something onto the paper but doesn't look up at Ivorie. "I don't know if he can see you today. We're full up."

Ivorie looks at the mostly empty waiting room; she's picking at that place on her thumb again. "I was told to be here by nine and I drove all the way from Morgan Hill."

The woman continues writing, talking down at her desk. "Take a seat. We'll see if the doctor can squeeze you in but I can tell you it won't be anytime soon."

Ivorie leads Peter to two wooden chairs next to each other and sits with the dinner sack on her lap. "She wasn't a friendly sort at all," she says, whispering. "And her face rivaled a titmouse. She's all eyes and nose. She's got all the charm of a bullfrog, too." He smiles and she leans into him. "That was bad. I shouldn't have said that. She's probably a fine person, despite it all. I might have scared her. I know I look like ten miles of country road." Ivorie looks up at the couple and their son, who are staring at her, and smiles, clearing her throat. "What does she mean *if the doctor can see us but I wouldn't count on it?* If *if* and *but* were candy and nuts, every day would be Christmas!" She looks around the waiting room. "Well, this sure is a plain-Jane room. You'd think somebody would hang a picture or slap a color of paint on the walls to cheer the place up."

She taps on a book. "We may as well do some letters and spelling while we wait in this bland place." She takes the first-grade primer and opens it to the page with all the letters and points to them. "P-E-T-E-R. Know what that spells?"

He doesn't.

She pulls a piece of paper from her pocketbook and writes the letters. "That spells *Peter.*"

He studies the name and looks back at the alphabet, wondering how his name magically came out of there.

She points to the letters again. "P-E-T-E-R. That's a good-looking name, isn't it?" He nods and she puts the pencil in his hand. "Here. I'll help you. Everybody should be able to write his own name." She wraps her hand around his and talks him through it.

"Make a post. Long and straight, just like a fence post. There you go. Now put an *O* off to the side of it so it sticks out like a bubble, like so. See? That's a *P.* Try it yourself."

He tries and the bubble looks skinny. It doesn't look anything like the one she wrote.

"Good, good. You're getting it. Now onto the *E.*" She talks him through every letter; thankfully each one of them needs a post so he gets lots of fence post practice. When he finishes, it looks like spiders are crawling on the paper but Ivorie takes the paper and folds it. "I'm keeping this one forever." She hands him a clean sheet of paper and turns the page in the primer.

"Run, dog, run," she says reading. "R-U-N. That spells *run.*" She shows him the letters at the front of the book where the alphabet is printed in neat rows. She taps the letters with her finger and spells new words. "Look at these words that sound like *run. Fun, sun, bun.* They all rhyme. That means they sound alike." They are still going over letters and spelling words long after the couple and their son leave and a new batch of waiting folks arrive.

"I'll be right back," Ivorie says, putting the book in his lap.

He tries to hear what she's saying to the big-eyed woman behind the glass but she's keeping her voice low.

Ivorie marches back to the chair and it sounds like she's leaking air. "They're behind. Let's keep reading." She rubs the back of her neck and tries to smile. "Sit, cat, sit." More letters are pointed to, more words are written on the paper, and more people come and go, each of them glancing up at Ivorie when they think she isn't looking. When the glass window is shut and a sign is taped up saying everybody is eating dinner, Ivorie's face pinches up. "Well, we sure got the short end of that stick! How do you like that? Miss Mouse shuts that window like she can't even see us sitting out here." She snatches up the paper sack and opens it. "Well, we'll just eat our dinner, too, and when she opens her fancy window again she'll see us still sitting here." She sets a peanut butter and jelly sandwich wrapped in waxed paper in his lap and pulls a small plastic bowl filled with blackberries from the sack. "Peanut butter and blackberries! A feast for any king."

When she finishes her sandwich, Ivorie wads up the waxed paper and puts it back into the empty sack. She steps to the glass window and cranes her neck to see if anyone has returned yet. "Takes her sweet time eating," she says, mumbling to herself. She

335

worries her hands together like a colicky infant and whistles some unknown tune. Her shoes clack against the speckled floor and she bends over at the waist, looking at it. "Isn't that something! I can just about see myself in this floor. Looks like the janitor does better at his job than Miss Mouse behind the window there."

Peter holds up *Homer Price* and Ivorie claps her hands together. "All right. I'll read while you finish your dinner. You can have the rest of those blackberries. I saved them for you."

He pops two into his mouth and taps the book.

"I know, I know," she says, opening *Homer Price.* Although she started reading the book days ago, she hasn't gotten through the first chapter yet because she stops to explain things like what a camp is or a contest or why someone would want a skunk to live in his house, and she points to words like *the, he, she,* and *and,* saying them several times. It takes a long time to read a story like this but every time he recognizes a word he feels something swelling up inside him.

Ivorie stops reading when she hears voices, and she hands the book to Peter and rushes to the window. "Hi!" she says, like she just bumped into an old friend on the street.

"We're still waiting out here."

"We'll get to you as soon as we can," Miss Mouse says.

Ivorie bends forward so her mouth is talking into the hole again. "I noticed there were a lot of people who came in after us, and they got to see the doctor." She's smiling, but Peter knows it's not one of her real smiles.

"Hon, that's because those people are patients and had appointments. Sit on down and we'll get to you when we can."

Ivorie's put-on smile gets bigger. "But we're the only ones in here right now. Can't the doctor see him?" She stands there looking in the window as if she's rooted to the floor and her finger starts picking at that place on her thumb.

"Hon, the doctor isn't back here right now and we're expecting a patient any minute. We'll work you in if we can."

Ivorie's face crumples and she sits next to Peter. She sighs, as if she's trying to blow the room up with air. "Some people try me." She finishes reading the first chapter of *Homer Price* and during that time two families filter into the room and take their places on opposite sides of the room. Ivorie closes the book and glances at the waiting faces. They are looking at her and her face turns the color of fall maple leaves. She stands and marches to the window, straightening her dress as she walks. "Excuse me. Is there a toilet?"

Miss Mouse takes her time shuffling back to her hole in the window. "Right out the door and down the hall, hon."

Ivorie holds out her hand for Peter and he sets the book on his seat. She opens the door and lets it close heavy behind them. "You know what she thinks? She thinks we're as poor as Job's turkey. I know I look like I've been beat with a bag of nickels but this is no way to treat somebody. And she thinks that you . . ." She stops and balls her hands up into fists, setting them on her hips. "Well, she thinks I'll give up and go home but I'm as serious as the business end of a .45 and I'm not going anywhere. And I wish she'd stop calling me hon!" She points to a sign on the bathroom and reads, "M-E-N. That spells *men.* You go in that one, and be sure to flush and wash your hands. I'm going in this one here. W-O-M-E-N. That spells *women.*"

He opens the door and can hear her talking to herself as she enters the women's toilet. Her voice echoes through the pipes and walls, and when he finishes and is waiting for her in the hallway, he can still hear her jabbering.

She opens her door and smiles. "Did you wash your hands?" He nods, and she leads him back down the hallway. "H-A-N-D-S. *Hands. Hand* is like the word *and* except it has an *h* at the beginning. *And* . . . A-N-D. Slap an *h* at the beginning: *hand.*" She opens the door and steps up to the window and, assuming Miss Mouse cares, announces, "We're back!"

As Ivorie reads another chapter, Peter leans into her and hears the words at the back of his mind bouncing and floating and taking flight. He crumples onto her lap, and sentences as cool as the spring breeze in the woods swirl around him. He drifts and falls and his feet touch the sludge bottom, creating dirty clouds in the water, so thick he can scarcely see the sun bobbing like a golden ball. He flails his arms trying to rise to the top and kicks his feet against the loose, watery floor, but it's no use. His body isn't rising. He thrashes his legs and feels a hand on his shoulder.

"It's all right, Peter. Wake up."

He opens his eyes and sees her face over him.

"You were having a dream. Come on. It's time to go home," she says, her voice dredged in weariness. "It's four thirty."

He sits up and the waiting room is empty.

Ivorie's dress is wrinkled and she's slump-shouldered as she walks to Miss Mouse's window. "We'll be coming back tomorrow."

"Hon, we may not be able to get you in."

Ivorie throws her hand up to stop her. "My name is not 'hon'! My name is Miss Walker. You may call me that tomorrow when I show up here again with my son."

"Miss Walker, the doctor may not get the chance to see —"

"Shame on you!" Ivorie's finger is through the hole in the window and her voice is ferocious, like a bear's. "Shame on you to cast judgment on me."

She grabs Peter's hand and walks out the door.

IVORIE

That woman! There I sat, looking damaged and frail, and her mind conjures up scenes of fornication and the bad fruit of a spoiled union. And I know full well what everyone in that waiting room thought — they looked for a ring; even the war widows wore their wedding rings. No ring and no man in sight, but obviously there was a sorry-tailed one at home who beat the soup out of me. The wind is hot through the cab of the truck but I scarcely notice. I feel as empty as a dry gourd. I blink back the tears and wonder how many briars and thorns will stick Peter and me throughout the years, creating more wounds, welts, and open sores.

My head is drumming and my throat is dry as dirt. I'm sickened by all of it — soul sick, a deep stabbing ache that I can't grease down with balm or saturate with homemade hooch. My thoughts take a serpentine path of what I will do to Miss Mouse tomorrow.

I have no idea how long I've been on the highway when Peter taps my arm. I look at him and it's as if he's shrouded in grave and tender silence in the middle of the shrieking wind. He smiles and I try my best to do the same. "I'm all right. Just thinking," I say above the noise. I can't bring myself to talk right now but hope I'll be able to love the accusing, the idiotic, and the thoughtless and that I won't punch her in her big, long nose tomorrow. Thankfully, my soul's shadow is broader, deeper, and more gracious than me.

It is six o'clock when I pull off at the crossroads. I pass the property Mother and Pop left me and try to picture a filling station on that beautiful spot. The thought of that land being misused makes me almost as angry as feeling condemning eyes on me in a waiting room. Henry's truck is in my driveway, and when Peter sees it he lets out a yelp of recognition. I am tired and feeling beastly. Henry and Loretta are on the porch, but I don't want to talk, and I sure don't want to explain what happened to my face. "We've been calling all day," Henry yells, walking toward us. "We just got here."

Peter leaps from the truck and as he and Sally run to Henry and Loretta, I remember that this day was about him. His name. His place. His voice. I get out of the truck and close the door. "We have great news," I say, seeing the horror in Henry and Loretta's eyes when they look at me.

"Lord have mercy," Loretta says, taking a step toward me.

I put up my hand to stop her. "I discovered his name."

Henry picks Peter up and I can tell Peter feels awkward but loves it. "Well, this is a day for the history books," Henry says. "What is it?"

I let the air get real full of suspense before I say it. "Peter."

"Just like the apostle," Loretta says. "Well, of course your mama named you Peter."

"That's what I said. It just seems fitting."

Henry's eyes don't betray his thoughts, and I nod, letting him know that I'm okay and will tell him everything in a few minutes. He puts Peter on the ground. "Well, how'd it go today?"

"We weren't able to see the doctor, so we'll go back tomorrow," I say, making it sound like this is as routine as milking. "But he's got lots of words under his belt now. He knows how to spell his name. Open that book and point to the letters in your name for Loretta and Henry. And he'll be reading a Dick and Jane book in no time."

Peter opens the book and puts his finger on top of each letter in his name.

"Well, that is something," Loretta says, crowing over him.

"Peter, do you think you can milk Gertie by yourself?" I need to talk to Henry and Loretta but can't imagine he's ready to milk alone. He nods, surprising me. "While you milk, I'll make us supper."

Henry and Loretta follow me inside and I plop everything down on the table. "What happened, Ivorie?" Loretta's eyes are solemn and round.

"Somebody turned the lights out last night and got a hold of me on the porch."

"And you're just now telling us?" Henry says.

"It was late, Henry, and there wasn't anything you could do."

He paces to the window and looks out at the barn, watching for Peter. "Did you call Wally?"

"I didn't want the sheriff here making noise. It was late!"

"Wally could have been out looking for him, Sarah!" Henry's voice is sharp and his back is stiff.

"By the time he got here the man would be long gone, and he'd wake Peter and scare him to death with all the talk of what happened."

"What *did* happen?" Loretta asks, falling into a chair.

"He grabbed me on the back porch and told me to get the boy out of here. That's all he said. I fought him and ended up looking like this."

Henry is quiet and Loretta wrings her hands together like she's trying to squeeze something out of them. "Somebody doesn't want him here," Henry says, watching the barn. Loretta sets her chin on her hands and nods, almost as if they've already come to this conclusion. "Somebody who wishes he'd never been born."

"His father wasn't the man at the shack," I say, not looking at them.

"What?" Loretta asks. "How do you know?"

"He told me. Whoever got his mother pregnant lives right here."

A rose-gray sky stands over the house, and although there's a small spray of sunlight left, I am worn-out and ready for bed. I wash my face and put some more salve on the big, bare spot on my cheek and under my eye. Mother swore by salve for cuts, knicks, scrapes, even goose eggs from bumping our noggins. My cheek and eye are sore and hurt at the touch. I take some headache powders to help the hammering in my head and hope it takes the edge off the pain in my face. I feel like a greasy mess when I cut off the lights in the house. When headlights brighten the kitchen, I feel my stomach lurch. I can't see anybody like this but assume it might be Sheriff Dutton, that Henry called him and sent him here.

I groan when I see George standing in the light of the porch. I stand in the darkened kitchen and talk to him through the screen door. "I know it's late," he says, trying to see me. "But I . . . What's on your face?"

"Nothing," I say, looking at the floor. "It's late, George, and I'm tired."

He opens the screen door and brushes past me to pull the string for the light over the table. "Good God Almighty! What happened to you?"

"I don't know. Last night someone came here and . . ."

His hands are flailing around the kitchen. "Somebody did this to you? Who?" He's getting loud. "Who?"

I gesture for him to lower his voice. "Shh. Peter's sleeping."

George lifts my chin to examine my face and looks down, disgusted. "What have you

346

gotten yourself into?" I am angry at his tone and feel water swelling in my bottom lids but he doesn't notice. "How'd this happen?"

I sink into a chair at the table and my voice sounds as flimsy as I feel. "A man grabbed me out on the back porch and told me to get the boy out of here."

He turns and puts his hands on the counter. I can see his shoulders rise and fall with each breath. "So it's done now?" He turns to look at me. "You've learned your lesson? You'll get rid of him?"

A storm blows through my lungs and I'm catapulted to my feet. "What are you talking about? What do you expect me to do? Just leave him alone?"

"Yes, Ivorie! That's what I want. It's what all of Morgan Hill wants!" He throws his hands in the air and raises his voice. "I thought we were going to be together."

"I did, too," I say, my voice weak and puny.

He reaches for me and holds my shoulders. "We can be." He looks at me like he's trying to see what he was attracted to in the first place. "We still can be."

"If," I say. He looks puzzled. "If I get rid of Peter."

He lifts my chin. "We can have our own children together. It is too dangerous for you to keep that boy."

I'm too numb to keep at this. "You need to get on home."

"What?"

I walk to the door. "Go on." Everything in me hopes he'll stay, ask me to forgive him, and then talk with me into the night about the last couple of days and our future ahead, but he doesn't. He walks past me in silence and the door snaps behind him.

I lie down, but I'm too weary to give George much thought because my heart feels like it could break at any moment. Theories whirlwind in my mind about who attacked me and who the father is but settle on nothing. I can't think straight. I listen to the hum of insects outside my window and close my eyes.

Images of the man's fist landing on my face shake me at three. My chest is covered with sweat and I fan the covers to cool me. I throw a leg outside the sheet and roll over to see the moon squatting low over the hillside. The man's voice and touch and smell play over and over in my head, like Maxine is reading it for the local news on the radio. *In Morgan Hill a man showed up out of nowhere,* she says in that pinched voice of hers, *and pushed Ivorie Walker's face*

*into the wall. Before running like a scared rab-
bit he told her to get rid of an innocent boy.
More details to come.* I throw my arm over
my head and look up at the ceiling. Shadows
from the oak are meeting up there and looking like dark, creeping vines. Why didn't he
come in the middle of the night when the
lights would already be off? Why didn't he
try to get in the house to get to me or Peter? He didn't want Peter to see him. I make
my way to the bathroom and wipe pee off
the seat before I sit down. Peter's trying, I
know, but he can't shoot a straight line of
pee to save his life.

I look at myself in the mirror and groan at
the sight. The cut under my eye has caused
swelling and the sore spot on my cheek is
glistening red under all that salve. I touch it
and remember the pain of my cheek crush-
ing against the house. Since it was dark,
why did the man go to such trouble to keep
my face turned away? I come to the conclusion that the man knew I would recognize
him and I fall back into bed with a sick-to-
my-stomach feeling.

The sun stands in the east, fanning out its
flame, and I figure I may as well do the
same. I slip on my blue flowered dress and
am determined that, come hell or high

water, we *will* see Dr. Culp today. Peter is already in the bathroom and I stand in the hallway and wait. He pees with less splatter this time and lets the toilet seat fall back down with a bang. The wounds on his back are all the color of a blister but the skin is healing and stretching itself back into place, just like he is. There are moments when his mind is far from this house, and he's back where the windows of his heart are closed against the breeze and he's breathing the shack's putrid air. I pray he'll throw that memory and the dreams that torment him onto the great heap of ruins outside that shack and set them on fire. Then there are times when he's pure boy, all energy and curiosity and running limbs, and I wonder what in the world I did before he started raiding my garden.

"Morning, Peter," I say, watching him wash his hands.

He turns and smiles and throws the towel in the general direction of the towel bar.

"Can you milk this morning while I start breakfast?" He runs for his overalls, and I realize he's always ready to work and wonder how much work he did each day up at that shack. I go through the routine of looking at my battered face and cringing. The colors are purple and green and dull yellow now, perfect if I were a rotting vegetable.

I make extra sausage and biscuits and pack them as sandwiches for our dinner at the hospital, along with another bowl of blackberries. I have neglected the garden and can't let the vegetables sit out there another day, so after breakfast Peter and I pick some beans, peas, cucumbers, tomatoes, and corn. "I'll take some of these to Henry and Loretta," I say. "I can't stand the thought of them going to waste."

Peter puts on his Sunday clothes again, and I make another attempt at makeup today but look ghoulish with all the grisly colors seeping through. I twist my hair on top of my head and grab the dinner, books, more writing paper, and my pocketbook. I look at the clock in my bedroom: seven ten. "All right, say your goodbyes to Sally and let's get on the road." Peter leans his head into Sally's and she follows us to the truck. "Stay," I say, putting my hand up in front of her to show how serious I am. I set the baskets of vegetables and the canisters of milk into the truck bed and drive off for Henry's.

Holt and Avis are pulling out of Henry's lot when I pull in and I slow down to wave. I hear Avis screech from inside their truck and Holt stops. "They law!" Avis says, leaning over Holt. "What happened to your face, Ivorie Walker?"

I feel Peter's eyes on me and smile at Avis. "Run-in with the porch swing."

Holt glances up and grimaces. "That looks real bad. Are you all right?" He looks at his steering wheel and I sense his embarrassment for me.

"It's just a little sore."

"Well, watch yourself before you knock yourself out," Avis says. Holt starts to drive the truck forward when Avis throws her hand up to stop him and gives him a scorching look. Holt stops the truck and withers in his seat. "How's the boy doing?" Avis asks.

"Well, I know his name is Peter. And he's doing fine."

"Good morning, Peter," Avis says, waving.

Peter waves and Holt and Avis both attempt a halfhearted smile before driving away. Peter and I take the milk and vegetables into the store and put them on the counter. "I can't work these up anytime soon," I say of the vegetables. "So you may as well have them."

Henry picks up the canister of milk and looks at me. "Boy, you are a sight today."

"Thanks, Henry. I wasn't aware of how I

looked until you and Holt pointed it out."

"Don't pay any attention to them," Loretta says. "You look fine. So you just go on and do what needs to be done today."

It's just before nine when I pull up in front of the hospital again and I take a deep breath, looking at it. "Today's the day," I say. "I can feel it in my bones." We grab our things and trek up the stairs and into the building, listening as the clack of our steps on the staircase echoes back to us. I open the door to Dr. Culp's office. Miss Mouse is sticking her nose out her air hole and sniffing at us. "We're here to see Dr. Culp," I say, as if I've never seen her or her twitching nose before.

"Take a seat, Miss Walker. The doctor will see your son when he can."

"Thank you," I say, making it sound like I have a mouth full of sugary syrup.

I pick out two chairs for a new angle in this plain-as-milk room and open the first-grade primer. I keep my eyes in the book as one patient after another goes back to see Dr. Culp. I feel my blood running hot — it's a combination of George, being attacked on my own porch, and this spiteful Miss Mouse. I catch her eye and put on a rubber smile for her. When she closes her window for the dinner hour I feel a hurricane sweep through my chest and snatch up the dinner sack. "Dinnertime!" We eat and do more spelling and I give Peter a quiz of sorts to see how many letters he can write on his own: eight! I then see how many words he can spell by pointing to the letters. "Twelve! My brother Caleb couldn't spell twelve words when he *was* twelve." I tousle his hair. "Smart as a whip, that's what you are!" The afternoon speeds by as fast as a turtle after eating a turkey dinner, and that hurricane keeps blowing against my lungs.

At two o'clock a thought knocks me upside the head: I never saw the doctor or Miss Mouse walk through the waiting room to eat dinner or go to the bathroom yesterday but can only assume they *do* go to the toilet, so they *must* have another door they enter and exit by. I grab Peter's hand and run into the hallway, where I spot a bench close to the stairwell and we sit down. "Listen, if we ever get in to see the doctor, you need to know that he's going to help you talk — so there's no reason to be afraid of him." He's getting better around men — he let Henry pick him up — but he's still mostly jitters and jumps.

Two hours later I am reading from *Homer Price* when I hear a door open down the hall. A tall man is heading toward the other end of the hall. "I'll be right back," I say, jumping up. "Dr. Culp!" He doesn't hear me and I run after him; my shoes are loud enough to wake the dead in this hollow hall. "Dr. Culp!" He stops and turns to me. His face is of an aging bulldog with glasses, all creases and jowls and gray muzzle. "I'm Ivorie Walker. I've been waiting two days to get my son in to see you. He has a cleft palate and has never been seen by a doctor."

He eyes Peter on the bench and looks at me with brown eyes that are soft and friendly. "Have you been waiting out here?" He sounds like he's from one of the Carolinas.

"In your office," I say, trying not to pick that sore place on my thumb. "We've driven from Morgan Hill two days in a row."

He scratches his beard and cocks his head. "Does Mrs. Goble know you're here?"

So that's her name. Goble. May as well be Lucifer. "She keeps telling me you'll get to me when you can."

He nods and says, "I see." He holds his index finger in the air and steps inside the men's toilet. My mind races, wondering if I should stand here and wait, but it seems indecent to hear him taking care of his business, so I tiptoe back down the hall to Peter. I sit and bounce my legs up and down. I could pull up oil with all this furious pumping. Dr. Culp opens the men's door and I sit straight up, watching him. "Come with me," he says, waving his hand in the air. "We are bypassing Mrs. Goble and going straight to my office." I scoop everything into my arms and run to him.

"This is Peter," I say, trying to balance my pocketbook and the books in my arms.

"Hello, Peter," Dr. Culp says, extending his hand. Peter slips his tiny hand into it, and he looks smaller and more afraid than he has in days. "Let me help you." Dr. Culp takes the books from me and I shove the dinner sack into my pocketbook. "Peter, would you open this door for your mother?" The sound of *mother* falling over his tongue makes me feel weepy but I pull myself together. Peter leans into a door without a nameplate on it and we enter a narrow hallway as bland as the waiting room. Dr. Culp leads us to a room with a long table and opens his hand. "Hop up here, Peter."

He climbs onto the table and his legs dangle over the front like ropes.

"Open up." Dr. Culp opens his own mouth as if he were talking to himself, and Peter opens his. Dr. Culp holds Peter's chin and shines a light into his mouth, feeling around with his finger. He presses his thumbs onto each side of Peter's nose and looks inside it with the same pointy light. "How old are you, Peter?" Peter doesn't say anything. "You don't talk?" Peter stares at him and Dr. Culp's face falls into serious ridges when he looks at me. "Tell me about Peter. Why hasn't he seen a doctor before now?"

I talk as fast as I can, telling him everything except for the abuse and neglect, which is no doubt obvious to Dr. Culp anyway. When I finish he hands Peter a set of clunky-looking headphones and asks him to put them on. He has to show Peter how to do it and explains he's going to do a hearing test. Peter closes his eyes and I watch his hand rise up and down throughout the test. Dr. Culp takes the headphones off Peter's head and writes something on a small sheet of paper. "Peter, would you please take this to Mrs. Goble right out this door?" He opens it and points to the back of her head. "See her? This tells her that I want you to have a lollipop. Now she'll be as surprised as the devil in heaven to see you standing there and that'll give her a good scare," he says, grinning. "Be good for her. Then you can sit on the chair right outside the door here and eat it."

Peter looks at me and I smile. "It's okay. Run get one."

He hesitates but takes the note and peeks around the door.

When Peter ambles off into the hallway, Dr. Culp leans against the exam table and crosses his arms. I can tell he wants to know why in the world I look like the backside of a mule but he doesn't ask. "I'll be honest, Miss Walker. I have never seen a child this old with a cleft palate. Ordinarily, we take care of children when they're infants, so that makes Peter's case not at all ordinary. The cleft runs through both his soft and hard palate." He points to a sketch of a roof of a mouth on the wall. "Frankly, I am amazed that he hasn't nearly choked while eating. And it will require several surgeries to get his teeth in order. Clefts this big affect speech — as you've seen — and can cause infections in the ears and sinuses. I can only assume he's had several infections by the looks of what I've seen in his ears, but his hearing is good. I am a bit amazed that he passed the hearing test." He hears Peter's footsteps in the hall and finishes: "Something needs to be done soon, Miss Walker."

The clouds are huddled together in whiteness for our drive home, and when I pull into the driveway, Peter jumps out to play with Sally as I walk to the mailbox. I pull out a small, plain envelope with nothing written on the outside. My heart gallops as I open it, hoping it's from George. Six words are scrawled in big letters, taking up the entire page: *Get the boy out of here.*

I crumple the paper and jerk my head around to see Peter. He's banging his hands together, looking for Sally. I spin around, searching for her. She's always here waiting when I pull up the driveway. I run to the edge of the garden and call out her name. Peter and I run to the embankment and I yell out toward the creek for her. My heart is hammering because I know something has happened to her. Peter looks up at me and I work at a smile. "She's out chasing rabbits, I guess."

My legs wobble as I walk back to the house. Sally's gone. I know it but I don't want to imagine what happened to her. My eyes are burning but I hold back the tears so Peter won't see. I don't want him to sense what's inside me or feel the terror that's sitting on my chest. He continues to run around the property, banging his hands and making a throaty noise, while I step inside and walk to my bedroom, closing the door. I slide down against it, and despite my efforts to hold them back, the tears fall onto my hands. Why would someone do this? Why hurt my dog? I bury my face in my knees and sound like a child, sobbing. All of this over one small boy! I want to call George but in my mind I see the disappointment on his face on his last night here and remember the way he was trying to dredge up some sort of feeling for me and I feel the anger picking away at my skin.

I wipe my face with my dress and stand up, noticing Refrigerator Lady peering out at me from the pages of *Redbook* on my bedside table. I snatch up the magazine and rip out the page on my way to the kitchen, tossing it and the magazine into the garbage can. Peter's pregnant mother was my own mother's greatest regret. I won't live like that. I pick up the phone, and when he answers I let the words rush out.

"I want to sell the land."

He and the Cannon kids swing out of the barn loft when they hear tires on the gravel drive. As if the sight of the cake on the kitchen table isn't agony enough, Henry is due any minute to make homemade ice cream for Peter's birthday. Ivorie is frying chicken with Fran, and she's made biscuits that are ready for the oven just as soon as Henry, Loretta, Joe Cannon, Doc, Pete, and Charlotte arrive. The anticipation is enough to kill anybody, let alone a new eight-year-old.

Peter stops running when he sees a man he doesn't know.

"Who in tarnation is that?" John asks.

Peter shrugs.

"Looks like a stranger to me," Milo says. "Maybe Miss Walker invited a mess of strangers to come to your birthday."

They run to the car and stand sided together like a posse. "Hey! Who do we have here?" the man asks. He is tall with a kind face and loose pants.

"We know who we are," Jane says. "Who are you?"

"Davis Carpenter," he says, offering her his hand. She pumps it up and down and squints up at him. "Is Miss Walker home?"

"Up yonder at the house," Jane says. "I've never seen you before. What do you want with her?"

He walks toward the house with the posse closing in. "I'm here on bank business."

Jane sprints in front of him. "Then you better let me tell her you're here." He stands in the middle of the yard, and Peter, John, and Milo circle him like lawmen around a criminal.

"It's his birthday today," John says, pointing at Peter with his thumb.

Davis is sweating under his arms and rolls up the sleeves of his shirt, as if that will help. "Is that so? Happy birthday. How old are you?"

"He don't talk much," Milo says, stepping in front of Peter. "But he's eight, same as me. We're having a party."

"Davis! How are you?" Ivorie is standing on the porch, wiping her hands on a towel and looking like she knows him, so the lawmen break their fortress. "Did you meet Peter?"

Davis ambles to the porch and makes over the flowers in bloom and the smells wafting out the door. "I did, Miss Walker. What a fine day for a birthday." He's wiping his neck and Ivorie gestures to one of the chairs on the porch.

"Have a seat in the shade, Davis."

"I'm obliged," he says, tucking his lanky body into the cane-bottomed chair. Peter, John, and Milo crouch behind the shrubs and listen as if they're some of Hoover's G-men on surveillance.

Jane sits on the chair next to Davis and stares at his face. "You shouldn't wear them long-sleeved shirts on such a hot day. You'll burn up. Mama says if you get overheated you can go plumb out of your mind."

"Jane, get in here and help me with all this chicken," Fran says, standing at the kitchen door.

"But, Mama, Miss Walker needs me out here to help with her bank business."

Ivorie smiles. "I'm all right, Jane. If your mama needs you, you can go."

Jane takes her time getting up, listening for any lulling moment where she can offer advice from her wide knowledge of financing. The screen door closes behind her with a snap, and Davis leans forward. "I just wanted to let you know that we haven't forgotten about you, Miss Walker. Mr. Lewis was at the bank yesterday eager to move forward with his filling station. If you've traveled the highway you know how few and far between filling stations can be."

Ivorie fans herself with the towel and leans her head against the house. "I do know that, Mr. Carpenter. I have traveled these roads several times in the last several days going to Knoxville."

His face is eager and childlike. "Then you know the need for filling stations in this area."

"I do, Mr. Carpenter. I sure do."

He grasps his palms and seems to be shaking hands with himself. "Mr. Lewis is ready to move ahead if you are, Miss Walker. We're just waiting for you."

Ivorie sits upright and looks at him. "But I can't help you, Mr. Carpenter. I don't own the land anymore."

He stands as if someone pushed him out of his seat with a mighty heave and reaches for his handkerchief. He's getting so red and hot in the face he looks like the ball of liquid at the bottom of the thermometer that hangs outside the kitchen window. "You don't own . . . Miss Walker, did you sell the land?"

"I did."

He looks like he'll pass out. "I don't understand, Miss Walker. Who did you sell the land to so fast?"

"Henry."

It is a dizzying day of sun and sweat and cops and robbers in the barn. Every few minutes Peter runs to the knotholes in the barn wall and watches for Ivorie or Fran to bring platefuls of chicken and potato salad out. When Ivorie calls out to them, her voice ringing through the barn loft, Peter is the first to swing down from the rope to the dirt floor below. With the agility of monkeys on vines, Jane, John, and Milo swing screaming from the rafters. The thick leaves of the giant oak form a cool shade for the picnic table, and one plate after another is carried out from the kitchen. "You all wash your hands before you dare touch any of this food," Ivorie says. It is with great agony that the children leave the smells and clamor together inside the kitchen, nudging one another out of the way of the sink.

"You all act like you got some sense before somebody takes an eye out," Fran says. "Have you heard a peep from George?" she says in whispered tones to Ivorie.

"Nothing," Ivorie says.

Peter looks up at her face and wonders who George is and why he isn't here for his birthday.

"Where's Sally Dog?" John asks. "She ain't been around all day."

Peter looks at Ivorie and she shrugs but tries to smile. "Maybe she met a boy dog and decided to elope."

Even though she's making light of Sally being gone, Peter knows she's sad to the quick. He is, too. He misses that dog something terrible.

Ivorie spreads a blue-and-yellow quilt on the ground, and the children fill their plates with too much food and plop down. Joe Cannon sets the baby on the quilt with a few bites of torn chicken and a biscuit on a plate. "Ah, Daddy," Jane says. "Do we have to have the baby? He gets into everything."

"He wants to be with you all," Joe says, rubbing Peter's head. Peter has noticed that Joe doesn't say too much, but he's quick to smile and offer a head or shoulder pat. Jane groans and guards her plate from the baby's reaching hands.

The grown-ups laugh easily. Loretta snorts when she gets to laughing hard, and Doc wheezes. Ivorie tells them the story of Davis

Carpenter and how he turned white as a ghost when she told him Henry bought the land, and Henry bangs the table. The children can't figure out how that's amusing in the least and talk about a man named Booger Jones who lives in Mosheim, and that gets them talking about poots and boogers and belches, which leads to actual belches.

Peter looks up into the hills and Jane catches him. "Did you ever see us from up there?"

He nods and takes a bite of chicken.

"Did you ever wish you were down here?"

His head bobs as he gives the baby a bite of biscuit.

"Well, now you are. And you're having just about as good a birthday that I've ever seen."

Peter lies back on the quilt and squints into the cottony sky. Can she see him? Does she know today is his birthday? Has she heard that he might talk someday soon? Something gallops from one side of his chest to the other and he smiles, reaching toward those cotton-candy clouds to touch his mother's face.

It's been a long time since he's heard the happy-birthday song and he watches their mouths, listening to their voices rise and fall and then come together with a great clashing at the end.

"Now close your eyes and make a wish and blow out the candles," Ivorie says.

He closes his eyes and makes the wish of a lifetime and blows with all his might. The paper is blue, just like she said it would be, and he's careful as he pulls on the tape.

"What are you taking your sweet time for?" John asks. "Just rip into it."

He eases his finger beneath the ridge of tape and the paper falls open. A cardboard box with CHEESE printed on the side of it sits in front of him.

"Go ahead, look inside," Ivorie says.

He lifts two of the brown flaps and smiles, lifting out a toy gun.

"With a holster!" John yells. "Can you see that, Milo?"

"I'm looking at it," Milo says.

Peter lifts a star from the box, and John smacks his hand to his forehead. "And a sheriff's badge! Can you see *that,* Milo?"

Milo says he most surely does see the badge. Henry pins the star to Peter's overalls and helps wrap the holster around his hips. "Now you are one fine-looking deputy," Henry says. "Sheriff Dutton might need somebody to help him and you'd be just the man for the job!"

Peter fingers the gun and pretends to aim it at John. John grabs his gut and falls to the ground. "Tell my mama I didn't mean to do it," he yells. "Tell her I didn't mean to turn no-good." Fran rolls her eyes and nudges John with her bare toe.

"And this is from me, too," Ivorie says, handing him a flat package wrapped in the same blue paper. He tears at it and pulls out a pad of paper and a pencil. "Your very own paper and first pencil." Paper and pencil. This is what Jane meant when she said birthdays are like Christmas.

"One more," Henry says, pulling a small gift from under the table wrapped in brown paper.

"I bet I know what that is," Jane says, with a smug, knowing smile.

Peter opens the package and lifts up a book, studying the words.

"That says 'The Three Musketeers,' " Jane says. "That's Henry's favorite book. It's got sword fights and chases and horses and all sorts of such stuff in it."

He flips through the pages and sighs.

"I'll read it to you the first time," Ivorie says. "Then one day you'll read it by yourself."

It's his birthday and Peter believes that

anything, even what Ivorie says about him reading this book with its too many words, could be true.

The kids strip down to their underpants and jump into the water together. The creek reflects the sky's puffy face and Peter stares long into the water, watching his reflection ripple and bob and then smooth out.

"It's all right," Ivorie says. "It's only waist high and we're all here with you."

He looks at the grown-ups taking off their shoes and decides to take a step, then another one, toward John and Milo. The water is warm and spreads over his legs like the blanket on his bed.

Fran steps into the water and bobs the baby up and down in the shallow end, listening to him giggle. Will Henry balances on a rock holding his daddy's hand, and Loretta makes it sound like he's as brave as a warrior the way she goes on and on over his rock-standing ability.

The sun slips behind a scrim of clouds as Jane, John, and Milo play Marco Polo, closing their eyes and chasing one another. The grown-ups are fussing over baby Paul and Will Henry and talking about tobacco crops when Peter slips under the water. He's out of body and drifting, the flames of the dream consuming him and filling his lungs, but the arms around his waist are strong, pulling him up.

"Put your feet down," Joe says.

Peter gasps and gags and tears mingle with water as he falls into Joe.

"It's all right, son," Joe says. "You just lost your footing. When that happens, put your feet down." He gives Peter one of those rubs on top of his wet head and Peter looks out to find Ivorie. She's right here next to him, her dress soaked through and her face sagging in sadness.

His head is hanging as he slogs toward the creek bank.

"It's too pretty a day to get out of the creek," Ivorie says, looking at his friends, who are staring at him in pounding silence. "If ever there was a day for creek playing, this is it."

"Come on, Peter," Jane says. "Everybody goes under. Watch me." She ducks under the water, her hands sticking up like waving flags before she breaks through the water's surface, smiling. John, Milo, Will Henry, Joe, and even Ivorie slip beneath the surface and come up grinning.

"Just put your feet down," Joe says, nodding at the water. "I'm right here if you want to try it again." An arthritic old man could dip into the water faster, but after three false starts, Peter gets under, keeping one hand up over his head and the other on Joe's waist. He does it again and once more, and by the time they all trudge waterlogged out of the creek, he has, according to Joe's count, baptized himself twenty-one times.

Lights sharp and bright as diamonds flicker against a backdrop of black when everybody goes home. Peter stands on the porch, watching them load into their trucks, and he wishes again the wish he made on his candles — that the day would never end.

"What a day!" Ivorie says, clanging the last of the plates as she stacks them in the cupboard. "Come on in, Peter, and get ready for bed."

He doesn't move; Henry's truck is just about out of sight.

The screen door groans and Ivorie sticks her head out. "Hey, birthday boy!" He turns and she raises her eyebrows. "Bath and then bed."

He trudges through the door to the bath-room. Clean underpants are on the com-mode waiting for him after his bath and he brushes his teeth, gagging like he always does (he doesn't know if he'll ever learn how to do this right). Ivorie is standing at the window, looking out into the dark. He stands at the end of the bed and makes that low, throaty noise to get her attention. She turns to him and he pretends to pet something in front of him.

"I don't know where she is," Ivorie says. "I keep hoping and praying she'll come back." She's quiet and turns back to the window.

He walks to her and taps her on the hip. When she looks at him her eyes are full of water. He pretends to pet something again and a tear sneaks down her cheek, quicker than she wants, and she hurries to brush it away.

"I miss her," she says. "She's been with me a long time."

He stares up at her but doesn't know what to do. He feels like running or hiding, afraid he'll make Ivorie sadder or angry or wish he hadn't come here.

"I bet she misses you," she says, reading his mind. "Her world got a whole heap better when you showed up. I bet she's a sad dog right now." She walks to the bed and crawls on top of it, leaning up against the headboard, and holds the books and paper. He sets his pistol, holster, and sheriff's badge on the chair and drapes his overalls across the arm. "Do you want to go over any words, or are you too tired?"

He gestures for the books and she pats the bed next to her.

"Climb on up here and spell your name for me." He takes his place and runs his fingers down the spine of books, looking for the one Henry gave him. "*The Three Musketeers* is right there on the night table," she says.

He puts his hand on top of the book just to make sure it's there and turns back to Ivorie, taking the pencil. He holds it and painstakingly writes each letter, each one taller than the last.

"Lordy day! You just keep spelling, Peter. And you are writing! Look at this!"

He looks at the words, as tall and uneven as trees, and feels his face getting hot with pride.

She spells *hat, cat, sat, rat,* and *bat* and writes each word on the page. "Point to the vowels," she says.

He does with a fluttery tap of the pencil.

She gathers up the books and papers and heaps them into her lap. "All right. Bedtime."

He doesn't want to sleep and pats the books.

"It's too late. More tomorrow. Do you know how much you've learned in just a few weeks?" He doesn't and she smiles. "We are just about through this first-grade primer. Your brain is like a sponge soaking it up because you are so smart." It feels like there's a spring inside his body that's about to release. "I can't even keep track anymore of the number of words you can read." *Boing.* "And then there's the ones you can spell! Who knows how many that is!" *Boing, boing.* "You are just as bright as the sun, you know that?" It's springing loose like a jack-in-the-box. "And someday real soon you're going to say those words."

She turns off the lamp, whispering words about his birthday and reading *The Three Musketeers* someday, and the whites of her eyes glimmer like fireflies in moonlight. She reaches for his arm but he's rising and drifting, too far away to reach for her before the room is snoring in sleep.

HENRY

Loretta and I walk to the store every morning. It's only a quarter of a mile, and on those mornings when I'm feeling stiff and brittle, the walk helps work out the kinks. From halfway down the road this morning, we see a car pull into the lot and stop so fast it bucks. Davis Carpenter's long leg tumbles out of the car first and pulls the rest of him out. He jumps onto the porch and paces back and forth, acting like a man about to be convicted. "He is fit to be tied," Loretta says, watching him.

"Mornin', Davis," I say, picking up my pace. "Hot and dry, isn't it?"

"Sure is, Henry."

"It's so dry the trees are bribing the dogs." Loretta laughs; she's always been an easy audience and says a quick good-morning to Davis before opening the door.

I walk onto the porch and gesture to the chairs. "What brings you out so early in the morning?"

Davis sits and crosses his right ankle up on his left knee and circles it round like a windmill. "Your sister said you now own the land out at the crossroads."

I sit next to him and teeter on the back legs of the chair, patting the deed folded in my shirt pocket. I've been keeping it there, knowing full well that Davis would be paying me a visit. "Sure do," I say, taking the deed out of my pocket and slapping it in the palm of my hand. "She sold it to me."

Davis takes his handkerchief out of his back pocket and wipes his face. "Your sister always likes to keep things interesting. You know that, Henry?"

I feel bad for Davis. He's a fine man, just trying to do his job. I don't know why I find this so funny. "She has been known to do that."

Davis stands and leans that lanky body up against the porch railing. "Henry, how much do you want for that land?"

It was Sarah's idea for me to buy the land. She didn't think they'd ever offer more money, not to a woman, anyway, and that's when she asked me to buy it. But here's the thing: I didn't buy the front acreage, what Davis wants. I bought the back fifteen acres, but Davis doesn't know that. She just wanted me to throw around the deed of property like I was the owner so Davis would offer more money. Once the price was driven up, Sarah would sell the front fifteen acres at that price. "Well, I hadn't put much thought to it, Davis, considering I just bought it and all. But if someone were interested in buying it, I'd say I'd let it go for four hundred an acre."

It sounds like something has exploded inside Davis. "Four hundred an acre! Henry, you know yourself that land right here in town sells for a hundred an acre!"

I scratch my head and let the chair fall forward onto its front legs. "Do you think I should ask for more?" Davis puts a fist right in the middle of his forehead and steps away from me, looking out over the parking lot. Loretta pokes her face in the screen door and tightens her lips into a straight line so she won't laugh. She steps back before Davis turns around and sees her. "Now I know that your client only wanted ten acres but if he still wants to put up a filling station he's going to have to buy a minimum of fifteen."

"Six thousand dollars!" He turns to me as slow as a pig on a spit and crosses his arms. "Henry." He's chuckling now. "You're as crazy as your sister. There is no way Mr. Lewis is going to buy fifteen acres of land at four hundred an acre."

"Well, I understand, Davis. I thought it might sound like a lot of money to Mr. Lewis."

He watches me, and try as I might not to, I feel like I'm smiling. I rub my face, hoping to turn down my mouth into a sorrowful, hounddog expression. "What do you mean 'I thought it might sound like a lot of money to Mr. Lewis'? Do you mean it doesn't sound like a lot of money to somebody else?"

I happened to run into Jess Herman in Greenville when I was there three days ago to stock up on chicken and horse feed for the store. Jess and his family have owned a warehouse in Greenville for fifty-plus years. They use it to hang and dry their own tobacco, but come auction time that place is chugged full of tobacco baskets from all over Greene County so great big companies like Philip Morris can come bid on it. I told Jess about the property down at the crossroads and told him it was for sale. "I'm thinking I should ask four hundred an acre," I said, hoping Jess knew more than I did since he lived in town.

"That sounds like a fair price to me," he said. "That's good, useful land there."

The way I figure it, Davis doesn't need to

know all that. "Well," I say, looking at him. "The owner of a warehouse in Greenville thought the price sounded fair. Said the land is useful. I hadn't thought on that much, but you know it is useful the way it sits right there off the highway. Some land, like that land over across from the tracks, is about as useful as a back pocket on a shirt. It's rocky and barren and just not fit for much."

Davis rubs his head like he's trying to smooth out a headache, and his voice sounds like air being released from a balloon. "Did you talk to Buddy Harper? He's been looking for land."

I don't even know Buddy Harper but play along. "I didn't know Buddy was interested, too."

Davis throws up his long, willowy hand and makes his way down the steps. "I'm leaving to make some calls, Henry. But I'll be back."

I stand and rest my hands on the railing. "I didn't even get the chance to ask if you want a cup of coffee, Davis."

"Too hot for coffee," he says, sliding behind the wheel. The car engine roars, and Davis backs out of the lot faster than green grass through a goose and, I admit, I laugh watching him.

■ ■ ■ ■

"Hey, Henry! Hey, Loretta!" Jane says, letting the screen door pop closed. She's here to help Loretta make sandwiches for the dinner folks.

"Mornin', pretty girl."

She pulls an apron down over her head and ties it behind her. It's way too big but Jane's never been fussy. "Where's Peter? Isn't he going to sweep up today?"

Sarah Ivorie hasn't brought Peter to the store since she got the tar slapped out of her. She's trying her best to stay out of sight to keep talk down. "I believe he's home helping Sarah today."

Jane opens a package of white bread and lines the slices up like big teeth across the countertop. Loretta reaches for some bologna and ham and cheese out of the refrigerated case. "That sure was some birthday he had," Jane says, over her shoulder. "Wasn't that some birthday?"

"Who's birthday was it?" Hot Dot says in that grainy voice of hers. She's looking particularly jowly this morning and her bosom is pushing up from underneath her dress like bread dough trying to rise out of a pan but stopped by a thin layer of cotton.

I work hard to shove that image out of my head.

"Peter's," Jane says.

"Who's Peter?"

"The little boy at Miss Walker's."

Hot Dot sounds like she's putting out a fire. "Is she still carrying on with that boy?"

"That makes it sound lewd, Dot," Loretta says.

An empty basket dangles off Hot Dot's arm. "Why is she pretending to be that boy's mama?"

Jane has stopped working and is facing Hot Dot, holding a butter knife slathered in mayonnaise. "She's not pretending to be his mother," I say before Jane gets going. "Sarah took him in because he doesn't have anybody."

"A single woman . . . a single woman her age . . ." She dragged out the word *age* for dramatic effect. "Can't afford to raise somebody else's child. Period."

"Period nothing!" Jane says, waving the knife in the air. Dots of mayo the size of bird poop splatter across the floor, and Loretta grabs a rag. "Why's everybody saying bad things about Miss Walker taking him in? That's the dumbest thing I ever heard." I can see clouds of smoke roiling up out of Jane's ears.

Avis Oxman opens the door and stops when she can't get past Hot Dot. She looks at Jane wielding that drippy knife.

"Grown-ups sure take up a lot of time thinking up bad things but don't take nary a second to think up something good," Jane says.

She's breaking out in blotches of red and I step toward her, putting up my hand. "All right, pretty girl. Try to finish those sandwiches before the dinner hour." Hot Dot rolls her eyes at me, as if she and I are in some secret society together that doesn't understand the youth of our nation, and begins rooting through the shelves. "Mornin', Avis. Where's Ox been lately?"

"Feeling puny," Avis says, like she just took a big gulp of vinegar.

"What's he got?" Loretta asks.

"That same old virus that plagues him from time to time. He's worn to the bone. He'll work for a spell and then have to lay down. He's been that way for days now. I need to get some chicken feed for him."

I move to the porch, where I keep a lot of the feed stacked, and throw two bags in the back of Avis's truck. When she rings out, I say, "If you can't come in and Ox isn't able, you just call and I'll bring out what you need."

"Thanks, Henry." She pulls open the door. "And, Jane!" Jane turns to look at Avis. "I agree with you. That little boy needs somebody to take care of him. Period."

Jane's grin is as long as that knife.

I drop Jane off at her house and then pull into Sarah's driveway so I can tell her about Davis's visit this morning. She's quiet as a stump, listening to me on the porch. She's gotten reed thin in the last few weeks, and she isn't any bigger than a minute to begin with. She's gotten behind in her gardening. I actually saw two tomatoes rotting on the ground because she didn't pick them. The thought of doctor bills is worrying her to death, and I know she's grieving for Sally something fierce.

She spends most of her time working with Peter and teaching him how to do things like wash a car, pick beans, shovel manure, fry an egg, pull weeds, fold a shirt, or learn his ABCs. From all the books she keeps bringing home, he knows the three types of elephants, which shows what I know because I thought there was just one flavor of elephant! Sometimes she's so busy out here you'd think she was twins, but I know in all the work that her mind is occupied. Her face looks like it's about to rupture.

"How you doing?" A small tear squeezes out the side of her eye and she rubs her forehead. "Now, come on. It'll all work out," I say, patting her on the back.

"Why'd they have to do something to my dog, Henry? I loved that dog."

"I know you did."

She pushes her fingers into her eyes and snaps her head up, shaking her head as if that'd settle the tears somewhere back in her eye sockets. "I've lost my dog, it looks like my man is gone for good, and I got the pudding knocked out of me. What's next?"

I wish Loretta were here because she could talk to Sarah better than I could about George and that whole mess. "They'll buy the land," I say, hoping to make her feel better. "I can feel it."

She looks over at me, and tiny spokes like rays of the sun shoot out from around her eyes. "What if they don't? Then what do I do?"

Contrary to what Loretta says, I really *don't* know everything and I don't have any answers or solutions for my sister, just a handful of silence.

IVORIE

I tuck Peter into bed at eight so he can get a full night's rest before the surgery. I have butterflies in my stomach, thinking about it. I kneel down on the floor next to his bed and rest my chin on the side, looking at him. "Are you ready for tomorrow?"

He nods.

"Me too," I say, hoping my voice sounds stronger than I feel. I reach up and play with his hair. "I sure am glad you chose my garden to ransack, you know that?" He smiles and I tap his arm. "I'll see you in the morning."

I walk to the kitchen and sit down at the table, reading through the papers Dr. Culp gave me. I finish and tuck them inside my pocketbook when I see headlights shine through the kitchen window. There's still enough light for me to recognize George's truck and I open the screen door. He looks handsome in his work shirt and blue jeans but it's not lost on me that he waited again till it was late and he knew Peter would be in bed.

He walks to the porch and stops, looking at me. He reaches his hand for my face and runs a finger over my cheek. "That looks painful."

"It is."

He shakes his head real sorrowful-like and murmurs low in his throat. "I hate to see you like this."

I reach for his hand and hold it. I'm so glad he's back. "I'm okay."

"I heard he's having surgery tomorrow."

"His first," I say, leaning against the porch rail.

He moves next to me and crosses his arms. "So there will be more?" I nod. He looks out toward the barn, and although he's right beside me, I feel him moving away. "It's hard to think that some kid you didn't even know a few weeks ago is inside your house, sleeping. He's living here with you, eating supper, working in the garden, and milking the cow just like he's always been here."

My mouth turns up a little, thinking about that. "It is like he's always been here. I hope you can meet him sometime soon."

There comes a day in the garden when I

know that a plant will no longer produce. I can walk through the rows of beans and know that they're done or when I've picked the last tomato of the season. There's always a sense of melancholy that sets in when I know the harvest is over. Neither George nor I says anything but I know there will be no more wondering or guessing or glancing to the window to see if he's coming up the driveway. We both know it's over, and that sense of melancholy begins to set in behind my ribs.

"I'll meet him, someday," he says, stepping away from the railing.

"I hope so."

He stops to look at me and we both work hard at mustering up a smile and hoping for something to say. "I just wanted to stop and say that I hope everything turns out real good tomorrow," he says. My hand is heavy as I lift it to wave and I watch him drive away.

I don't know why I bothered to go to bed. Dr. Culp told me to have Peter at the hospital at six thirty this morning, August fifth, and I awoke every hour last night with my heart pounding, thinking I'd overslept. At four thirty I creep to the bathroom and wash my face. I look like I've been pulled backward through a knothole. My eyes look grim and red rimmed, and the mark under my eye is just a dark bruise now, and the patch on my face is a hard crust of yellow and purple. I have a face only a mother could love, and she's not here. Words and thoughts flop around my mind, and there is something frozen, frantic, and foreign inside me, an odd feeling of hope or dread, I don't know. "Please give him his voice," I say out loud. I think of Peter's voice as a closed-off room, a hidden attic space that no one knows about until one day somebody pulls on just the right loose board and, lo and behold, a treasure trove. I picture that bounty of treasure in my mind as I make my way to the barn.

I milk Gertie and pat her on the side. "Today's the day." She swishes her tail back and forth. I finish milking and give Gertie a solid pat on her backside, sending her to the pasture. The air is spiked with the smell of honeysuckle this morning and I inhale deeply. Mother loved this smell early in the mornings. She'd walk out onto the porch and take a deep breath before getting to work, as if the scent started her engine. I wonder if she was inhaling honeysuckle the morning she saw Peter's mother. Was she back on the porch watching the sun come up and sucking in morning's familiar scents when that scared, pregnant girl happened by?

Peter ambles to the kitchen and his slept-on hair is poking out everywhere, making him look like a newly hatched chick. "This is going to be a great day!" Deep down in that heartsick place I really hope this is true, but my mind is frightened. Dr. Culp said Peter couldn't eat anything, so I forgo eating as well. We sit together on the front porch and wait for Henry and Loretta. I told Henry he didn't have to come, but he insisted, and truth is, I'm glad he did. Peter and I will stay the night at the hospital and Henry will come back home. When he arrives, he is all teeth and noise to our closed mouths and long stretches of silence.

"What a day! What a day!" he says, jumping out of his truck. We still haven't heard a peep from Davis Carpenter about the purchase of the land, and although I'm trying my best not to let it get to me, it's getting to me. Normally I can shut things off like a lamp, but the land, George, and Peter's father are eating at me. Dr. Culp said to pay what I could of the bill, when I could. Mother and Pop would squirm in their graves if they knew I was moving forward with this surgery and had no way to pay the bill.

Loretta bends down and hugs Peter to her. "I'll be manning the store today." She pushes him out at arm's length. "Let me look at you because the next time I see you you'll be chattering up a storm." She kisses him on top of his head and gets back inside their truck, waving.

"Well, come on," Henry says. "I'll drive if you want."

I do want that. I'm having a hard time focusing my thoughts; they're like trying to lasso a fish, let alone think clear enough to get us into Knoxville again. We cram into the cab of the truck and a clear, blue-silk sky stretches out in front of us. Halfway there, Peter slips his hand into mine. He has rarely touched me the whole time he's been with me and I know he's frightened. Henry sees it, too, and talks on and on in that way he has of easing people. He tells Peter the story of the time our old family dog thought Henry was a night prowler and cornered him up against the house, pulling off his britches. "Pulled them clean off me," Henry says. "Left me naked as a jaybird right there in front of God and Mother."

Shots of air pass over the roof of Peter's mouth and he leans his head back on the seat, smiling.

Henry always could tell a story much better than me. "No big boy of thirteen wants to be naked in front of his mother — that's just not right! I tried to cover myself and run but that old dog kept yapping and nipping in such a way that I was afraid I was going to lose something mighty important, if you know what I mean." I laugh out loud at this and Peter makes fast wheezing sounds. Henry is stretching the truth but tears stream down my face. "Well, there I stood, covering myself and shuddering like cannonballs are going off in front of me, and that old dog's yapping gets the attention of every single one of my brothers. Now you'd think brothers could come in handy in a situation like this, but they were as helpful as teats on a bull. They fell over on the ground and laughed at me, which I thought was mighty rude." I lunge forward in laughter and picture the scene in my mind. "My own mother couldn't keep from laughing, and all that laughing just egged that old dog on. He would have quit ages ago, but with an audience he just went on and on like he was in a moving picture and just doing his part. I was as busy as a stump-tailed cow in fly season trying to bat him away and cover myself, and I finally just took off for the kitchen door. I got there, but I'll be dog-gone if he didn't take a nip out of my hind end! I couldn't sit on that cheek for a week or more, and I sure wasn't going to let mother put salve on it!"

Henry pulls up in front of the hospital, and even though Peter is still laughing, my stomach flip-flops. We're sent to the surgical wing and I take Peter's hand into my clammy one. Henry leads us through the double doors and I walk to the check-in window, where an older woman with nutmeg-colored hair and cat-eyed glasses sits, writing. Her face is round and her eyes are wreathed in crow's feet. She looks at Peter, and her heart, all big and warm, pops out of her eyes. "You must be Peter!" He clings to me from behind, and her voice goes up a register as she stands. "Well, come on back." She opens the door next to her window and extends her arm, showing us the way. "You'll wait right in this room for Dr. Culp." The room is mostly empty with the exception of a few chairs and a wooden puzzle on a small table. "I have coffee. Would you all like some while you wait?"

I can't drink in front of Peter; it feels unfair, so I pass on it. "Maybe later."

"I'll tell Dr. Culp you're here."

She disappears, and a ball of nerves rolls

393

up inside me. Peter puts a finger on the puzzle when the door opens. Dr. Culp looks different than the day we met him, when he was wearing trousers and a button-down shirt. Today he's in soft gray lightweight pants and a gray short-sleeved shirt with a white doctor's coat over it. He extends a hand to Henry. "Dr. Culp."

"I'm Henry. Sarah's brother."

Dr. Culp doesn't make small talk but sits down next to Peter and pats his leg. "I hope you're as excited as we are, Peter." I smile at Peter and he nods at Dr. Culp. Another man appears in the door, short and solid with a dark crew cut. "This is Dr. Sanders and he'll be helping me today. He's going to take you to another room and give you some special clothes to put on, and then your mother and Henry will be with you. Okay?" I indicate that it's okay and Peter follows Dr. Sanders. "In the next few minutes we'll give him some anesthesia while you're still in the room with him. Once he's under, we'll take him back to surgery." The ball is rolling faster inside me and I can't figure out if I want to scream in excitement or vomit from nerves. Dr. Culp seems to hear my inner voice and smiles. "We do a lot of these, Miss Walker. This team has been together a long time. Again, I'll be moving tissue from the edges of the cleft into the cleft area." He mentions the name of the surgical dentist and what he'll do, but I catch only bits and pieces of it. I'm hoping Henry can fill me in later because he's doing a lot of nodding like he understands what's what.

Peter is swallowed up in the surgical gown but I make it sound like he's the handsomest thing I've seen this side of Clark Gable. He hops up onto the rolling bed and sits on his hands, as if they'll fly away if he doesn't, and I smile, standing next to him. Dr. Sanders talks him through what he'll be doing and how the ether will help him sleep through the surgery, and my stomach flip-flops more violently than before. Peter lies back, and when Dr. Sanders comes near to take him, I hold up my hand. "Wait." I stroke Peter's hair, and the same eyes that peered out from my garden late one night weeks earlier look back at me. "This is the day that your mother dreamed about." My voice catches and I hear Henry clear his throat. "She would be so proud of you." I squeeze his arm and feel water gathering in my lower lids. "I am, too. I'm just as proud as I can be." I run my finger under my nose and pat his hand; the small bones feel like chopsticks under my palm. "You go on now.

We'll be right here waiting for you." Peter looks at Henry, and Henry nods, mute for the first time in his life.

There comes a time when you don't know what you're capable of anymore. Looking back, say five or even two years ago, you can remember what you were capable of then — how you thought, what you did, who you loved, who people said you were. Then something happens and takes all that away; the basket of good intentions you've been toting around, the trunk of dreams you've been pulling behind you — all of it is gone in an instant, and it's just you, naked, bare, exposed. So many names and faces are marbled into my past, but looking back two years ago, even six months ago, I can't recognize any of them. I can't even recognize the woman I was. All I see is Peter's face flagging me down along the way, his voice an alarm going off, urging me to slow down so I wouldn't miss him. I am overcome with a feeling of having been here before, although I wasn't, but it feels familiar. I look down at his serene little face and my heart pitches into my throat. He came making no conditions or demands. He was a gift that came with no strings attached. When he sits in my home, it is no longer my home, but ours. Mine and his. When I look ahead, it's no longer at just my future, but his, filled with school and dreams and a woman to marry. When I go through doors, I no longer see the next view with just my eyes, but his. Two months ago I had no idea I was capable of this.

Dr. Sanders gives a knowing smile and pushes part of me out of the room.

PETER

She is there when I open my eyes, and it feels like a sock is rolled up in my mouth. Something like spider legs brush up against my tongue and I wiggle it back and forth, feeling their legs around the top edge of my mouth, but my tongue stops. I lift it and feel a wall instead of the big empty space. Her eyes are huge and scared-looking. I open my lips around the sock and try to say, "Mama." It doesn't come out the way I hear it in my head.

Her hand flies to her mouth, and tears shoot like rapids down her cheeks. "What did you say?"

I try it again, hoping it will sound like a word this time. Inside my head I always knew how to say *mama* just like little Will Henry says it to Fran, but I never could. The word is muffled because of my big cotton tongue, but Mama understands what I'm trying to say.

She's reaching behind her, flopping her hand up and down. "Henry. Did you hear . . . ?"

Henry steps beside her and smiles at me. His gray eyes are filling up, too. "I heard him . . . Mama." He says that while patting her shoulder.

It's all I can say for now, and by the way Mama is carrying on, it's enough. I'm pooped and close my eyes when the doctor comes in to talk.

Mama's still sitting there when I open my eyes again. "Hey there," she says, wiping her nose with a handkerchief. "I don't know why I can't stop carrying on. I've just been sitting here blubbering." She laughs and blows her nose, jumping up on the side of the bed with me. Her eyes are puffed up and red, and she smiles, letting the tears roll over her face. She throws up her hands. "I am just a mess!" She wipes her eyes and squeezes my arm the way she always does. "Henry went home. He had to get back to the store. That's what he said, anyway. Truth is, he's a great big caterwaulin' baby like me, and I think he needed the drive home to settle down." I wish Henry were here. I want to hear one of his bad jokes or made-up stories, the ones that make Mama shake her head and make a hissing sound when he's done telling them.

"Ma-ma." I'm whispering because my throat hurts, but the sound of my voice makes me stop. I always wondered if I'd sound like John or Milo but I don't sound like either one of them. I don't sound like anybody I've ever heard. My voice sounds faraway and full of wool, and my tongue feels so heavy. It's never moved like this, but a word is trying to slip right out of my mouth. My own mouth!

She throws her head back and laughs and presses the handkerchief into her eyes to stop the new flow. I know it's because I called her mama. But the first time I ever snuck into her garden I wanted to be a part of that place, and the first time I saw her I wanted her to be my mother. I always thought of her as mine. Even when she didn't know my name it was all right, because she knew me and I knew she wanted me. I could always tell she wanted me by how tight she held my hand, or fussed over my blankets, or held me wet out of the bath still stinking like poop, or how she wiped up my pee, or cleaned up my wounds, or when she'd cry but didn't think I saw her, or when she rode Miss Kitty up into the mountains to get me in the rain.

Only a mother would do that. Only my mother would face the devil himself and ride away with me.

"Listen to that voice, would you?" She shakes her head and lays a hand on my chest. "The doctor said it went much better than he thought it would. You'll stay two nights here in the hospital so they can make sure you don't get an infection."

I don't want to be here and I try to say no. The sound surprises me again; all I ever heard myself make was groans or grunts, and I feel tears on my cheeks. These sounds have curves and ridges and beginnings and endings.

"I'm staying, too." She uses her handkerchief to wipe my face. "Normally, they wouldn't let me stay in the room with you, but Dr. Culp signed some papers and said, 'By doggone, she's staying with him.' So that's that." I don't want to, but I cry again and Mama crawls right up next to me and lies down on the bed. She puts her nose in my cheek and starts sniffling. "Lord have mercy," she says, flapping open the handkerchief. "We are a sight!" She leans up on her elbow and wipes my eyes. "I never thought in a million years that I'd carry on in such a way after hearing somebody's voice, but I tell you what, that is the most beautiful sound I've ever heard." She kisses me on the forehead and I try to stick my finger in my mouth. She pushes my hand away. "Dr. Culp said not to do that. You don't want anything to infect what they've done up there. Open up." I open my mouth and Mama opens hers, angling her head this way and that to get a good look.

"Ah . . ." I can't figure out the sound. "Ah . . . ?"

"What does it look like?" she asks. I nod. Mama fans herself because she's crying again, and she looks up at the ceiling, trying to pull herself together up there in that bright white paint. "It's just pink and red and there's little black threads holding it all in place. Does it hurt?" I shake my head. "Try to say *no*."

I smile because when I try to say it I can hear the *o* sound.

"Hey!" Her eyes are big, looking at me. "I've been thinking about a middle name and I think I came up with one." I listen and wait. "David. Like the giant slayer himself. Peter David Walker. What do you think?"

I've never thought of myself as being a giant killer before and that makes me smile.

"I heard you were awake." Dr. Culp walks into the room and Mama shimmies off the side of the bed. "I also heard you said *mama.* Any truth to that?"

Mama nods at me and I open my mouth to form the word again. "Ma-ma."

I sound like a monster, but his face wrinkles up and he pokes his fist in the air. He sits on the edge of the bed. "It's all going to start pouring out now, Peter. You know, most of our patients are just learning to talk when they have this operation but you've heard these words for years. They are all in there like snow on top of a mountain. As soon as one word tumbles out, so does another one and then another one and before long . . . avalanche. All those words are going to come racing down that mountain." He bangs his hands together and smiles. "What do you think of that?" I smile, nodding. "Not good enough. Use words."

I struggle, reaching for the sounds. "Eh . . ."

Dr. Culp pokes both fists up into the air and grabs me by the shoulders. "Yes!"

They only let me eat what Mama calls broth for supper, and it's not very good without anything in it. "Solid foods could jar one of those stitches loose," she says. "Once it heals up more, I'll get some good food into you. How about some biscuits and gravy?"

I think about that throat-call noise I used to do and reach for it.

She smiles and taps my cheek. "You need to stop making those noises and use words now." I try but it feels like a mangled mess of wire trying to fall out of my mouth.

She squeezes my leg and pulls out the first-grade primer, opening it to the ABCs. "We've gone over these umpteen dozen times. Now it's time to *say* them. Are you ready?"

I am so excited I want to bust open like an egg. When I learn to say these letters I'll be able to talk to Mama and yell things out to Jane and John and Milo when we play cops and robbers and I'll be able to read the book Henry gave me. I'll be able to do anything I want.

Henry

I darted away from that hospital faster than a fish when you poke your finger in the water at it. When I heard Peter try to say *mama,* it did me in and my sister was beside herself. He turned up that little mouth and I expected him to make those sounds that I was used to; I didn't think he'd make a noise that I could make out as a word. I'm still shook up over it and want to tell Loretta and Jane and whoever else is inside the store. I look down on the seat and realize I still have some iodine that Avis Oxman called about yesterday, so I decide to drop that off first.

Ox's boy Len is in the yard when I pull into the driveway. Between the dairy cows, tobacco, and garden, Ox has some of the hardest-working kids I've ever seen. I wave in Len's direction and hold up the bag of groceries. "For your mama." Len runs and snatches it out of my hands, running for the house.

"Ox is in the barn," Avis yells to me from the porch.

I make my way into the barn and breathe in that milk-damp smell. Ox and his son Rayburn are finishing up milking the last of the cows and they can't hear me over the noise the machines are making. Ox glances up and he looks like death on a cracker. His dungarees are falling off him and he's the color of mold. Every part of him is shrunken and slumped. Whatever he's got is taking him right down to the grave. He walks down the center of the barn and motions to Rayburn, letting him know he's stepping outside.

"How are you, Henry?"

"Well, I'm good, but you look bad, Ox. Real bad. You're a bag of bones."

He mops his face and squints up at the sun. "I've never been so sick in my life. My bones hurt; the slightest breeze pounds at them like the air is made of ice. I can't even move without feeling the pain in my joints. I sleep ten hours but it's not enough. Avis tells me to eat but I can't. It comes right back up. These cows are wearing me down but the kids and Avis can't keep up with everything on their own." He coughs into his handkerchief. "I b'lieve I'm over the worst of it."

He's sick and doesn't want to talk. I don't blame him. "I'll let you get back to work. I brought out some iodine that Avis said you need."

He turns to head back into the barn. "Wish she hadn't bothered you, Henry. I thought we had a whole bottle of iodine. I 'preciate your time."

I take a step toward my truck and stop. "Hey, Ox! Peter got his voice today." It doesn't register with him. "The boy at Sarah's. We took him into Knoxville for surgery on his cleft palate!" He smiles in a way that makes my stomach clench. He's sick to the marrow and slinks back into the barn.

I walk to the truck and see Avis leaning against the porch post. A statue in a cemetery couldn't look more stiff or sad. Something in her eyes makes me uneasy but I pass it off. Avis sometimes has a way of making people feel uneasy. I wave to Len and get into the truck. I'm hungry enough to eat the tail out of rag doll. I put my hand on the key but stop when I see Avis walking toward me. She stops in the middle of the yard, staring at me. She's ghost pale and solemn but doesn't come any closer. She looks to the barn, then back to me, and something quivers down inside me. Ox told me they had a full bottle of iodine. Why did she want more with a full bottle in the house? Why did Ox's smile make my stomach clench up the way it did? Why is his smile so familiar? Looking at her staring a hole through me, something snaps in my head and I realize she *wanted* me to come. Ox's nose. His mouth. They're the same. Avis has come face-to-face with that nose and mouth in recent days and that's why she wanted me here.

When Ox comes out of the barn twenty minutes later, he looks surprised to see me standing here looking at him. A locomotive could drive through the silence between us. "Ox." It doesn't sound like my voice, and when I think about saying more it makes my heart buck and stop a little. I sure am assuming a lot here. Avis walks out on the porch and looks our way. "I've been studying on something and I'm hoping you can set me straight." My stomach lurches and rolls, and I hope with everything in me that I'm wrong.

Ox is breathing but he hasn't moved. He's quiet for the longest time. "But what's made crooked can't ever be set straight again. Isn't that what they say, Henry?"

"But sometimes it can get straighter.

Maybe not all the way but some." He's not looking at me. "Might be time to start, Ox. Lay the whole mess out on the table." It looks like blood drains from his head and he falls against the truck next to me. There's a low humming sound in my ears. Avis moves inside the house.

His voice is uneven and small when he starts. "Avis and me got married right out of high school. I was the youngest and working the dairy with Dad but he was getting old. It just made good sense to marry and start a family so we could all work on the farm together. I had four sisters who all married off and my younger brother Gray didn't work on the farm because my parents drove him away." I reach back in my memory, trying to remember Gray; he's been gone so long that his face is fuzzy to me. "Mama and Dad named him Gray because it was a gray day when he was born and Mama said it matched his personality. He was always turned different than the rest of us. He'd fight and argue with Mama and Dad and cuss them out. He could beat the living tar out of me with one hand tied behind his back. One day the preacher came calling, and out of meanness, Gray picked up the bottle of milk that was setting on the table and smashed it over the preacher's snow-white head. Gray laughed and Dad punched him right upside the head, knocking him out." He squeezes his eyes with his fingers like he's trying to push the memory of that day further back in his brain. "That was the final straw. Gray woke up outside, a suitcase packed beside him. I was left to work the farm, and that suited me — I was made for farming.

Over the years Avis and me always used help out here, you know."

I nod. Lots of farmers used extra help.

"One day a family moved to Bony Creek, and a man and his daughter, Ruth, came out here because he was looking for work. Avis had a lot of trouble when she had our last boy, Len, and was in bed with him. She heard me talking with the man out on the porch and hollered for me to come inside. I went into the bedroom, and she lay there looking puny and pale and wanted me to ask the girl about helping her around the house.

" *'Just till I'm up and able again,'* Avis said. *'Doc says it won't be longer than two weeks.'* "

"So Ruth came to work for you?" I ask.

He nods, looking off someplace beyond us. "She took over what Avis did in the house and helped me with the milking and farming. She called me Holt; nobody calls

410

me Holt, nobody ever has except Ruth and Ivorie; even Avis calls me Ox." My limbs feel heavy, listening to him. He crosses his arms as if he's fighting a chill and pinches up his face. "I was thirty-eight and she was a girl of nineteen. We were never alone; I made sure of that. Rayburn or Stella were always working with us, but after she was gone for the day I couldn't blast the images of her out of my mind." He looks up at me, searching my face for telltale signs of hope or forgiveness; I don't know.

"We were finishing in the tobacco one day when Rayburn and Stella ran off to play back at the house, leaving me and Ruth alone. We were working the far patch that day, back by the line of oaks." He gestures toward the trees and I notice them standing tall and thick in the distance. "If I could go back to that day, Henry." His voice tightens and then snaps. "Everything in me wanted to do the right thing. I could hear my own children playing in the distance!"

He stops talking, and I bend down to pull out a weed from among the gravel, rubbing it between my fingers. "She was a girl, Ox. You were old enough to be her father. What did she . . ."

"See in me?" His face is closed and scowl-ing. "I didn't bother to know then." He puts

411

his hands over his face, hiding from the thoughts, from me, and from himself, I suppose. "Sometime during her fifth month with us Ruth told me she was at least three months pregnant. It felt like somebody took a tire iron to my stomach. She said her daddy would run her off." He lifts his arm and coughs into it, a wet, gravelly sounding hack. "She was young and fine and had her whole life ahead of her until she came here. I'd ruined her, Henry. I knew it even then."

"How'd she and the boy end up in those hills?"

He closes his eyes but more memories come seeping in, like water under a door. "Gray took to living in the hills after Mama and Dad drove him off. He wanted to live alone and that was fine with them. Dad gave him what money they had and said he could stay up there and rot for all they cared. I hauled planks up to him and helped him build a shack no bigger than my and Avis's bedroom. He chose a spot near the top of the hill in a grove of woods that was pretty as can be but I knew Gray would make it ugly before long."

I hold up my hand, looking at him. "I thought your brother ran off to California."

"That's what my folks said. They would have said he was dead but you need a body

412

for that." I look out toward the hills, listening, trying to wrap my head around it all. "He killed his own grub, grew what he could in a small patch of sun, and kept some chickens. He wasted away like any old hermit would and looked viler every time I saw him. A year or so after Mama and Dad were both dead he showed up on my porch. After that, he showed up from time to time. Avis hated the sight of him." I look over at his face and it's knotted up in pain. "He came here one day after Ruth said she was pregnant. Ruth didn't pay any attention to him but went to work in the tobacco. He watched her and I knew what he was thinking. Gray had been alone for lots of years by then. I told him I had work to do but he asked if I'd bring him some lumber and some other supplies sometime soon. I told him I would just so I could get him off the property."

He stops and slides the back of his hand over his upper lip. "He was drinking moonshine on the porch of the shack when I took him that lumber eight and a half years ago. I jumped off the horse and sat next to him, taking a swig of moonshine that set my gut on fire. Gray laughed and took another swig to prove he was a bigger man than me. His teeth were as gray as his name and I felt my stomach roll, watching him drink."

" 'Who's that fine little piece of tail you got on the farm?' he asked.

"He looked over at me and my liver shook. I told him her daddy had come looking for work for her. He stood up and laughed so hard he stumbled off the steps.

" 'Did her daddy know the boss man would be beddin' his little girl?'

"The moonshine rose to my throat and I wanted to puke. He got his red, bloated face close to mine and I could smell the filth of who he was.

" 'You're screwin' that little girl, ain't ya, big brother?'

"I told him I wasn't."

" 'Horseshit! You knocked that girl up!'

"My skin was crawling because Gray knew but I wouldn't admit to it. He held himself up against a tree and pointed his finger at me."

" 'If Mama and the old man could see you now!'

"Every time he opened his mouth I felt bile rise to my throat. I kept my voice steady because Gray's fuse was short. I told him he was wrong. He was swaying while he laughed and I hated him.

" 'Is she any good?'

"I couldn't feel my legs. My stomach

lurched and I leaned over the rail of the shack, vomiting. The moonshine burned more the second time through my throat. Gray cackled and slapped my back.

" 'You are a weak-gutted thing, big brother.'

"He took another swig and wiped his mouth before he leaned down to talk in my ear.

" 'You only got one way out of this mess, big brother. You bring your whore up here to be with me.'

"I vomited again and felt my hands shaking. I told him I wouldn't bring Ruth anywhere near him. He laughed and fell against a tree, sliding down the trunk to the ground.

" 'You'll bring her because you're chickenshit. The thought of your wife finding out scares the piss out of you. And she will find out, big brother. I'll make sure of that.'

"I wanted to throw up but there wasn't anything left. He looked at me and his eyes said he knew — he knew he had me."

A wave of queasiness hits my stomach.

Ox is slope-shouldered and his chest looks like it's collapsing. "I tried every which way to figure out a better way but there wasn't one. As I rode down through those hills that day I wanted to take it all back: her dad pulling into the farm that day, Avis's sickness and asking me if Ruth could help, my sins against my wife and children and God and Ruth. But I couldn't take one thing back. Our thought was she'd stay there till the baby came and then we could take the baby somewhere, to someplace where people would take care of it." He moves to the shade of the oak tree and leans against the trunk.

"I remember her folks," I say. "They weren't here long. Moved back wherever they came from."

"Florida. She left a note saying she was running off. They never knew anything. She didn't even tell me that she was walking up into them hills alone."

I shuffle my feet and clear my throat. "Did you ever see her again?"

He looks up into the branches and shuts his eyes. "Once a month I'd ride up and take her some clothes or dish towels or a pan I thought she could use, maybe some bacon, flour, or coffee. We met at the base of the hill. I saw her about two weeks after she first went up and I knew by looking at her that she was different. He'd done it to her. I'd done it to her." Tears trickle out the corners of his eyes and he pushes a fist into each eye. "I sent her up there to live with . . ." He laughs at himself, at what he did. "I rode down out of those hills with my skin stinking with her dried blood on it."

I can't think of one thing to say to him. He looks at me, hoping I'm surprised or disgusted, but I can't put a finger on what I'm thinking. I'm just here, listening and looking at him. "And you never took the baby someplace after he was born?"

He shakes his head. "Never even talked about it. Gray said he'd kill the baby if she ever thought of stepping foot out of the hills."

"Did you ever see Peter?"

Tears fall on his hands and he brushes them off. "After he was born. I brought Ruth a Bible as a gift. A Bible, Henry!" He laughs at the thought. "A book that says *don't commit adultery* and encourages good living so you don't go through hell on earth!" He bends over, laughing. "She hadn't named him yet but I wrote his birth date in it. I wasn't even sure if she kept up with the day of the week or the month or anything else up there."

"Did you hold him?

"I didn't want to and she didn't offer. She'd shut down. She was cold. Hard. I couldn't blame her. She was like a bear protecting her cub from me and Gray. When I'd meet her once a month the boy was always up at the base of the woods. She never brought him down to see me."

I look up toward the house. "Did Avis ever know about Ruth? About her living in the hills?"

He has a sick look in his eyes. "No. If she knew about that . . . well, who knows what Avis would be capable of? She's never known anything, but it's there. Hanging between us."

I glance at the house and see Avis watching us through the screen door. "I have a notion she knows now, Ox." He runs his hand through his hair, crying. "Do you know when Ruth died?"

Tears fall again but he doesn't brush them away. "I don't. I went up to take her some clothes for the boy and some food over a year ago but she never came to meet me. I kept going but she never came." He's laughing again, the stench of it all stinging his eyes. "I was too afraid to go up there and see what I'd find. I finally stopped going and hoped they'd all gone away." A long spell of quiet fills the space between us. "I killed her, Henry. I took her life."

He slumps over and I watch his shoulders. "You gonna be sick, Ox?" He shakes his head and I step back. He's just weary from hiding and covering up and living in shadows, his mind spewing sick and terrifying thoughts at him day in and out.

Tears are springing out of his eye sockets when he stands up. "I dropped by Ivorie's one day and she told me about the boy and how his mother was dead. I thought I was going to be sick right there on Ivorie's porch. Then somebody said they saw Gray and it felt like a tire iron hit me. I knew he was coming for me."

"He's running, Ox." A tear drops off the end of his nose, leaving a wet streak along the top of it. He turns his head slow to look at me. "The sheriff went up there but the shack was empty. Maybe someday they'll find him in Georgia or North Carolina but he's long gone from here."

He tries to laugh but more tears fall off his nose. "The first time I went up to see Ruth I took her some barbiturate powder I got from the vet in Greenville. I'd had it for years — got it for two sick cows I had to put down. I knew a little bit in Gray's coffee or moonshine would knock him out and he wouldn't touch her. I had hoped that one day she'd give him enough to put him underground." He takes a deep breath and looks up, squinting. "I hoped she'd just kill him so she could get away from all of us." It's like somebody has just kicked him in the chest; the sobs take him right down to his knees. He arches his neck to see me and reaches his arms out like a man begging for his life. "I didn't mean to hurt Ivorie that night on her porch. I just went to her house to scare her. You have to believe me, Henry."

"I believe you, Ox. Desperate men do desperate things." I move a foot over the knotty ground.

He turns his face away and waves a hand at the air in front of him. "Every day I've asked the Lord to forgive me for what I did to Ruth. Every day, Henry!"

"Once was enough, Ox."

"The first time I saw her up in the hills I begged her, too. But she didn't say a word." I'm dead quiet. "I can't live here and look at him. I'll see Ruth and be reminded again of what I've done . . . what I didn't do . . . what I've never been man enough to do. . . ."

That knot in my stomach lunges to my throat and I answer him with a voice full of gristle. "There's more at stake here than what you think or what you see or what you did or didn't do, Ox! Think about your family. Enough lives have been ruined." He sobs into his hands, thinking of them. "Life's hard, Ox. A lot of times *we* make it mighty hard, but you don't have to make it worse. You need to try to live the rest of your days without guilt and shame eating you alive. Almost a decade of that has nearly killed you." He stays on the ground and is the most pitiful sight I've ever seen. "Truth is, if you catch a glimpse of Peter in town from time to time you'll see what a fine boy he is. You can tell his mother loved him. You can tell he's got her inside him. You know better than anybody what he lived with up there, and he survived it! If ever there was beauty from ashes — he's it. If you ran away you'd never see the fine kid he is or how's he turning out, and that'd gnaw away at your bones till there was nothing left." I take the handkerchief out of my pocket and wipe the back of my neck. I look at the house, wondering what the kids are thinking, why they aren't running through the yard. 'Cause Avis told them to stay put, that's why.

"Ivorie's a good person, Henry. She took him in and opened her home. She's good." He can barely get the words out. "I don't want him to know me. I don't want him to turn out like me."

"Ox, you're raising fine kids here. You've kept this farm running long after your pop died. You've got a wife who has lived in a haunted house for close to ten years but she's still in there, waiting. You're a hard-working man who made a big, big mistake. We all have."

He rakes his fingers through the blades of grass and shakes his head. "He's better off not knowing."

I kneel down in front of him. "My sister needs to know."

He nods and I walk to my truck without saying another word. I slip behind the wheel and drive away, feeling sick. Avis isn't all bristles and mites that people have made her out to be; she's a woman who has lived with ghosts and kept her family together despite them, kept them from drowning in sinkholes of shame, regret, and betrayal. All this time I thought Ox was the green shoot that busted through the hard, dry ground of a thorny marriage, but he wasn't. Avis was.

People are messy. When we're left to ourselves we can make a gollywhopper of a mess. Nothing but sadness sloshes around inside me as I drive home because it all could have been different. Ox could have told Avis what happened. It would have been ugly, but uglier than this? Uglier than a young girl living with an animal and trying to raise a child? Ruth could have told her parents. It would have been hard, but harder than their never knowing what happened to her? I think of Ox walking back into his house to face Avis and can't imagine what that will look like. The mishmash of thoughts makes me angry and sad and worn clean through.

Loretta's in the garden when I drive by and I honk the horn, turning into the driveway. She waves at me and I fish around in my head, wondering where to begin. We'll be up half the night.

Two days later, I'm at the hospital by eight in the morning. When I peek in the room I see Sarah Ivorie sitting on the bed with Peter. "Well, how'd you like sleeping in the hospital?" Peter looks up at me and smiles; I see Ox's grin and feel a slow, dull jerk on my heart. He's smiling and I swear he's a different kid than the one I left here two days ago. He looks all pink and proud and bright eyed and bushy tailed.

He points his thumb down and tries to say no.

It sounds like something is in his mouth with his tongue, but I understood him! "You didn't like it? Well, I'll be! I thought that'd be considered adventure sleeping."

"No," he says. It sounds garbled, but it's still *no!*

I slap my head. "Listen to that! More words!" He smiles and I hear the buttons on his chest popping. "I've told everybody in Morgan Hill that you are talking up a storm. So, are you ready to go home?" He smiles. "Well, come on! The taxi's waiting."

The doctors have already told Sarah everything she needs to know, so they and the nurses make over Peter one last time before he leaves. "We'll see you back here in a few days to check on you," Dr. Culp says. "Then we'll talk about that next surgery. In the meantime . . . keep talking."

The nurses give Peter one final hug and he carries a gift of jacks and a deck of cards through the hallway, waving as he goes. He and Sarah are bounding down the stairs. "Come on, old man," she says. "We want to get home." I hurry as fast as my weary bones will take me.

The driveway is full of cars when I pull into Sarah's and she cranes her neck to see who's here. Jane, John, and Milo come screaming through the yard, followed by little Will Henry, who has no idea why they're screaming, but he joins them. "Hi," Jane says, sticking her head inside the truck's cab. She's looking right at Peter and waiting. If he doesn't hurry, her head is going to pop.

"Hi."

"He talks!" she screams over her shoulder to the crowd gathering like clouds behind her. I see Fran and Joe and Joe's folks, Del and Helen. There's Loretta, Doc, Pete, Charlotte, and Dolly Wade and her mother. Hot Dot, Gabbie, Haze, Clayton, and some more folks behind them. "Hurry! Come out and tell us all about it." Jane opens the door and is dragging Peter over Sarah's lap. John and Milo tug on him, too, and they stand him in front of everybody like a prize pig. "I'm Jane," she says, sticking her hand out to shake.

Peter slaps his hand into hers and concentrates. "Pe . . . ter." It sounds like his mouth is full of marbles, but the small crowd erupts in all sorts of sounds and I hear things like, *"Well, I'll swan! If that don't beat all! That is something!"*

Fran and Loretta are already making enough fried chicken to feed the rest of Morgan Hill, and the kitchen table is covered with potato salad and green beans from Charlotte and rolls and corn from Del and Helen Cannon, and the house smells like cobbler. "Peach," Loretta says, batting my hand away. I pour a cup of some of Loretta's world-famous floating-pistol coffee and take a gulp. It's the least painful way to drink it. I look out and see Peter talking to

Milo; his mouth is just jabbering away. I walk out the door and join Sarah in the yard.

"He talked about his mother last night," she says. She's watching Peter play and her arms are folded the way she stands when something's on her mind. "It was hard to understand him but I think I pieced most of it together. His mother got sick and just kept getting sicker till one day she was gone." Her voice trails off and she glances over at me. "The man took her off and buried her." She wipes her face and looks back at Peter. "That's what he called him . . . *the man.* He never knew his name. But he had a name. Right?" She looks over at me. "Everybody has a name. The man had a name. Peter's father has a name." She digs her foot into the grass and twists it side to side.

I see Pete and Charlotte and the rest of the folks out of the corner of my eye and know I better talk fast. "Sarah. There's something you need to know."

"Really, Henry?" She's looking at me with those sizzling blues. "Do I really need to know? When I look at Peter's face and see a familiar smile, do I need to know whose it is? Will that help me raise him?" Her voice is fading. "For over eight years somebody tried to bury a secret. But now that secret's out," she says, looking at Peter. "And he's mine. Enough people have been ruined. I have a son. That's all I need to know."

We are halfway through dinner when I hear tires on the gravel. I step away from the picnic table to see Davis Carpenter getting out of his car. "Big day, Davis! Big, big day around here."

"You all are the partyingest people I've ever met, Henry." He walks up the stone path and waves at everybody under the tree.

"Peter there had an operation on his cleft up here," I say, pointing to the roof of my mouth. "And now he can talk. Well, he still sounds mush-mouthed but I'll be doggone if we can't pick out a word or two!"

Davis looks over at Peter eating with the kids on top of the quilt. "Well, that is some cause for celebrating, isn't it?"

I walk toward the picnic table. "Come on. Fix you a plate and get some tea. It's been so dry my duck don't know how to swim anymore."

He stops and his face gets long with seriousness. "Henry, I spoke with Mr. Lewis." I wipe my mouth, waiting. "He won't pay four hundred an acre." I start to say something and Davis flaps his hand in front of my face. "But he'll do three fifty."

It feels like I'm doing cartwheels but my big feet are still under me. "What do you say to that?"

"I say we have a deal." I won't tell Davis that Sarah Ivorie has owned the property all along. No need to put a damper on Davis's day. We'll go over that when the papers are signed.

Sarah walks onto the porch holding a pitcher of iced tea and smiles toward Davis. "Hey, Mr. Carpenter."

"Miss Walker! I hear there's good news at your house."

She covers her eyes with her free hand. "There sure is! It seems every time you come out here we're celebrating something. Why don't you grab a plate and join us this time?"

He does, and we never talk about land or money or even who died or was fixing to die. We talk about blue skies, ripe vegetables, pretty tobacco, and the sweetest voice any of us has ever heard.

Four days after Peter came home from the hospital a truck I'd never seen before pulled up the driveway. Peter and I were in the garden working and I stood up to look at the driver. The sun was in my eyes but I made out something bounding toward me and barking. Peter ran past me lickety-split and Sally knocked him clean to the ground. I threw my peck basket on the grass and ran after them, laughing my fool head off. I even let her lick me right on the mouth! "Miss Walker?" I looked up to see an old farmer twisting his hat between his hands. "Somebody said this might be your dog and it sure looks like she is!"

"She is!" Sally pinned Peter to the ground and wouldn't let him up no matter how hard he yelled uncle.

"Somebody dropped her off at my place a few weeks ago. Her leg got banged up when she was thrown out of the truck but me and the wife nursed her best we could. She's doing good now."

I tried to keep Sally off me so I could talk to him. "Where do you live?"

"Out past Burly Crossing. Nobody knew where she came from but we could tell she belonged to somebody." He didn't know who came by his place that morning and told him Sally was my dog, and I couldn't talk with Sally pushing me to the ground, so he drove away and left the three of us rolling around on the ground like we'd all lost our minds.

Sally sleeps every night on the porch now and is sitting at the door, looking in, when Peter and I make it to the kitchen in the morning. There are days I still can't believe she's back. But then she pushes her wet nose up under my hand and I talk to her like I always did before and I know she's here to stay.

I ran into George a few days ago at the store. He smiled down at Peter and we made small talk that made my heart sore. He paid for his groceries and left without taking another glance at me. "Oatmeal. Right, Sarah?" Henry said, looking at me. I smiled, but that spooned-out place under my ribs ached. "Don't forget, you got your dog back."

"Some women would say you got the better end of the deal," Loretta said, making me laugh.

I lie awake some nights and wonder what would have happened if George and I had been married when Peter showed up. Would he have strong-armed me into not doing anything for Peter? Or would I have convinced him that we needed to do something to help this child? I don't think George would ever have accepted Peter. That's hard to think about, harder to believe, but it's true. He wasn't the man intended for this house. Peter is.

I don't know where the summer has gone. My garden is picked over, the well house shelves are full, the chest freezer is bulging, and school starts in two weeks, just after Labor Day. Peter and I have borrowed so many books that we've worn a hole in the hall leading to the school library. We eat breakfast spelling and reading and doing simple math and do it all again at dinner and supper and when he jumps into bed at night. Every day his words come out clearer and Dr. Culp says the second surgery should help round off some of those garbled edges even more. I socked the money from the land away right inside Davis's bank and that's where it will sit for all of Peter's medical bills.

They're digging down at the crossroads now, and Peter and I sit in the truck with Sally sometimes and watch them move the earth. I don't get a knot in my stomach watching them, which means, I guess, that I've come to some sort of peace with The Big Q.

I take Peter to church every Sunday. I figure I've been pouting at God long enough about Mother's death. We sit on the second row, the row where our family always sat, where Pop would keep his hands on the back of Caleb's and James's necks to keep them in line during the service. Jane, John, and Milo always plop down beside us. The first time I took Peter, John let him know in no uncertain terms that church *ain't what it's all cracked up to be.*

At the end of the service today I tell Peter we need to get home to spell and read some more. "You sure are making a big to-do over reading and spelling and such," John says. He looks at Peter and whispers, "Trust me, that ain't what it's cracked up to be, either."

"I want to read," Peter says, swinging his legs.

John slaps his hand to his head. "What in

tarnation for?"

"Because he doesn't want to be ignorant all his life," Jane says.

Peter holds on to my hand on the way home, teetering on top of the rails that are shimmering in the heat. His shoes are squeaking as he angles his feet just so. "Boy, it's been so hot and dry," I say.

"It's so hot my chickens are laying hard-boiled eggs."

He's still a little hard to understand, but I get the gist of it and hiss through my teeth. "Where in the world did you hear that?"

"Henry."

He starts to laugh and I shake my head. "That sounds like one of Henry's dumb jokes."

"It's so dry the Baptists are sprinkling, the Methodists are spitting, and the Catholics are giving rain checks."

I take hold of his hand and start walking again. "You have got to stop loafing at Henry's store."

"What is a Catholic anyway?"

I laugh out loud and rub my hand over his newly buzzed hair. "We don't have any of them around here!"

He almost loses his footing and sticks his arms out like an airplane. "How many more operations am I going to need?"

I shrug. "I don't know."

"But I'm talking pretty good."

I swat a bee away with my Bible and push the hair back off my face. "Well, I can figure out most of what you say, but if Dr. Culp says you need another surgery, then that's what we'll do. They'll start working on your teeth next. Open up." He stops and jumps off the rail, tilting back his head and opening wide. "Uh-huh. Just what I thought."

"What?"

"Bunch of words in there waiting to be spelled."

He steps back onto the rail and takes my hand. "Am I ignorant?"

"No."

"Was I ignorant?"

I glance up into the hills. "Never."

"What was I then?"

"Illiterate."

He falls off the rail and looks up at me with drops of sweat resting on his forehead. "What's that mean?"

"Means you can't read or write."

He bangs his hands together, and we wait, watching for Sally to scamper down the embankment toward us. "I'm not that anymore, am I?"

He rushes off to meet Sally, and they run back to me before bounding up the stairs and leaving me on the tracks. I stand, looking up into the hills. When did I go up there? What did I do before that day? All I recall is skies and trees, a patch of garden, and lots of lonely space. I remember the days were dark and sad and full of shadows, with a sense of gloom pushing away any brightness. Nothing surprised or amazed me anymore, and that was part of my problem. Nothing took my breath away.

But then he came.

PETER

Mama is almost finished reading *The Three Musketeers,* and Jane was right. This is the most exciting thing I've ever heard. Mama looks like she's about to drop over when she pulls the sheet up under my chin. She kisses me on the forehead, we say our prayers, and then she says, "Get some sleep now. I'll see you in the morning." She says that every night, making sure I know she'll be here when I wake up, but I've never doubted her.

I try not to think about the shack or the man, but I see my mother's face a lot, especially in Mama's. Mama wants me to talk about my mother and I try, but it's hard sometimes. She says she understands, and that it will all come with time and that we have plenty of it.

I don't wake up thinking I'm drowning anymore. All that time I thought I was having a nightmare but that's not what it was

at all. It was just a dream, the best dream
— one where Mama pulls me up out of the
dark water and sets me down in the bright
of the day.

ABOUT THE AUTHOR

Donna VanLiere is the *New York Times* and *USA Today* bestselling author of *Finding Grace, The Angels of Morgan Hill,* and seven Christmas books, including the perennial favorites *The Christmas Shoes* and *The Christmas Hope.* She lives in Franklin, Tennessee, with her husband and three children. Connect with Donna on Facebook and Twitter and at www.donnavanliere.com.